ALICE'S SECRET

TYLER PIKE

TYLER PIKE BOOKS

BEFORE YOU BEGIN

Please consider signing up for Tyler's mailing list for free Alice Brickstone novellas and details on future releases. There's a quick signup on www.tylerpikebooks.com.

Enjoy *Alice's Secret*.

CHAPTER 1

THURSDAY, 3:00 P.M.

SEVENTY-TWO HOURS BEFORE THE END

Alice was furious. A tall and broad-shouldered seventeen-year-old, Alice harbored a fury that thrashed and rumbled inside her like a hurricane, her anger commensurate in force with her powerful nature. As she stormed away from her parents' cabin, she felt oppressed by the huge cliff face that enclosed the small rural Colorado property she now called home. Today it felt like a tomb or a damp hole here, rather than a family home. But she knew it wasn't the cliff's fault she felt so trapped.

Glancing over her shoulder, she saw her vacant-eyed mother close the front door, probably to return to bed. In the throes of her postpartum depression, Mom was the real cause of Alice's anger. Once again, Alice had been asked to postpone all her plans in order to go into town and pick up her four-month-old sister, Connie, from day care because Mom was unable to rise to the occasion. Alice's parents were familiar with her routine—a five a.m. start, hours in the pool in town, followed by a full day at school—but somehow, Mom was still oblivious to her exhaustion. It was too late for Alice, but her sister needed a mother. A real one, not this vacant shell.

Alice considered going back to shake her mom out of her

lethargy. She and Dad had both been begging her for weeks to go back to her doctor and get some different meds, but she had grown more evasive and vacant every day. These days, her only reaction to Alice's angry interventions and Dad's pleading was to defend her right to choose what she put in her body.

Alice was just done. What her mom was doing was so ... irresponsible! She punctuated her thoughts by kicking a loose piece of firewood into a flower bed. Above the pines and beyond the cliff that marked the beginning of the national forest, she saw dark clouds gathering. Perhaps in response to the ones roiling within her.

Alice stormed across the gravel to the barn she and her father had converted into her space. She pushed open the creaky side door, walked by her car, and plodded up the steps to her bedroom, which still smelled of new carpet and recently applied wood stain. She looked at herself in the mirror and saw a mess of short light-brown hair and dark shadows under her eyes. Dad had once told her that her eyes resembled those of an ancient Egyptian princess, whatever that meant. Now they just looked tired. The rest of her looked as solid and muscular as ever. At seventeen, she had grown into her six-feet tall, two-hundred-pound swimmer's body. She was powerful and grace-ful. Besides the anxiety and exhaustion that showed in her face, she generally liked the young woman in the mirror.

She ate two energy bars and managed to text an apology to Madison for being late to meet up before flopping down on the bed and immediately falling into a deep sleep.

Alice dreamed she was in the rare books room in the local university library with her friends Madison and Karan. Although they were only high school students, they had gotten permission to hang out there. It was reliably private, too, as virtually no one else used that room. The stone walls and thick carpeting usually made the place feel safe and secure.

Not now. In her dream, the space felt wrong. Alice felt like someone or something was watching her. Her dream-vision transported her to the source: a gaping cavity in the top of a mountain. Shaped like a cat's eye but serving as a mouth, the hole was animated by a hunger to consume everything around it. Alice felt her energy draining.

She heard a hellish rumble from deep underground, which resolved into a cough, and then into a strangely eloquent voice, which seemed to come out of the hole itself.

Your filthy secret is out. I know you are a freak. Magic is a relic of unholy times, and abominations like you were snuffed out long ago. Humans are not meant to fly. Humans are not meant to read minds. I will suck your unnatural powers out of you. You will suffer. Your friends and family will suffer with you. <u>*The end is coming.*</u>

CHAPTER 2

THURSDAY, 6:00 P.M.

SIXTY-NINE HOURS BEFORE THE END

W aking with a start, Alice rose and scolded herself for eating so much processed crap right before lying down. It always gave her nightmares. Her swimming coach was constantly on her to eat real food more often, but she just never had time.

She quickly drank a glass of water and set out to pick Connie up from day care. She was going to be late because of her unplanned nap. The day care manager would be standing at the door with Connie in her arms, the last child on the premises. Again.

Worse, she was going to be even later than she'd thought to meet Madison and Karan at the library. She knew Madison had some important things to talk about, and she had made Alice promise to be on time. And Alice had genuinely wanted to keep that promise. Madison and Karan were among the few people on the planet whom she didn't fear or hate. Friendships were very, very hard work for a socially anxious person like her. Basically, she just showed up and hoped for the best over and over again, never sure she would be able to bust through her selective mutism to even say hello. And being late today would be one more thing that strained their relationship.

Madison and Karan did not yet know that she was more than a tall girl with selective mutism. Much more. A freak of nature, really. Sure, they had caught glimpses, like the time Karan *might* have seen her new friend dive off a cliff. But Karan had been a prisoner in a speeding car at the time, looking at Alice through the rearview mirror. Could she trust her memory of what she had seen? When she tried to find out more about it later, Alice threatened to end the friendship if she kept asking questions. Madison had never seen Alice do anything uncanny, but she knew her strange friend seemed to cheat the normal rules of space-time. She had grown particularly suspicious last year when Alice managed to travel from Hardrock to Laramie in an hour. She had agreed to accept the lie that Alice had taken a ride share, afraid of how their friend would react if they pressed her.

And Alice had good reason to hide her secret. As far as she knew, nobody else on the planet could do what she could do. Alice could fly. She could read minds, though it generally made her hate the people who owned them. She had visions. Her body began to heal instantly from terrible injuries. According to Mr. Rao—an old Indian man who had lived in her parents' cabin before he died in a fireball while saving Alice's life—all this was because she could see and feel the elementary life force in nature, while other people could not. Mr. Rao called it "prana," and it was everywhere, countless crystalline currents flowing most strongly from beautiful places and through the clearest skies. Now, Alice could make the magical energy flowing around her respond to her wishes, even when they went unspoken and unthought.

Mr. Rao had explained that her supernatural abilities were called "siddhis," and they were known and appreciated in ancient India, though they had largely disappeared now. He theorized her abilities might have first been triggered by the death of her twin brother when they were five. Thomas had been murdered while the family was in India, and Alice, in the bed next to him, had only just escaped with her life. Ever since then, the traumatized little girl had fallen into silence, and in that silence had discovered prana. It was only last year when Alice had finally broken through her silence to try and make friends with anyone, and she was still struggling with it on a daily basis.

Anyway, all she could do was keep trying. Better late than never. As a wise man had once said, 90% percent of life was just showing up.

She dropped Connie at home and rushed to the university library, through the big atrium, and up the stairs past the librarian's office, and was soon facing the familiar door to the rare books room.

This room was her sanctuary and had been for the past three or four years. As a little girl, she had often accompanied her dad when he worked on his doctoral dissertation in this room, and she had fallen in love with the atmosphere, and with the library in general. It was a place she could feel anonymous and safe. While other kids met at the mall or went to movies, she got permission from her mom and dad to wander the halls of the library alone. After a few thefts occurred at the library, her dad begged her to confine herself to the rare books room, wandering the stacks only when she needed new material. The rare books room was like a little fortress, because it was closed to the general library public behind a locked door. What she hadn't known until last year was that her dad had made a special arrangement with Brian, the librarian responsible for that space, to look after her and report on her movements. Brian, a middle-aged man who always dressed like a golf pro who escaped from the 1980s, had turned out to have secrets of his own. Alice had discovered some of them, and now she and Brian had an understanding. He had even given her a key.

She unlocked the solid oak door and breathed in the

familiar smell of leather furniture, wool carpet, and old books. Her friends were indeed there, but the books dominated the room like a crowd of silent watchers. The shelves were dour, dark mahogany, rising all the way to the twenty-foot-high ceiling.

The room was furnished with heavy, overstuffed leather armchairs and warmly lit by art deco lamps. On one side of the room, the shelves gave way to a cold stone fireplace, enclosed by a black metal grate. The opposite wall featured a grand stained glass window, through which the afternoon sun shone, hitting the lustrous dust in the air and the main feature of the room: an enormously heavy table, at which Madison and Karan sat.

As Alice's friends lifted their heads at the sound of the creaking door hinges, Alice suddenly remembered her nightmare—the horrible eye, the hellish voice. "The end is coming ..."

Madison stared at her with dark eyes, her thin lips pursed.

Alice held her breath, waiting for her chastisement.

"Alice, you're late again. You promised to pick up Connie early so you could meet us here at four thirty." Madison's criticism carried a bit of weight, because she was always able to pick up *her* sister, Billie, from day care and make it to places on time. Alice had always simultaneously admired and hated Madison's ability to be so damn organized. Billie was three-years-old, and as far as Alice could tell, the toddler pretty much thought of Madison as her mom, not her sister.

Apparently sensing Alice's discomfort, Karan smiled at her.

Alice thought Karan was pretty when she smiled. It helped hide the network of thin, angry red scars all over her face. Karan had put on some weight since they'd met over the summer, and Alice thought it suited her. Big, strong, and a bit round. Attractive. She had told Karan so multiple times. Hadn't she? Maybe not in the most explicit terms. Maybe not at all.

She should remedy that; it might make a difference to her self-esteem.

Karan was fragile because she had been through hell. Like Alice, she'd had a miserable childhood, but for different reasons. Born as Katie Fremantle, her mother had died when she was young, and her father acted more like a coach than a doting dad. He had trained Katie ruthlessly, and she'd become one of the most promising young swimmers in the nation, on track to attend the next Olympics. But that had all ended a year ago when Katie and her dad were in a car accident with another man and his daughter. Their vehicle plunged deep into a river, and Katie's dad died instantly. The other vehicle remained on the land, but the other girl died on impact. The driver managed to keep himself together long enough to dive into the freezing river and rescue Katie, who was unconscious and severely injured.

Then, in his grief and shock, the other driver suffered a psychotic break. He re-entered the water and belted his own dead daughter into the submerged vehicle, then concealed that car's tire tracks to hide its presence. He did everything he could to make it look like his car had struck an animal, rather than another vehicle. When the paramedics arrived, he lied that the injured girl was *his* daughter, Karan. When Katie Percival and her father were eventually reported missing, he thought he was in the clear. "Karan," who had severe amnesia, underwent extensive reconstructive surgery and a bit of brainwashing, and her "dad" hoped they would live happily ever after.

Until Alice came along. She met Karan after the amnesiac girl had largely healed, at least on the outside. She managed to piece together what had happened to Karan, extricated her from her captor, and worked with her social workers to move her to Hardrock, where Madison's parents agreed to foster her. Karan's memory still hadn't come back, and she chose to continue going by that name as a testament to who she had become. Neither Alice nor Madison could understand why she didn't revert to Katie, but they respected it, along with all of Karan's other oddities, and the three girls quickly became fast friends.

Smiling back at Karan, Alice sat down in a heavy, high-backed wooden chair at the table. "Sorry. I just had to have a power nap."

"You okay?" Madison asked.

"Yeah. Just tired."

"I know what you mean," Karan said. "This town exhausts me too. Terrifying place."

Madison rolled her eyes. It accentuated the length of her face and the prominence of her long nose, making her look even more like a bird. "Karan, we've been through this. Hardrock is no worse than anywhere else. Statistically speaking, you're just as safe here as you were in Arizona. You're just new. It will grow on you."

"Yeah?" Karan retorted. "But how safe is that, really? I read that one in four girls in America will be sexually assaulted at least once. That doesn't make me feel all that safe. And there are way more meth users here than I ever saw in Arizona. And pot is legal in Colorado. I smell it everywhere."

Sighing, Madison replied, "Not everyone does drugs here, Karan."

"Seems like they do," Karan blundered on, lifting her blond bangs with both hands. "I know nobody wants to date a horribly scarred girl like me, but the boys in this town all seem to have just crawled out of the woods. They all look like that guy in *Into the Wild*. Not even I could date any of them. The only boy who doesn't wear a T-shirt to school is that one who deals Xanax." Dropping her hair back into place, she added, "That guy is hot."

"I heard he isn't even a high school student," Madison said. "He's the school IT technician."

"Out of my league, that's for sure," Karan said. "Wait, is 'hot drug dealer' a league?"

"Seriously?" Madison exclaimed, pinching her nose and shaking her head.

"You've got a guy who's interested in you, though, Karan," Alice argued. "I thought you went out with Dave, like, yesterday."

"It was nothing like a date," Karan said, blushing. "He's only helping me adjust to life here. His dad works at the sheriff's office." She turned to Alice and added, "By the way, Alice, what was your mom doing at the sheriff's office last night?"

"What?" Alice asked, shocked.

"She wasn't, like, arrested or anything," Karan quickly assured her. "She was just in the front atrium by herself."

Alice thought hard, coming up with no theories that would explain her mom's presence there. As far as she knew, her mom had hardly left home these past few weeks.

"I'm sure it's fine," Karan said awkwardly. "Like, maybe she was turning in a lost ring or something."

After a few seconds of silence, Madison pulled her long black bangs out of her eyes and announced, "I do have a reason for making sure you were both here this afternoon. Two reasons, actually ..."

"We're all being arrested?" Karan interrupted cheerfully.

Madison rolled her eyes again and folded her hands in front of her. Down to business. "I presume you've both received the same email?"

Alice appealed to Karan, who shrugged. "I don't check my phone every three minutes, Mad. Sorry," she added pathetically.

"Well, aren't you going to look now?!" Madison's businesslike manner cracked, and her face showed some rare childlike excitement.

Still unnerved by the news about her Mom, Alice tentatively picked up her phone and read the email. It was from the head coach of one of the best university swimming programs in the U.S. Some time ago, Madison had compelled Alice and Karan to send out countless emails, together with videos and stats, to all the best swimming programs, with the idea that they could get an early start begging for scholarships. This email was their first response.

DEAR MS. BRICKSTONE,

Thank you for the email and video you sent last month. I also received emails from Katie "Karan" Fremantle and Madison Percival. It is highly unusual that three such promising young swimmers are in the same town! Your coach is an old friend of mine, and I have spoken to him about attending your afternoon practice next Tuesday, provided each of you gives written consent. After practice, I would like the opportunity to discuss our program with you. I hope very much that the three of you will visit our university. Please respond at your earliest convenience."

"Wow," Karan said. "That's great, Madison. The only problem is ..." She leaned in for emphasis. "I'm not on your swim team. I haven't trained in almost a year. I don't even remember what it feels like. I know I told you I'd try to get back into it, at least to use swimming as a way to get a scholarship into college. But I've decided I just can't do it. I can't fool people like that recruiter. I haven't trained. Mad, I think I'm done."

"Oh, get a grip, Karan," Madison said dismissively. "You're one of the best high school swimmers in the nation. You just need some more time to recover from the accident."

Alice's heart was beating fast. "I'll meet this lady," she said uneasily. "But, like I've said a million times, I'm planning to stay in Hardrock for college. My stupid parents would probably kill Connie in about ten minutes without me monitoring them."

"Oh, that's a great plan, Alice," Karan quipped. "You'll meet lots of guys at Connie's day care. Or maybe you can settle down with one of those skinny meth addicts who works at a dude ranch."

Madison regarded Alice and Karan with her usual disappointed mom look. Then she brightened. "You guys will change your minds when we all get full scholarships. Just think: we could be college roommates!"

Alice was skeptical that she could ever be anyone's roommate because of her secrets, her selective mutism, and her introverted personality. It suited her to live alone above a garage.

She was also worried she would never have any kind of normal life at all. She had never had a partner, never had sex or even been on a date, and had only just managed to maintain these two friendships. And even if she found someone who was attracted to tall girls with speech problems, how could she ever reveal her secrets or her traumatic past? She couldn't imagine having a partner or a family of her own. It was unthinkable. And her career prospects were equally bleak. Because of her social anxiety and selective mutism, she could hardly stand to be in the same room as anyone else, let alone work with them. The mutism was particularly debilitating. She was improving slowly, with help from her therapist, but Alice still had no idea when she would be able to speak and when the mutism would prevent her. It was like the words were there, at the tip of her tongue, but she couldn't find a way to speak them. She could speak normally to her parents, and now to Madison and Karan, but everyone else was just a big question mark. What career could accommodate that? Maybe she could be a writer (because she loved the library), or just an athlete, or one of those people who sits in a tower watching for fires? Do they have those anymore?

But the email was interesting. It was her first real proof that someone thought Alice Brickstone had promise. Her club swimming coach was always encouraging, but college was different; it was part of the adult world, so it meant more. But on a deeper level, she feared the attention. What would happen if someone on campus found out her secrets? No thanks. Not worth the risk. If she stayed local for college, she could minimize risks by just living at home and remaining more or less a loner. She hoped to persuade at least one of her new friends to stay with her, but judging how excited Madison was about this email, it didn't seem very likely she'd stay at Hardrock too.

Just then, there was a timid knock on the door.

Madison ran over, smiling graciously as she opened it.

"Your guest, ladies," Brian said ceremoniously. "I'm heading home now."

CHAPTER 3

THURSDAY, 7:00 P.M.

SIXTY-EIGHT HOURS BEFORE THE END

Brian turned to go, leaving a terrified-looking boy at the door like a lost dog.

Alice's inner warning bells went crazy; Madison had no right to invite anyone to their sacred place. And what if Alice's mutism kicked in?

Madison pulled the boy inside, glancing at Alice. "You need this," she whispered ominously.

He looked to be around eleven or twelve years old and was tall for his age, but still a head shorter than Madison's five eleven. He wore jeans and a ratty T-shirt. He had his hands behind his back, and Alice noticed that he was trying to hide a manila envelope.

"I'm sorry it is so late," Madison cooed, as though speaking to a far younger child. As the heavy wood door closed, sealing them off from the outside world once again, Madison guided the boy to a seat. "You okay?" she asked.

"Yeah, of course I am!" he said in a high voice not yet touched by puberty. "My mom is fine with me hanging out in the library. She's coming to pick me up at eight. I'm just ... it's cool you could meet with me." He stared at Alice as he sat down across from her, next to Karan. He put his manila envelope on the table in front of him, drawing everyone's attention to it.

Madison sat down next to Alice. "No problem, Asher," she said, looking nervously at the envelope.

"Cool place," he added, appearing to relax a tiny bit. "It's like the Hogwarts library."

"What's in the envelope?" Karan asked with her usual bluntness.

"Well," Asher began, "my mom knows Madison's mom, and that's how I got Madison's number. I'm in this drone club—we fly drones together, you know, like, on missions." Asher's blue eyes shone as he said the word *missions*, but the shine disappeared as quickly as it had come. "And one of the kids in my club went missing this morning. Wyatt Zhang."

"How do you know he's missing?" Madison asked.

"He didn't show up for school. He never misses school. He's a nerd, like me. I just know he's done something crazy. He was—"

Before Asher could say what crazy act Wyatt was considering, Alice interrupted. "Call the cops. This is their job. Their phone number is 911." It came out ruder than she had intended, but she was uncomfortable with the whole thing and angry with Madison for inviting him here.

But instead of shrinking back at Alice's harsh tone, Asher turned to her, his eyes sparkling again. "That's just it—his family called the police already. I went over when they were at his house. I already told them everything. Except ..."

Alice interrupted again, this time attempting a softer tone. "Asher, we're just high school kids. We can't do anything."

He almost smiled, looking up at her with puppy eyes. She tried to stare deep into them, to draw out his thoughts, but she failed. Kids had always been impossible for Alice to read.

"It's ..." Asher looked back at Madison, as though asking permission. She nodded at him to continue. "You found that girl, Kirsty somebody, in the woods last year when no one else could. When not even the police could find her."

Alice felt like throwing the kid out the window, perhaps just to avoid talking about this subject. But she couldn't fault him for knowing about it. It was a small town, and Kirsty's disappearance, followed by her miraculous rescue by Alice, was common knowledge, almost local legend. Afterward, Alice knew some of the stares and whispered comments directed at her were about that miracle rather than her height and speech difficulties. It was nearly a relief, but not quite. Alice was terrified people would eventually find out the truth about how she had managed to rescue Kirsty. And the truth—that she had used her paranormal abilities to find her—was something even Alice herself couldn't fully grasp. All she knew was that she never, ever wanted it to come out.

"What makes you think your drone buddy is lost in the woods?" Alice asked. "Maybe he ran away from home."

"This," Asher said, pushing the envelope over to Alice.

Madison grabbed it before Alice could. She slipped her fingers in, withdrawing a piece of old-looking paper.

Alice leaned over to see. It was a peculiar document. It was about the size of a standard piece of paper, but it was heavy and rough, like parchment. Like something on which you'd find the Declaration of Independence written. The whole top of the page was taken up by a line drawing of a familiar-looking mountain: a twelve-thousand-foot peak in the wilderness north of Hardrock. Alice knew that peak reasonably well. It was named Witchat Mountain because it looked exactly like a lopsided witch hat. It flopped to the right, where a series of massive cliffs fell away into a deep valley. Some of them were popular among rock climbers. The place was a regular feature on Hardrock postcards.

Below the line drawing, someone had sketched some strange figures in the style of Native American petroglyphs. One of them showed a powerfully muscled man with a blank expression and an oversized head like a potato with a thin protrusion on top that leaned to one side. His potato head exactly matched the shape of Witchat Mountain. It seemed he was supposed to be the mountain personified, perhaps the god of the mountain. Next to this strange figure was a much smaller one, crouched down, placing something on a pyramid-shaped pile.

In fancy script, someone had written a rhyme:

I GRANTED YOU HIGH POWER,
  but this came at a cost.
  Those around you grew ill;
  soon, they may all be lost.
  But save them you can!
  Travel to that place
  you learned to conceal
  and leap from the heights
  to embrace the void.
  Only then will you find
  the divine power to heal.

AFTER THE GIRLS passed the parchment around, Karan handed it back to Asher. She turned to Alice and gave a big dramatic eye roll Asher couldn't see. Alice tried to smile, but she was still nervous the discussion would turn to how exactly Alice was supposed to find Wyatt.

Madison folded her hands and gently asked Asher, "Where'd you get this ... paper?"

"It's an important document, and it's Wyatt's. He gave it to me for safekeeping yesterday. He said he'd found the 'place concealed from view' up on Witchat Mountain and was going to skip school today to check it out. He never came home. I think ..." Asher fidgeted. "I think he did it. The leap, I mean. Off a cliff."

"But Asher," Madison said slowly, carefully, narrowing her eyes, "why would anyone believe you could gain healing powers by jumping off a cliff?"

Asher quickly blurted, "I think he was planning to outsmart it. Using a drone, I mean. He only weighs like seventy pounds; he has a huge drone that he rigged up to carry him in a harness. It's the coolest thing I've ever seen. He can totally fly himself anywhere."

"Yeah, I'm sure that's totally safe," Karan commented. "What could possibly have gone wrong?"

"Those cliffs are hundreds of feet high," Madison said, aghast.

"For Wyatt," Asher said, "that risk was totally worth it. His dad died of cancer last month. He can't save his dad, of course, but maybe he thinks he could save other people who have cancer if he had the powers. I don't know."

As soon as Karan heard that Wyatt's dad had died, she stifled a cry and rose abruptly from the table. She turned and took the first book she could find off the shelf and stood there reading, her shoulders shaking.

"It's just how she is," Madison said to Asher as she got up, walked over to Karan, and patted her back gently. "Don't worry, it will pass. Now, what did the police say when you shared this ... document?"

"I can't show them this!" Asher said quickly, still staring at Karan's back. "I mean, I just can't. They'd take it away. They'd think I'm crazy." Asher turned to speak to Alice. "It's, like, Wyatt's prized possession. I don't even know how he got it. He made me promise never to show it to anyone outside our club.

Ever."

"So why are you showing us?" Madison returned to her seat. "We're not in your drone club."

Asher began fidgeting again. "Because ..." He paused, looking down at the parchment. Then he looked up with total desperation in his eyes. "Please, just help me find Wyatt. He's a really nice kid. And he's my friend. Really. Please! You found that other girl, and—"

"We will try, Asher," Madison said quickly, glancing over at Alice. "But, as Alice said, we're likely not going to produce any miracles. And the first thing we should do is to show this paper thing to the authorities to aid their search."

"No," Asher said emphatically, putting it back into his envelope and holding it close to his chest.

Madison urged, "At least you can tell them you heard Wyatt talking about going up to the cliffs."

Asher shook his head and pursed his lips like a five-year-old who wouldn't eat broccoli.

"So if you didn't tell the sheriff any of that, what *did* you tell them?!" Alice asked.

Asher remained silent. Perhaps he was overwhelmed? If so, Alice could relate. But it seemed more likely he was just hiding things from them.

Okay, Asher," Madison consented at last. "But all we can do right now is make one of those lost boy flyers. We can all pass them out at school tomorrow. After school, we can hang them around town."

"No! He's not just lost. He's up there. What if he's all splattered at the bottom of a cliff? Can't you go find him right now?"

"If he's splattered, the only one who can help him is your Mr. Potato Head god," Karan said, still standing with her back to them, her nose in the book.

"If he hasn't come home or been found by the weekend, we

can ask if the search and rescue teams need more volunteers," Madison added.

Asher was gripping his envelope so hard it curled at the edges. He nodded, then left, dragging his feet, clearly disappointed.

CHAPTER 4

FRIDAY, 3:00 P.M.

FORTY-EIGHT HOURS BEFORE THE END

The swim team wasn't meeting this Friday afternoon after school, so Alice, Madison, and Karan fulfilled their promise to Asher and taped up lost boy flyers all over town. Hardrock isn't a big town, and they were able to hit pretty much every traffic light pole, streetlight, transformer box, café, and odd wall where flyers could be hung.

The sun was already threatening to fall behind the ski mountain, and the mountain air was cooling. As they walked by the cheap bars along the river, Madison crossed the street to hang one last flyer, and Alice stayed with Karan. Alice noticed her friend seemed to be shivering and looking around warily.

"You okay?" she asked.

"It's freezing," Karan said, her brow creased. "Also, there are some scary guys following us."

Alice had noticed neither the cold nor the scary guys. It was early fall and she and Madison were still wearing summer clothes. For Alice that meant any old T-shirt and jeans, while Madison wore her usual nerdy goth outfit, consisting of a black skirt and fitted black shirt with some lace. Karan was wearing a shirt with a "WTF?" print. She looked cute, but as a newcomer from the warm Arizona desert, she should have worn more.

Swiveling her head around, Alice saw Karan's guys. They were two local cowboys who had made fun of Alice regularly since she was a little girl. *Fat oaf* was their favorite insult to hurl at her.

One of them raised his eyebrows, gave a fake smile, and waved. It was tiny motion with his fingers like he was a shy little girl.

"Why is it always the skinny guys?" Karan mumbled.

"Hey," Alice said, "they're after me, not you. I know those guys."

"No, they're making fun of me, actually. At least this time."

"Exactly what did they say to you?"

"Nothing loud enough for me to hear. But I bet they were saying I'm a fat circus freak with a face like a baboon's ass. If I had to guess. And they were taking pictures of me. I just ... I wonder what they'll do with those. Is there a dark corner of the internet for misogynist dude ranch laborers?"

"You're not a freak, Karan," Alice said, stooping to pick up a large rock about the size of a brick and heaving it at the guys.

Alice had a strong arm, and her rock was right on target. The cowboy idiots just managed to jump out of the way, acting all puffed up for a second, like they were going to come fight. Then they thought better of it, shouted the usual "Fat oaf!"— and walked away toward the nearest bar.

Karan gave a humorless smile, and they walked along quietly for a moment.

"Alice," Karan asked tentatively, "what would you do ... I mean, how would you feel if someone posted a video of you ... doing what you do? You know ..."

"I would die," Alice responded icily, and meant it. It was the first time Karan had brought this up. They had only known each other for three months, but she was sure her friend knew damn well that discussing Alice's "abilities" was off-limits. Taboo.

Madison's tape gun screeched behind them.

"Who's going to die?" she asked, finishing taping her flyer to a streetlight.

Alice didn't answer, her attention caught by some graffiti on the pole above the flyer. Graffiti was entirely out of place here by the river in a ski town. But even for graffiti, it was disturbing. It was a boy's face, haunting, sallow. And the eyes weren't right. They were too large, and one of them had a vertical, catlike pupil. It reminded her of that eye thing in the Lord of the Rings films. Underneath the eye, the boy's cheekbone was stylized to look like horns, framing the eye. Something about the shading of the whole face made it pop out like it was in 3-D. Alice leaned closer and saw that it was textured with a network of tiny dots rather than solid lines and shapes. She couldn't even imagine how it had been sprayed on, it was so delicately wrought.

As Alice stared at the haunting eye, she suddenly recalled the sucking hole in the mountain in her dream and started to feel sick, like she had eaten something heavy and inedible. She closed her eyes against the face, and yet the nausea continued to grow. Then, just as suddenly as it had come, the feeling dissipated.

Alice sighed and opened her eyes. She suddenly knew that she had dismissed yesterday's nightmare too quickly. It must have been a vision, rather than a nightmare. It had ingrained itself deeply into her mind. So deeply, it was replaying now, as though reaching through time to tell her something about this graffiti.

But what was it telling her? Alice's visions were usually more precise than yesterday's had been. An energy-sucking eye in the mountains somewhere? That could speak? Her messages were often abstract, a mashup of feelings and images of places, but she was sure she had never seen a talking cave before. Certainly not one that wanted to suck her powers out of her. And what did this weird graffiti face have to do with her vision?

"What?" Madison asked, noticing Alice's discomfort while reaching up and contemptuously covering the graffiti with another flyer.

"Nothing," Alice said.

Madison looked from Alice to the flyer. "We never used to have graffiti," she said tentatively, as though probing for the reason behind Alice's *nothing*. "Things have gone downhill a little," she continued.

"Nailed it," Karan said eagerly, rubbing the scars on her cheek. "Yes, this town is crap. But look at the bright side— maybe we're developing an awesome underground art scene. Maybe the tagger is some genius who's going to get famous, and people will come from Paris to visit this streetlight and say, 'Wow, ooh la la, what incredible street art. Better than Banksy.'"

They turned to walk away and were startled by a tall, well-dressed boy who had appeared from nowhere. He had dark hair, close cropped by the ears, longer on top, luxuriously combed over. He wore a black, long-sleeved T-shirt, expensive-looking tight jeans, and shiny leather shoes. Over his shoulder was a leather computer bag that exactly matched the leather on his feet.

Alice recognized him immediately as the Xanax dealer from their high school. He also sold kids other anxiety drugs, but he was mostly known for Xanax. Nobody knew how he managed to get away with it, as he was technically an employee. Maybe other staff didn't know he sold drugs?

Alice thought the skinny cowboys who had stalked her and Karan would take one look at this guy and peg him as an outsider, maybe from the East Coast. Maybe New York. And they would treat him with utter coldness and possibly hostility.

Alice found herself feeling attracted to him. Up close, he even smelled good, like cologne and leather books. It was like he was a walking, talking version of the rare books room. No, that was ridiculous. But there was something about him. Like … like he knew something.

He looked at Alice, and his eyes seemed to confirm that they shared a secret.

"Ladies," he said smoothly. As he smiled, his eyes grew a shade darker. "It appears you have lost someone."

"Huh?" Karan blurted, gaping at him. Did Karan have the same feeling about him as Alice?

As he lifted his chin to the flyer Madison had just hung, his hair bounced slightly.

Finally, one of them found her voice. "His name is Wyatt Zhang," Madison said. "Last seen yesterday morning. His family thinks he's lost in the Knifespur."

"I'm glad you covered up that nasty tag," he said. "I admire you for ignoring all the rumors."

"What rumors?" Alice asked.

"Just a bunch of superstition about black magic. People are saying it's bad luck to cover them up."

"What black magic?" Alice demanded. She really wanted to ask him if he felt the same thing she did when she looked at the tag and a million other questions. That feeling of kinship with him was growing by the second.

He smiled at her gently. "It's just superstition."

"Don't patronize her," Karan commanded, narrowing her eyes.

He turned his dark eyes to Karan and put on an even broader smile that seemed to invite her into his world. "I just heard that if you obstruct one of those graffiti faces, something bad happens to you or your family."

"Oh, come on," Karan exclaimed in exasperation.

"Ridiculous, isn't it?" he said. "There are even rumors that poor kid Wyatt sprayed over a tag just before he disappeared."

Karan guffawed, evidently having overcome her awe of him.

"Yeah. I bet he did, because I totally believe every rumor I hear from drug dealers."

Alice loved Karan's audacity, but she sensed the accusation had hurt this guy. She almost felt a little bad for him. Selling Xanax, after all, wasn't the same as pushing heroin.

"Tyler Rowley," he said, holding out his hand to Karan.

"Hermione Granger," Karan said, shaking his hand vigorously. "And no, I don't require any Xanax today. It is immoral to buy and sell drugs illegally."

"Hey," he said with mock defensiveness. "There are stressed kids out there who need to keep their conditions from their parents. I only point them in the right direction to get some help."

"You should point them toward their doctor. I'm stressed too, but I see my doctor about it. And you know why I'm so stressed?" Alice saw Tyler take a cautious step back. "Because I don't feel safe. What about global warming? Why does everyone in this town have to drive those huge trucks and SUVs? Nobody talks about it. And isn't it fun that one of the largest coal mines in America is located right in our county? Nobody talks about that either."

Tyler took another step back like he was about to leave. "Global warming?" he stammered. "Were we speaking about global warming?"

"Stresses me out, man," Karan added, apparently noticing the effect her tirade was having on Tyler.

"Well, I've got somewhere to go. Pleasure meeting the three of you. And good luck with your flyer hanging. I hope the lost boy turns up." Then he turned and strode away down the street. His butt was quite a sight.

The three girls looked at each other, hesitant to speak for a moment.

Madison finally broke the silence with a "Yuck."

As Alice watched Tyler turn the corner and disappear, she

felt a kind of longing, then shame for feeling something for this guy. A drug dealer, at least five years older than she was. But she remembered his eyes ... could he have felt something for her?

"Let's go," Madison said, packing away her tape gun and remaining flyers of Wyatt. "We have to drive up to Witchat and search those cliffs, and then meet someone tonight."

CHAPTER 5

FRIDAY, 4:00 P.M.

FORTY-SEVEN HOURS BEFORE THE END

While Madison and Karan drove to check out the only section of the infamous Witchat cliffs that was accessible to vehicles, an area popular among rock climbers, Alice stayed back to pick up her sister from day care. Again. As she skated to the other side of town, she began to loosen up and enjoy the sensation of speed. She was riding her electric skateboard as fast as it would take her. A big, tall girl on a long skateboard always drew stares, especially when she passed cars, but she didn't care. It was like she was going fast enough to outrun their judgments.

The day care center, a converted St. Anne-style house on the edge of town near the river, was surrounded by aspen trees, dense and golden with autumn leaves.

Throwing her skateboard onto her back, where it thwacked firmly onto the powerful magnets she had sewn into her backpack, Alice began to walk under the aspens toward the front door. Suddenly, she felt chills run down her back, overcome by the unmistakable feeling that she was being watched.

She spun around and caught sight of a kid across the street. He immediately dashed behind a big pine tree. Even though she got only a glimpse of him, Alice was sure it was a tall kid.

Skinny. Wearing some kind of camera strapped to his head. He looked like Asher.

"Hey, Asher!" she shouted.

When he did not emerge from his hiding spot, she knew something wasn't right.

She pulled out her phone and saw she still had ten minutes before the day care closed. That was enough time to confront him. Alice Brickstone would not put up with some kind of preteen surveillance program.

As she strode across the street, the kid poked his head out and saw her. He bolted from his hiding place, dashing between two houses—definitely Asher.

Alice knew there was a hiking trail back there. She followed and was soon running full speed up the narrow dirt path, lined on both sides by aspens and pines. Despite the heavy load on her back, she began to gain on him.

Asher looked over his shoulder and saw that Alice was going to catch him. He still had options; he could dash into the woods. But that backward glance was his undoing. His foot hit a rock, and he face-planted hard in the dirt. Even from fifty yards away, Alice heard the thump of his head hitting the ground. She sped up, now intending to see if he was okay. But he was more resilient than expected. He picked himself up quickly and dashed haphazardly into the thick marshy grass next to the trail.

It was the perfect evasive maneuver. It had been a wet summer, and the grass was well over the kid's head. By the time Alice got to the place he had turned off the trail, she couldn't see any movement in the grass. It would take her ages to find him in that marsh, and she would be muddy and late to pick up Connie.

She turned and saw something shiny on the trail where he had fallen. Picking it up and turning it around in her fingers, she felt slightly sad for the kid. Not only had he smacked his head pretty good and was probably going to have to explain a fat lip to his mom, he had also lost something precious. It was a replica of something from a Harry Potter movie.

"Hey, Asher," Alice shouted at the grass. "I have your Dumbledore watch." She didn't see any movement. "It's nice. I wouldn't want anyone to take it." Still nothing. "So, I'll hold on to it for you."

She watched the grass for a while longer. It occurred to her that Asher could have passed out, so she extended her feelings toward him. But she sensed nothing terrible, so she left him to his bruises.

She pocketed his Dumbledore watch and walked back to the day care. After signing Connie out, she gave the baby a big sloppy kiss on her rosy cheek and received a glowing smile in return.

As she bundled Connie into a carrier on her chest, Alice cursed her parents for not fulfilling their duties to this innocent little thing. She loved her sister, but she was not her mother.

At least she could offer Connie a thrill. She knew it was a stupid thing to do, but flying her home from day care had become a habit. It had begun as a gesture of defiance, proof to herself that she would never sacrifice her happiness even though her parents were using her as an unpaid caretaker. She was okay with being a sister, but not a nanny. She was no Madison Percival, able to be a model student, a star athlete, and her little sister's nanny all at once. Nor was she like most other kids she knew, who expressed their anger at their parents by taking drugs or breaking curfew. Alice could, however, leap over buildings in a single bound. Well, sort of. Technically, she had to get quite a lot of speed up first, then swim hard through the prana until she could get enough lift to vault a building ... but it was close enough. And she could do it all with a four-month-old baby attached to her chest.

Thankfully, Asher was not hiding behind his tree, filming

her. She hoped he was on his way home to eat a bowl of cereal and ice his head. Taking one last look around, Alice detached her longboard from her backpack and set it on the ground.

Just then, Alice heard an annoying, screechy voice from the door of the day care center.

"Young lady, you are not taking that baby on a skateboard." The day care manager had just emerged. She was tall, thin, and matronly.

"Excuse me?"

"You weren't seriously planning to take her all the way home on that? You live ten miles out of town, do you not?"

"Dad's waiting around the corner for us," Alice lied.

"Walk, then. I won't allow a baby to be carried on a skateboard. Stunning disregard for the child's safety. Just stunning."

"Yes, ma'am," Alice said, just to escape. The lady was technically right; it probably was dangerous for an ordinary person to take a baby on a little piece of wood with a few wheels on it. But Alice was no ordinary person, and the skateboard was only her launchpad.

After Alice rounded the corner, she tossed her electric longboard down again and pushed off down the empty street. She reached into her pocket, took out the hand control, and launched them forward at top speed.

The back street led to a paved bike trail that followed the Hardrock River west toward Alice's house. Alice skated through the more populated areas until the path delivered her safely out of town and out of sight. From there on out, there were no homes, no golf courses, no businesses. Just this paved trail and nature. Maybe a few random dog walkers or the odd fly fisherman, who were easy to spot. The riverside path was lined with overgrown cottonwood trees, shielding it from view of anyone who may be watching from a distance.

Alice stopped and stepped off her board. She pulled a polyurethane leg rope out of her backpack and Velcroed one end around her ankle, then fed the other end through an eye she had bolted to the back of her skateboard. The leg rope was designed for surfboards, but it served her purposes well. She tightened Connie's carrier and gave her a big kiss on the top of her fuzzy head.

As always, visible currents encircled her playfully, whisps of blue and white enticing her into flight. Prana: the magical, energy-like substance that she alone could see and feel. She observed as fast-flowing crystalline currents pushed along the surface of the river, like water above water, and then occasionally jetted upwards, where they mingled with cottonwood branches and then joined powerful pranic jet-streams in sky.

She scanned her surroundings carefully and saw no one—no skinny kids with cameras strapped to their heads, no hikers, and no dog walkers. Alice stopped breathing and listened for any noises. Not hearing anything but the soothing babble of the river and the babble of a baby, she stepped onto her board and kicked hard. Pressing the throttle of her handheld controller, Alice waited until her electric motor pushed the board to top speed, about twenty-five miles per hour. Then she checked the path in front of her and behind her again. Seeing no one, she squatted down on the board, paused, then sprang up, diving straight into the air, trailing her board behind her on the leg rope.

Flying through the air, she felt with both outstretched arms. Prana was there, as always, reaching out to her as readily as she reached out to it. She felt it like a warm, loving presence that would never let her down. It was like water to her, and as usual, she began to swim through it, increasing their speed. She pulled down with a powerful butterfly stroke to propel her and Connie about ten feet up so that they were almost above the trees.

With a practiced movement, she jerked her leg against the

rope, swung her board up in front of her, grabbed it, and reached behind her to attach it to her backpack.

Alice briefly thought about the day care manager and was glad she didn't know about this. If she had been there to see how Alice really brought Connie home, she would have simply dropped dead from cognitive dissonance.

Alice concentrated on feeling the prana against the skin of her arms and her stomach, and the awareness of it intensified. Then she swam as hard as she could for a few more strokes and burst above the cottonwoods. A vast pink sky opened up in front of her. Connie kicked against her stomach, perhaps an expression of her own elation.

Alice gazed at the distant peaks of the Knifespur and decided to take Connie on a detour over Witchat Mountain and do a quick aerial search of the cliffs. Maybe she could find Wyatt safe and sound and get this over with today so they could stop hanging flyers and meeting with strange kids in the library. She didn't know how she would get close enough to the cliffs to see a small boy without risking being seen by him or someone else below, but she wanted to try, at least.

There wasn't a cloud in the sky, so her priority was to fly at least a few thousand feet higher so that no one on the ground could see her. Up there, the air was thin enough that she worried about Connie's breathing, but during past flights, she had noticed no ill effects on the baby.

Once she reached her cruising altitude, she let herself be overwhelmed by the sensation of being alone in the cool pink sky. Vast miles of clean air surrounded Alice on all sides, shimmering lightly with prana and cut by mountain peaks that stretched toward the horizon below. She felt as if she could see forever.

Alice swam along in a relaxed rhythm—something like a slow freestyle crossed with a casual, mermaid-like kicking motion—conserving energy, cruising along at what she knew to be about sixty or seventy miles per hour. She rested her neck by looking down at the tiny homes and ranches that comprised the outskirts of Hardrock. The fat cattle wandering around were little ant-like dots. She could see a few miniature toy cars on the highway, probably heading home.

Soon they were above the Knifespur wilderness, an area designated by the federal government as a minimally managed, vehicle-free and road-free area. Wild, like Alice. She traveled toward Witchat Mountain, just beyond the wilderness area, where she began to see evidence of mining. The Bureau of Land Management owned most of Witchat and leased it to the coal mine. The mining area had all the usual signs of human use. Rather than the dense green-and-brown tangle of the wilderness, here were winding access roads for logging and mining, carefully cut forest firebreaks, and more meandering cattle.

As she crested the summit of the mountain, which was well above timberline, she still neither saw nor sensed anything unusual.

She banked east, where the peak of Witchat flopped toward the south and was cut by a series of massive cliffs. She flew as low as she dared, but the landscape was too fragmented and full of shadows for her to make any kind of careful search.

Thinking it would serve the search effort best to take Connie home and return later, she arched her back and banked sharply around to the southwest. Witchat Mountain gave way to a broad valley.

She circled back over the wilderness area and toward home, murmuring reassuring words to Connie, who was getting cold and restless. She soon started her final approach to her usual landing spot. She descended to the level of the pine trees, scrubbing as much speed as she could. When she was just five feet above the ground, she lifted her chin and arched her back hard, flaring slightly upward while stalling her flight. The practiced maneuver left her a few feet above the grass and slowed her down sufficiently to land in a jog.

Alice took a deep breath, trying to shake off the giddiness of flight, and looked down from the high cliff at her family's cabin, careful not to be seen by anyone below.

Out of habit, Alice walked over to the steering wheel she had planted in the ground nearby. It used to belong to an old VW bus that had been consumed by a fireball. Its owner, Mr. Rao, was the old Indian man who had served as her mentor last year before he had died in the bus, trying to save Alice's life.

She marveled at Mr. Rao's strange life. He had, after all, lived well over a hundred years and had demonstrated a few powers like hers. Well, something like hers—he had never found out about her ability to fly or to heal. She walked behind Mr. Rao's altar and picked up her bike. The bike was just a prop to fool her parents into thinking she had brought Connie home in a standard way.

After strapping Connie into her child seat on the back of the bike, Alice cycled them through the meadow, along the cliff face, and then home on a trail, well worn from daily use.

Dad was out front doing something stupid, as always. Or rather, doing ten stupid things at once. Today, it looked like he was watching a YouTube video on a laptop sitting in the dirt. It was guiding his desperate attempt to fix his old crappy truck. At the same time, he was splitting logs using his massive second-hand hydraulic splitter—which should have had all of his attention, to avoid the inconvenience of losing limbs—while also talking on the phone. The call was probably unrelated to the wood or the truck.

"Hi, Dad," Alice shouted over the hammering of the wood splitter.

"Alice! Hi, darling! Hi, Connie, my little baby! I'll be off the phone in one second."

Alice stood there, listening to him shout into the phone. It sounded like he was talking to a property manager for one of the low-income houses in Detroit in which Dad had invested the last of their savings. He had hoped these investments would produce a steady passive income for them to live off while he worked part-time in a university lab for peanuts. From the tone of his voice and the stress on his face, Alice suspected Detroit wasn't going well.

Then she looked at the pile of split wood and the bigger pile of unsplit wood. She knew Dad was hoping to cut all the wood they'd need for this winter in order to save them money. It was also a point of pride for him. He was trying to be a rugged provider, a capable woodsman, a DIY expert, a car mechanic, the perfect dad, the ideal husband, the frugal head of the household, all at once. He had been none of these things for the past ten years, but Alice knew his heart was in the right place. She was just worried his heart wouldn't last much longer under this kind of strain.

"Looks like that thing just puked a pile of red stuff, Dad." Alice shouted, pointing at the ground under the truck when he had clicked off his call.

"No, no, no, no," he shouted back. "I'm changing the differential oil. I just can't get all the new oil in there. It's awkward, and it keeps spilling out. But not to worry." He looked worried. Very worried. Alice couldn't tell if his biggest concern was the Ford or the rental properties. "By the way, honey, you'd do well to learn this stuff too. Your differential oil will need changing someday."

"I'll take it to Mike to change the barfy red oil properly," Alice shouted, referring to the TV mechanic who had restored her Mustang. "He said nobody but him is allowed to touch it unless it's an emergency."

Her dad reached over and killed the engine on the wood splitter. The silence was sudden. But rather than give Alice his full attention, Dad was staring at a text that had just arrived; probably some lousy news about a property.

Anger surged through her. "Um, excuse me, Dad, but I think Connie needs a change. Is Mom up for something so physically and emotionally taxing?"

"Don't be so hard on your mom," Dad said without looking up. "You know she has postpartum depression. It's no laughing matter."

"Whatever," Alice said. "Dad, I was hoping to go out to dinner with Madison and Karan tonight. We want to go to the old Roadhouse near Witchat Mountain. Would that be okay?"

"Sure," he said, finally looking up from his phone and attempting a smile at Alice, who didn't return it. He let his unnatural smile disappear. Looking squarely at Alice, he said, "I want you to be very careful out there. The Roadhouse can draw some rough characters. And drive very, very carefully. Locals know the police don't go out there, so they don't mind drinking and driving." Dad reached for Connie. "And I'll change Connie myself. But go say hello to your mother before you leave."

"Thanks, Dad." Alice didn't meet his eyes as she handed Connie over.

CHAPTER 6

FRIDAY, 6:00 P.M.

FORTY-FIVE HOURS BEFORE THE END

Having no intention of going in to see Mom, Alice pushed her bike over to her barn.

She opened the insulated garage door to reveal her burnt-orange '67 Mustang. She wasn't into cars in general, but she knew this one was as fast as a Ferrari. It was the last frivolous thing Dad had bought before he had lost his high-paying job at a pharmaceutical company. It was a ridiculous gift for a sixteen-year-old girl in a mountain town with roads that required four-wheel drive half the year. But she liked it. When she looked at it, she got a feeling not unlike the one when she thought about that guy Tyler Rowley from earlier today.

She got into the car and turned the key, and it coughed and hesitated because she hadn't driven it for a week or so. But it roared to life on the second try and settled into its throaty purr after a few minutes. Today she had to drive rather than fly in order to avoid answering difficult questions from Madison and Karan about how she'd gotten to the Roadhouse in the middle of nowhere. Karan's hypothetical about how Alice would respond to someone posting a video of her online had seriously unnerved her. Karan had not come out and said a "video of you flying," but Alice suspected that's what she meant.

She liberated her car from the garage, like letting a primordial beast out of its cage, and accelerated hard down the dirt road that led to the highway.

In autumn, it got dark at about 5:00 p.m., and Alice had to be mindful not to hit a deer crossing the highway toward the river to bed down for the night. It took all of her concentration to drive, for which she was grateful, because it meant she couldn't worry about all the garbage that was in her head. As she neared the Roadhouse, she caught a glimpse of the drilling project through a clearing in the pine trees. During her flyover this afternoon, it had just looked like a big tent and some cars. Now, at ground level, she could see it was some kind of giant canopy over a considerable quantity of shiny machinery, lit up by unnaturally bright spotlights and surrounded by large vehicles. The light from the site reflected off the mountainside like the eerie, silvery glow of a full moon.

Next, a motley collection of houses on five-acre lots came into view. One of them was Wyatt and Crystal's home. These properties were adjacent to a large log building that came to be called the Roadhouse, the only bar and restaurant between Hardrock and the mining town of Johnston.

Alice parked next to Madison's Subaru and let the silence wash over her. No cars were driving by on the highway. She listened for heavy machinery noises from the drilling site up the road but could hear nothing. It was an ominous silence. She recalled the sucking hole in the mountaintop, then put this indecipherable vision out of her mind.

Alice got out of her car and walked warily up to the worn front doors of the Roadhouse. She pushed through into a babble of male voices, which quieted on her entrance. Rough-looking men stared unashamedly at her from their slumped positions on bar stools.

She tried to ignore them and scanned the cavernous room. It was decorated with three retired snowmobiles, which doubled as benches. Oddly, there was no music playing. There were American flags everywhere, and a wall of license plates, and dusty old Wild West memorabilia scattered around. There was a pool table surrounded by men in flannel. Some of the walls were decorated with skis, apparently gifted by famous skiers. There was a massive stone fireplace, which was smoke-stained, cold, and unlit, and a gigantic elk head mounted above it. The lighting was inconsistent; cheap chandeliers lit the center tables, while darkness held the booths around the edges of the room.

Alice reached out with her senses and perceived some kind of unspecified danger. She stared down the drunks at the bar, all of whom eyed her back with undecipherable expressions, and decided they were harmless. The younger-looking men playing pool were too hard to read.

Then she saw a table in the darkest corner of the Road-house. A shadowy figure was staring back at her from beneath unkempt bangs. He looked dirty, unshaven, and unsmiling.

He broke her gaze and looked down at his mug.

Tearing her eyes from this mysterious cowboy, Alice saw her friends on the opposite side of the room. They were beck-oning her to come over.

She waved back but turned away to search for the bath-rooms. She needed to pee and think.

Walking inside the ladies' room was a relief. There was nobody there—no noise, no one staring at her. Except ... as she sat on the toilet, she was shocked to see a terrible face on the wall. It was, she realized instantly, the same graffiti Madison had covered up that afternoon, but in this darker space, lit only by cheap fluorescents, it took on an even more sinister appear-ance. The cat eye was leering at her like ... like it saw something in Alice that she herself could not. Her shock at seeing it trans-formed easily into anger. She flushed the toilet and unraveled a huge amount of toilet paper, wet it in the sink, and stuck it to the wall to cover the face.

As Alice emerged from the bathroom, she found that rogue in the dark corner staring at her once again. She had had enough of people staring at her in this place, and decided to put a stop to it. She strode straight up to him.

"Who are you?" she demanded.

He didn't say anything, but slowly lifted a leathery hand and gestured for her to sit down.

She did not sit. "Well?"

"You should be more careful," he said slowly with a deep voice. Surprisingly, he had a posh British accent, which contrasted strongly with his full cowboy attire. "There are many eyes here. It's dangerous."

"Thanks for the awesome advice and for caring so much. That's called sarcasm in America, by the way. Answer my question. Who are you?"

"My name is Dean. Very pleased to meet you." He didn't offer a hand and didn't seem pleased.

Alice didn't reciprocate with her name. She had a strange feeling this man already knew it. In fact, she suddenly suspected he knew a lot about her, just as she had felt about Tyler. With Tyler, it had felt good. Not with this guy. She asked, "You gonna tell me there's some black magic haunting the graffiti in the bathroom or something?"

His eyes widened.

"Or some dark, evil eye in the mountain?"

He smiled at her for the first time. The smile said, *We're on the same wavelength. You're like me; you feel things that other people cannot feel.* It also communicated a surprising amount of warmth and kindness. His eyes sparkled with an intelligence he had not exhibited before. Then his smile disappeared back under his dirty, rough cowboy mask. "Actually, I was speaking of the normal kind of danger. People in this bar, for instance."

"Who exactly is dangerous in here, besides you? Those guys on bar stools?"

"I'm no danger to you. And those men at the bar work at the drilling site; they're from out of town. They're drunk but mostly harmless."

"I thought coal was dead."

"Don't tell that to those men, and they'll leave you alone."

"Dude, I'm getting impatient. No more games, or I'm calling 911 and reporting that you threatened me."

He looked over at the group of younger men playing pool. "Those boys, for example. They're online trolls, and they post regularly on incel subreddits."

"You mean incel like involuntary celibate? Like, computer geeks who are mad because they can't find anyone to have sex with?"

"Correct. But it's worse than that. In recent days, they have been trolling the family of that poor boy who went missing."

Alice tried to disguise her surprise. "Wyatt?"

"Ah, you know about him? Then you know his father died, but while his mother and sister have been scrambling around on the mountain looking for him, those two gentlemen have been spreading racist stories about them online." He gazed across the room at them. "Very dangerous men indeed."

Alice narrowed her eyes and looked Dean up and down again. "You a cop?"

"No," he said, bringing his attention back to Alice. "I'm a university recruiter. It's my business to know who the most promising young students in the area are, as well as the threats and obstacles they must overcome."

Alice couldn't help but laugh at his claim. "Yeah, I'm sure that's what you are. A recruiter. That's why you're here in a bar in the middle of nowhere, dressed like Roy Rogers."

"I represent an old university in the UK. My recruitment

territory stretches from South Dakota through Wyoming and Colorado and down to New Mexico. I'm based in Hardrock."

"Bullshit," Alice said, smiling and gesturing toward him and his clothes, as if his appearance and presence in the Roadhouse were enough to prove her point.

He remained stoic, his face no longer reflecting the warmth it had earlier. "I have a very high success rate. I believe in quality over quantity." He looked squarely at Alice. "Right now, I know there is a very unique recruit in this area. All signs indicate that this young person will do great things, if provided with the right education."

"By your, um, university, presumably."

"Yes, in fact."

Alice looked into his eyes and tried to read him, but failed to lock onto his thoughts. She shook her head and turned to leave. "I have no idea who you are or what you're up to, but I hope you have a nice time stalking kids on the internet."

"Alice," he said in a low, serious voice that halted her in her tracks. "Be very careful. Those boys are not the only dangerous people in the area. In my experience, great evil is always attracted to its opposite. And I ..." Pausing, he appeared troubled for the first time in their brief conversation. Then he set his jaw and said, "Those boys are acting on behalf of someone else. A person who is highly agitated. And because of that agitation, they are taking big risks. That person is dangerous. Especially to you." He leaned back as though he thought he had said too much, which he definitely had. "I'm sorry for frightening you," he finished, his face resuming its dark cowboy mask, and he cupped his hands around his coffee mug.

Alarmed, Alice demanded, "How do you even know my name?"

"It's my job," he growled without looking up.

"Your job is to know my name and tell me there are guys

after me? But of course, you're not like them. You're here to save me."

When he didn't respond, Alice glared at him, thought about dumping his coffee over his head, realized that would probably make him happy, and wrote him off instead as some kind of delusional weirdo. Perhaps he was an old, psychotic British tourist who used this conspiracy story to pick up young girls. She left him to his coffee and walked to her friends' table.

"Hi, guys," she said, as though she had not just chatted with the scariest-looking man in the room.

"I thought you'd never been here before," Madison said as Alice sat next to her. "Who's the scary cowboy in the corner?"

Alice didn't answer and picked up a menu.

"Seriously, Alice. Who is that guy?" Madison put her huge bony hand on top of Alice's menu, demanding a response.

"I thought I recognized him," Alice said defensively. "I was wrong."

"He looks like Strider from Lord of the Rings," Karan commented brightly. "Maybe he can fight wraiths." She looked to Madison for encouragement, but Madison gave her a hard stare.

Alice smiled at Madison as kindly as she could, then flicked her eyes at the fourth woman sitting at their table in an effort to say, *I don't want to talk about it in front of a stranger.*

"Alice," Madison said, somewhat more formally, "this is Wyatt's sister, Crystal."

Alice nodded at her. She recognized her from around town, as there weren't many Asian people in Hardrock. She was about the same age as Alice and her friends. The dirty jeans, boots, and T-shirt and her smell marked her as someone who worked with horses. She was very beautiful beneath the tragedy written all over her face.

"Hi," Alice said awkwardly. "I hope he turns up." She immediately regretted how flippant she sounded. "Your brother, I mean."

Madison explained, "I asked Crystal to meet with us tonight so she could tell us how best to help her search for Wyatt."

Crystal said desperately, "He's been missing for thirty-five hours." Her voice was hoarse.

"So, have the cops come up with any leads?" Karan asked.

"Search and rescue guys are actually not police," Madison corrected in a pedantic tone. "They're partially funded by the sheriff's department but are an independent—"

"Nobody has found any trace of Wyatt," Crystal interrupted, impatiently knitting her brow. "The only clue we have is his horse. I found her all saddled up yesterday afternoon, wandering near our barn. And then ..." She squeezed her eyes shut.

"And then what?" Madison encouraged.

"We filed a report with the sheriff's office, and then we looked for him all night up on Witchat. This morning, the search and rescue team set up camp near the drilling site and started getting organized to help us search. But they left a couple of hours ago. They pretty much stopped the search. Now I just don't know what we're going to do ..." Crystal covered her eyes with her hand. Alice couldn't tell if she was crying silently or was just exhausted.

"What happened? Why did they stop searching?" she asked, incredulous. She was thinking of her friend Nancy, a scrupulously virtuous but practical officer in the sheriff's department. Nancy would definitely keep searching for Wyatt day and night until he was found. Day and night.

Crystal pressed her eyes with her hands, took a deep breath, and explained, "The sheriff said he had a reliable witness who saw a young Asian boy hitchhiking west last night. There are no other Asian boys in this area, so they think it was Wyatt, and they no longer think he's lost up here in the mountains. They've passed it off to some other department in Utah. And those guys told me they think Wyatt will probably get lonely and come home by himself. They say most runaways do."

"And you obviously don't think that was Wyatt hitchhiking in Utah." Madison rested her chin in her hand.

"It's bullshit. Wyatt wouldn't leave us. Ever. Believe me."

"Why not?" Madison asked.

"Because … because of Mom. After Dad died of cancer last month, Wyatt knows she needs him. We're a very close family. We stick together no matter what."

Alice thought about her own dysfunctional family and wondered what it would be like to stick together no matter what. Then she noticed Karan had turned her head and was quietly sobbing.

"Oh Jesus, Karan," Alice muttered.

Madison went behind Karan's chair and rubbed her shoulders for a second. Then Karan stood up and headed to the bathroom. Alice hoped she wasn't too disgusted by the huge splotch of toilet paper Alice had stuck to the wall.

"Don't worry, Crystal," Madison said quietly as she returned to her seat. "She's had a hard year. So, what do you think really happened to your little brother?"

"Look, Wyatt is ten years old," Crystal said. "Dad's death was hardest on him. The counselors keep telling Mom to have patience with him because everyone grieves in their own way."

"So, what's his way to grieve?" Alice asked.

"Wyatt's been spending lots of time alone in his room, working on his drones. It was a thing he used to do with Dad. He takes after Dad that way—both of them love to solve hard problems, like how to do things with the drones that nobody else has done before. And they were explorers. Before … he wanted to be an astronaut."

"He'll still be an astronaut," Madison reassured her.

Crystal didn't seem to hear. "Yesterday morning, I took him to the bus stop as usual before driving into town for college. I'm an engineering student at Hardrock State, and Dad made me promise I wouldn't drop out after he was ... gone. Mom is a guest manager at a dude ranch up here, and she was already at work that morning. And that was the last I saw of Wyatt. It was thirty-five hours ago."

"What do you think happened after the bus stop?"

"I don't think he got on the bus. I'm sure he doubled back and got his horse, Xingxing, and rode her up Witchat. Something happened up there. Xingxing wandered back home on her own, where I found her when I got back in the afternoon. She had her saddlebags on, and some of Wyatt's drone gear was in them."

"You think he fell off his horse?" Madison asked.

"I don't know. It's possible he was a victim of some kind of targeted racist attack."

"Seriously?" Madison exclaimed.

"You think that's a joke?"

"No, I'm just—"

"As the only nonwhite family up here, we cop a lot of abuse. Just tonight in the parking lot, I got told to go back to China."

"By whom?" Alice demanded, her eyes narrowing.

"Doesn't matter. Look, I gotta go."

Madison held up a hand to stop her. "And what did the sheriff say about that when they called off the search?"

Crystal looked agitated now, and she rose from her seat. "Look, I really gotta go," she said.

"Wait," Madison urged. "We may have some new information. We spoke to a kid in Wyatt's drone club. A kid called Asher."

Crystal froze. "What? Wyatt isn't in any drone club."

"But, um, is he friends with a kid called Asher?"

"No," Crystal said. "I think I know all Wyatt's friends. I'd remember a name like that."

"Tall skinny kid? About eleven?" Alice offered. "Wears a Dumbledore watch?"

"Nope."

"Anyway, Crystal," Madison continued, "Asher claims he knows Wyatt and that Wyatt told him something disturbing on Wednesday, the day before he disappeared."

Madison had Crystal's full attention now. She sat back down.

After Madison described the strange piece of parchment and Asher's suspicion that Wyatt had tried to use a big drone to carry him off a cliff in order to obtain magical healing powers, Crystal seemed even more confused.

"But," she said, eyes narrowed, "Wyatt isn't superstitious at all. He's like a little scientist. He wouldn't ever believe in magical healing powers. This just makes no sense."

Madison didn't have an answer for that. Asher's story had sounded outlandish.

"I'm sure your Asher is just a kid playing games. There's a lot of that going around." Crystal began to get up again. "Look, I've got to go. My mom and all the neighbors who are helping search for Wyatt have decided to meet every evening at this time to compare notes about where we went and what we saw. Tonight is the first meeting, back there in the private dining room. We have a lot of ground to cover, and we have no help from the authorities, so we have to be organized."

Just then, Karan returned from the bathroom looking somewhat refreshed. She tried to smile at Crystal as she elbowed by her.

"We'll help you search too, Crystal," Madison offered. "Karan and I already checked the areas below the Witchat cliffs. You know that rock climbing spot? We didn't see him."

Alice thought that wasn't a very tactful thing to say. The

implication was obvious: the girls had been looking for a body. Maybe with magpies and foxes feeding on it.

But Crystal seemed unfazed. Pulling something out of her back pocket, she said, "Great. Let me show you something." She unfolded a local topographical map and smoothed it out on the table. It featured some carefully drawn colored lines, each with dates and times written next to them. "Here's what you can do. Go buy one of these local topo maps from the bartender. Note exactly where you searched, like this. Come to the back room and show us when you're done, and we'll assign you some new areas to cover tomorrow. If you have time."

"How many miles of trails are up there?" Karan asked.

"There's one main trailhead up past the drilling site. But there are dozens of smaller unmarked trails that cross private property. Overall, there are more than two hundred miles of trails to cover. Probably more like three hundred, if you consider all the little game trails up there. There are five of us, plus you guys."

More like four hundred miles, Alice thought to herself. Game trails—those made by animals—were literally everywhere in places like Witchat Mountain. This search was going to take more than a week. At least from the ground.

CHAPTER 7

FRIDAY, 7:00 P.M.

FORTY-FOUR HOURS BEFORE THE END

Alice could still feel the anxiety that had radiated from Crystal's body, as if it had left an imprint in the air.

Then she saw the guys at the pool table pulling back the corners of their eyes with their fingers and strutting around in a bad imitation of what might have been Asian fashion models. Some of the drunks at the bar were leaning over their beers, shuddering with laughter while pretending not to.

Karan had obviously seen them making fun of Crystal too, and she abruptly jumped up. Before Alice or Madison could stop her, Karan strode over to the pool table and accosted the young pool-playing clowns. Alice couldn't hear every world, but she thought she heard Karan say something to the effect of, "One more racist or misogynist gesture, and I'm going to report you to the police for harassment,' at which the guys guffawed. Then, as Karan stood there unwavering, towering over them, they grew a bit serious. One of them pointed a pool cue at her and said they were "true patriots" defending the great "U.S. of A" from "you lefty jokes."

Alice got up to support her, but Karan seemed to have sensed the violence in the air and walked away, fury written red all over her scarred face. She sat down and boiled for a moment before asking, "Am I a lefty joke?"

"Are you serious?" Madison said. "You just did the bravest thing I've ever seen you do, defending Crystal like that. You're definitely no joke."

"How 'bout the lefty part? How would they even know anything about my politics?"

"No idea," Madison said. "Maybe because you defended Crystal. Plus, they probably think everyone from Hardrock is politically left-leaning, at least compared to the people from Johnston. It's a coal town. They all rely on the mine for their jobs. Naturally, their political views on energy and climate change are different from ours. Don't worry about it."

"Yeah, but even if they're from Johnston, why would they assume I'm from Hardrock and not from Sweden or the moon or Topeka? I was prepared for them to call me a mutant ass-faced cow, not assault my politics." After a pause, Karan smiled a bit. "I'm actually kind of flattered, all things considered. Wait, is that twisted and wrong?"

Choosing not to think about whether Karan should be flattered for being called a lefty instead of an ass-faced cow, Alice looked at her phone. The email from the coach of the vaunted swimming program was still open. It seemed distant now, forgotten like a weather prediction from last month that was demonstrably wrong.

Without discussing it with Madison first, Alice dialed her friend, the deputy sheriff.

"Hi, Nancy," she said, looking sideways at Madison. "Why did you guys quit looking for Wyatt Zhang up on Witchat?" She put the phone on speaker so the girls could hear Nancy's response. Which wasn't going to be pretty, she predicted.

Nancy paused, then growled into the phone like a wild animal before finally saying, "Alice, if I find out you're interfering in police business again, I will literally kill you."

"Look," Alice said confidently. "All we've been doing is hanging lost boy flyers. It's just that Madison knows Crystal, Wyatt's sister. Crystal says her brother would never run away. She says the hitchhiking story is crap."

Nancy didn't respond to this, but at least her growling stopped.

Alice took that as encouragement for her to continue. "And we also know this kid, Asher, who says he's in a drone club with Wyatt. Asher claims Wyatt was obsessed with the cliffs up on Witchat. You guys should totally be looking at the bottom of all those cliffs. There are miles of them up there. You need a helicopter or something."

After a pause and a deep breath, Nancy finally answered in a clipped, robotic voice. "Alice, thanks for the information. Please send me Asher's details. And I'm choosing to take this as a tip rather than an egregious breach of trust. Because you know I am trusting you and your friends to stay out of police affairs, to leave policing to the police. I am trusting you not to act as a vigilante ever again. I'll see you at your parole tomorrow." She was referring to Alice's mandatory weight lifting sessions with Nancy twice a week. Last year, when someone at the sheriff's office was insisting Alice be brought in on obstruction of justice charges, Nancy defended her on the condition Alice committed to these gym sessions.

Alice stared at the phone. Nancy had hung up.

"Wow," Karan said, having recovered from her argument with the incel guys.

Alice leaned back in her chair, overcome once more by her nightmarish sense of impending doom. It had nothing to do with the call with Nancy or the racist jerks, who had gone back to their pool game. It had nothing to do with Crystal, who had disappeared into the back room, either.

Alice looked toward the dark corner where Dean was sitting

and saw him sit up straight, looking at Alice with apparent concern. She wondered if he could feel it too.

Just then, Alice's phone rang, and she picked it up with a sense of foreboding.

"Hi, Dad," she said uneasily.

"Honey," he said in an urgent voice that startled Alice even more, "where are you?"

"I'm out with Madison and Karan. What's wrong? You don't sound like—"

"Alice, something's happened. Can you come to the hospital right away?"

"What is it, Dad?" she said with alarm, rising from her chair. Her heart was beating fast, and she could feel adrenaline surging through her.

"Connie is sick," Dad said, his voice breaking.

"She was fine an hour ago," Alice said like an accusation, the panic taking over. She couldn't help but feel some of the trauma caused by the murder of her brother ten years earlier. Was it all starting again? Had someone tried to kill Connie?

Madison looked at her with alarm.

"We're in the ER. The doctor thinks she ate something off the ground. A pill ..."

"I'm on my way." Alice pocketed her phone, already moving toward the door.

She felt a firm hand on her wrist from behind.

"What happened?" Madison asked.

"Connie's in the ER. I gotta go."

"I'll come with you," Madison said.

"No," Alice said firmly. Because she planned to fly there, not drive. Alice took a deep breath, focused all her energy, and gave Madison the most reassuring smile she could muster. It took a nearly inhuman effort to do so, and she probably looked like she'd stepped on a nail.

Madison responded to Alice's effort with a smile of her own. Something wordless passed between them, and she finally agreed. "Okay. We'll wrap up here and be right behind you."

Alice ran out the front door.

CHAPTER 8

FRIDAY 7:30 P.M.

FORTY-THREE AND A HALF HOURS BEFORE
THE END

Bursting out of the front doors of the Roadhouse, Alice scanned the area for some way she could gain the speed she needed to take off. She didn't have her longboard, and there were no cliffs nearby. The Witchat cliffs were a two-hour hike away. She thought of the suicide spot, which was only a five-minute drive, but she balked at the thought of leaving her car parked there. Her friends would see it from the highway and think she had jumped.

Resigned to driving instead of flying, she ran to her car, got in, and started up the V8.

She almost reversed straight into an old man who had appeared right behind her parking spot. She slammed on the brakes, but he seemed not to have even noticed her car. Which meant he was either blind drunk or deaf (or both), as Alice's car was very, very loud. He just kept walking while staring intently at the ground.

She looked at her phone, and the clock said seven thirty p.m. Her heart skipped a beat as she thought of her innocent, cherubic baby sister dying in a hospital. Maybe already dead.

Then she got an idea.

Killing her engine, she jumped out of her car and ran to

where the drunk guy had gotten in his own truck. It was an old Dodge with an oversized flatbed, currently with nothing on it.

He pulled out of his parking spot, put it in gear, and began to drive slowly toward the highway.

Alice following him stealthily on foot, and before he accelerated onto the highway, she lightly jumped up onto his truck bed. There she squatted low, holding on to a nylon tie-down.

As she suspected, the old man didn't seem to notice anything unusual. Alice was impressed he could actually drive straighter than he had been walking. He simply accelerated to about fifty miles an hour, the speed limit on this stretch of road.

It was all the speed Alice needed.

She took a deep breath, feeling for the prana around her. Then she pounced straight up into the air, catching the wind and prana full force with her chest and stomach.

After two strong strokes, she was climbing steadily into the sky, picking up speed. Far below her, she saw the truck driving straight as an arrow along the highway, getting smaller every second.

Thinking of Connie, who was perhaps taking her last breath right that second, Alice tried to speed through the air faster than she ever had before. The effort failed, and she lost contact with prana. This had happened a few times in the past in moments of panic. She knew her connection to prana depended upon her being relaxed and focused. She was currently anything but relaxed and focused. As she dropped from the sky, she thought of Connie, dying in the ER.

She took a deep breath and closed her eyes against the sight of the ground coming up to meet her. "Come on, Alice, concentrate."

Immediately she could feel prana again. Rediscovering its warm, reassuring presence on her skin, she opened her eyes, ignoring how close the ground loomed, and resumed her long, steady strokes. She swooped so low, she nearly scraped her stomach on the highway—not too far, in fact, in front of the drunk in his flatbed truck. She hoped he was too blind drunk to see anything out of the ordinary.

Soon she regained altitude and was back up to her usual top speed, perhaps even a bit faster.

She reached the hospital after a ten-minute flight. Descending as quickly as she dared, she saw the circular marks of the helicopter pad. She headed straight for it, knowing it would be located close to the emergency room.

She made a very clumsy landing, failing to flare correctly, and tumbled roughly to the concrete. But she rolled, gracefully jumped to her feet, and ran toward the doors near the helipad.

"Where's Connie Brickstone?" Alice asked the night receptionist while tripping over her own feet.

"I'll buzz you through," he responded without even glancing at her.

She immediately saw her mom and dad near a bed and ran over, somehow managing not to trip again.

Connie was a terrible sight, but she appeared to be alive. She had a respirator over her mouth and nose. It looked huge compared to her tiny head, highlighting the puffiness of her eyes. IVs and wires snaked around her.

Alice's dad jumped out of his chair and took her into his arms.

"She's okay, she's okay," he repeated in her ear.

Mom was hugging her too now. Alice didn't welcome her mom's embrace, as she felt a rush of anger at her. Last time, when Thomas was murdered, it had mostly been her Dad's fault. He had gotten involved in a situation in India that had fatal consequences. Alice guessed this time it was just pure negligence by her mom.

"What happened, Mom?" Alice asked accusingly, trying hard to arrest her own crying. She stuck a finger into Connie's little hand but received no reassuring squeeze in return.

Her mom had obviously been crying desperately before Alice arrived, and the tears began again now.

"It was *not* your mom's fault, Alice." Dad's face was stern, his eyes dry.

"It was my fault," Mom finally said, her face twisted in self-recrimination.

"Of *course* it wasn't," Dad said firmly. "Your depression just got worse. It was my fault for not—"

"No!" Mom shouted, then covered her face with her hands, as though disgusted with herself. She quickly recovered and got a determined look on her face. "I … I have to tell you both the truth. I …"

"What truth, Mom?" Alice glared.

"Nathan," Mom said, apparently unable to meet Alice's eyes, "I stopped taking my antidepressants two months ago."

"What? You mean when you went to see that Ayurvedic doctor? What was her name? Claire?"

Mom nodded.

"But you told me she just gave you some natural remedies to replace your antianxiety medicine. We agreed your antidepressants were essential."

Hearing Mom trusted some fake doctor over a real one made Alice livid. She wiped her eyes and stared fireballs at Mom. "You've been trusting some witch doctor with your health? And Connie's?"

"It's traditional Indian medicine, Alice. Please let your mother talk."

Mom continued, still avoiding Alice's eyes. "Claire was horrified by the toxic cocktail of medications they had me on. I was so embarrassed. I'm supposed to be a yoga teacher! Why should I pour all those chemicals into my body? She convinced me to stop everything, and … I took all of my meds to the drug drop box at the sheriff's office. "

"Everything?!" Dad asked. "Even the antidepressants?"

"Yes. But Nathan, it worked! I was feeling like myself again. Even *you* noticed."

"Well ..." Dad said, obviously conflicted.

Alice had NOT noticed any improvement, and suspected her mom had just been fooling herself. "So, if you were miraculously cured, Mom, what turned you into a total zombie a few weeks ago?"

"After starting Claire's new program, I started having panic attacks again."

"And you didn't tell me?" Dad asked.

"But Nathan, the depression was still gone! It was only the anxiety that came back. I really thought I could handle it. I wanted to prove to myself I could do this on my own."

"How did you *handle it*, Mom?" Alice asked, her voice dripping with scorn.

"I ... it sounds so stupid now. The website Claire suggested I use to buy my Ayurvedic remedies ... I saw that they also sold Xanax. I bought a small amount to help me get back on track."

"But honey, why didn't you just go back on your original medications? Or at least go see Dr. Johnston to prescribe something else?"

"I told you, Nathan—I *hated* all those chemicals. And I didn't want Dr. Johnston or anyone else to tell me to take even more. Who knows what he would have thought if I'd told him I wasn't taking the antidepressants anymore?"

Alice suddenly remembered Karan saying she'd seen Mom at the sheriff's office just last night. The timing didn't make sense.

"Wait, Mom, you're saying you took all those medications to the drop box a month ago?"

"Yes."

"Then why were you there again last night?"

Mom broke down again and began crying so hard she couldn't answer the question. Dad patted her back while Alice fumed, listening to the ventilator that was keeping Connie alive.

Finally, Mom wiped her eyes and said, "There was ... something different about the new Xanax I received. It turned me into ..."

"A frickin' zombie," Alice offered.

"Yes. I knew something was very, very wrong, but I couldn't stop taking it. Nathan, you can't imagine the torment. I hated it so much. I knew those pills were eating away at my soul. I knew they were taking me away from you three. I could see it. But I couldn't stop."

"So what did you do, Mom?"

"Last night I was desperate." Mom finally met Alice's gaze. "I saw the look on your face, Alice, after I asked you to pick up Connie from day care. Your eyes said everything. Your eyes told me what I had become. I felt like I was about to lose you. All of you. I knew I had to do something drastic, or I would disappear into those pills forever. "

"Victoria, what happened?" Dad had a terrified look on his face, like he was unable to accept what he was hearing.

"I took a hammer to the pill container. It was senseless and stupid, and I can't even explain it. It sounds so ridiculous."

"So you're an addict, Mom."

"Worse, Alice. I'm a killer."

"Victoria! Don't be—"

"I tried to clean up the stupid mess I had made of the pills, and I took them to the sheriff's drop box. But I must have missed one ..." Mom was lost in her tears again.

Alice looked from Mom to Connie. "I want to speak to the doctor," she demanded.

"We're waiting for her too, sweetheart," Dad whispered as he held his shuddering wife. "We're about to get some test results back."

"I have some news for you," a voice said from behind them.

"Doctor Leppan," Dad said, turning.

"Are you the sister?" she asked Alice, who nodded.

"Okay, so we know what Connie ingested," she said. "It was a combination of Xanax and the potent synthetic opioid fentanyl."

"But … fentanyl?" Dad said stupidly.

Dr. Leppan looked at Alice's mom. "Who is your doctor?"

"Doctor Johnston over at Hardrock Medical," Mom managed.

"Are you suffering from any pain? Were there any complications with Connie's delivery?"

"No," Alice's mom said meekly.

"Xanax is a common antianxiety medication, but fentanyl is a highly addictive opioid painkiller. It's a hundred times more potent than morphine. It's only prescribed legally in patch form; powders and pills have been prohibited as part of the battle against opioid addiction. Xanax laced with fentanyl is highly addictive and quite illegal." After a pause, she asked, "Which pharmacy fills your prescriptions?"

Mom's face crumpled again. "Those pills weren't from Dr. Johnston. I … I bought them on the internet. But I was just trying to buy regular Xanax, I swear."

Dr. Leppan nodded solemnly, as though Mom's answer was the one she had expected. In a reassuring voice, she said, "Unfortunately, we have seen quite a bit of this stuff in the ER lately. You are not the only one who has fallen prey to those online schemes—not by a long shot. The people who sell this stuff are predatory and very smart. They don't sell the laced product to everyone for fear of attracting too much attention. Instead, they choose a few of you, get you hooked on their product, and hope you'll stay alive and keep buying from them. What I'm saying is that you seem to have drawn the short straw."

"What about Connie?" Alice asked. "What does that fentanyl crap do to a baby?"

Dr. Leppan looked gravely at Alice.

"The fentanyl your sister ingested caused an instant overdose. By the time first responders arrived, her brain had probably been starved of oxygen for a minute or two. But she was lucky. Your mom's 911 call happened to get patched through to a neighbor of yours, an off-duty firefighter, who rushed to Connie's aid. He saw something that made him suspect an opioid overdose, and he administered a small dose of naloxone, which saved her life. He is a hero. He successfully resuscitated her and brought her in. She is, however, in a coma, and only time will tell whether she will improve." Dr. Leppan looked at Connie, motionless and exposed in the oversized hospital bed. "I'm optimistic. She seems like a strong kid, and her angels are obviously watching over her."

The doctor looked back at Alice's mom. "Mrs. Brickstone, may I speak to you privately?"

Alice's mom and Dr. Leppan walked away, leaving Alice and her dad and the beeping and sucking noises of the equipment keeping Connie alive.

"I'm sure there's another explanation," Dad said to Alice. His voice was weak now.

"That is so ... !" Alice thumped her leg hard and stifled an angry scream. "How could Mom be so stupid? How could you not have noticed? Why are your kids always paying for your mistakes?"

Alice saw that Dad looked ready to implode or burst into tears or both, and she realized she was going to have to be the strong one. She went and got three disgusting instant coffees from the kitchenette attached to the ER.

When she returned, Mom was back, looking even more embarrassed and unwell. She was grateful for the coffee and probably even more grateful for Alice's silence.

"The doctor is recommending I get ... tested for fentanyl in my system. She suspects I may be addicted, judging from my symptoms. If so, I'll need treatment. This is going to cost so much money ... I just can't believe this happened." She turned to Connie, covered her mouth with her hands, and crumpled into Alice's dad's arms.

"This is not the time to think about money," Dad lied. Alice knew he was thinking about money as well. They didn't have much. She knew they had health insurance, unlike lots of people she knew. But their policy had a large deductable, and she suspected they'd be paying a ton of money for all that methadone. And what did being in a coma cost? She was glad, at least, that she didn't have to figure that out.

Watching her parents in their despair and feeling a large amount of it herself, Alice began to grow faint. She walked back to the kitchenette to get some packs of sugar cookies and suddenly thought of Tyler, their high school Xanax dealer. Could he have anything to do with Mom's pills? But no, he couldn't—she'd gotten hers from some dodgy website, not from someone in town. But that stuff he'd said about the graffiti, how defacing it brought bad luck ... could there really be a curse on that graffiti face with the weird eyes? Was that why Connie was in a coma? But surely Alice didn't believe in black magic, did she?

Alice rushed back and demanded her mom tell her what website she used to buy the laced Xanax, and her mom meekly complied. Alice called it up and saw it did, in fact, look like a normal online shopfront, with 100% quality guarantees, secure purchasing, and fancy branding. It could have nothing to do with the Xanax sold by a local IT guy at her school.

Then, re-pocketing her phone, she thought of Dean, the weird English cowboy at the corner table. He had warned her there were some "really dangerous people around" and that he thought something bad was about to happen to Alice. Had he foreseen what happened to Connie? And another thing—just before Dad had called with the news, Alice had been overcome by a powerful sense of foreboding. She had looked at Dean and noticed that he seemed to sense something too.

She ate her sugar cookies and tried to shake off these useless thoughts. There was no such thing as dark magic. Nobody shared her ability to read prana. Not some Xanax dealer named Tyler, and not an English cowboy named Dean. She was just tired and grasping for answers.

She filled a foam cup with water and drank it down, feeling a bit less faint. She closed her eyes and took a deep breath, but all she could see in her mind was that awful graffiti face.

CHAPTER 9

FRIDAY, 9:00 P.M.

FORTY-TWO HOURS BEFORE THE END

After pacing around the hospital for a while, Alice realized she just had to know. Was there some kind of black magic around the face? Had it caused Connie's accident? What did Tyler know about it? What did Dean know?

She had no way of finding Tyler, but she knew precisely where Dean was. And if he knew something—anything—about how Connie had ended up overdosing tonight, Alice wanted to know. Now. Anything was better than hovering here in this bleak place with her mom and dad.

"Guys," Alice said to her grieving parents, "I have to go move my car. I may grab a bite to eat too. Can I get you anything?"

"No, thanks, sweetheart," Dad said.

Mom didn't say anything.

Alice chucked her instant coffee into a garbage can with a thunk, and coffee splashed onto the wall. She found an elevator and took it to the top floor. This mountain hospital was only four stories tall, but that would have to do.

She stepped out to the roof, and without even looking down, she flung herself out into the dark night.

A ten-minute flight later, she landed at the Roadhouse and

found her Mustang where she'd left it. Madison's car was gone. The Roadhouse's lights were still on, and there were four old trucks out front. She noticed that the flatbed she had hitch-hiked on was back in its spot; the driver must've been inside putting away more beer. She was impressed with his stamina. She hoped one of the other trucks belonged to the English cowboy and that he was still at his corner table.

Pushing inside, she found much the same scene as before, only quieter.

There were four guys at the bar, one of whom was the old guy with the flatbed. The same football games were playing, and the same bartender was shuffling around behind the bar. As before, the conversation went quiet as soon as she entered, and all eyes were on her.

She didn't care; all she wanted was to talk to Dean.

Unfortunately, he was no longer hiding out at the corner table.

"Do you know that cowboy who was sitting in the corner?" Alice asked the group at the bar.

"You mean that Brit?" the bartender asked warily, sizing up Alice.

"That's the one."

"He's here on occasion. Mysterious wanderer."

"Can I talk to you in private?" Alice asked the bartender.

He nodded grimly at her, then looked at his customers. "You boys all right for a moment?"

All the drunks nodded without falling off their stools, grinning hugely at the bartender as though they were all in on some private joke. The bartender sat with Alice at a table in the middle of the room.

"What did he do to you?" the bartender asked.

"Nothing. I just need to speak with him."

"Ah. That's different. I assumed you—"

Alice locked eyes with the man, who froze mid-sentence.

Reading minds was something she understood to be a highly unique ability, almost as rare as flying. It involved reading prana as it flowed through the person's thoughts. It came easy to her, but the process was always disgusting.

This guy's head was no exception. She wasn't surprised to see he was mentally undressing her, and it was not pleasant. Yet she pressed on. He thought she was ... beautiful. He especially admired her eyes, like those of a much older woman, like a movie star. Dismissing these as thoughts of a lonely bartender, she searched for what he knew about Dean. She saw that he had the impression Dean was a criminal. No one knew where he lived. Up north in Wyoming, rumor had it. Drove a green Ford F150 truck with Wyoming plates. He'd left the Roadhouse about thirty minutes ago, probably heading north to Wyoming.

Alice broke the link and watched as the bartender shook off the fogginess her reading had caused. He wouldn't remember spacing out for a moment; no one ever did (except Mr. Rao).

"All I can tell you, young lady, is that you should stay far away from that man." He stood to return to the bar. "And by the way, how old are you?"

She ignored his question and walked out of the Roadhouse.

She wanted to get airborne again.

A glint of metal caught her eye near the back corner of the Roadhouse. She ran toward it and was gratified when it revealed itself to be a ladder leaning against the roof. She recklessly scampered up. She crawled up the steep slope of the roof to the pinnacle, making enough noise that even the drunk guys inside probably heard something. She looked down the roof and surveyed her best approach. Finding none, she simply began to run and took a flying leap off the eave.

It was just enough speed and height to allow her to find purchase in prana, and she swam through the air just above the ground. She gained enough momentum to swim upward and above the trees. A few grazing horses watched her with alarm, but no humans seemed to have borne witness to her latest small victory over gravity.

She must find that weird cowboy and learn everything he knew. A voice in the back of her head told her this was stupid and that she should go straight back to the hospital, but she ignored it.

She began hunting above the highway like a predator. Like a raptor. She knew Dean drove a green Ford truck, just like her dad's. It would be easy enough to inspect every single vehicle on the road from this height.

There were only a few people out tonight. The cloudless sky was bright; the moon even cast shadows of the roadside pine trees.

After checking each vehicle up close and finding no pickups, Alice reached her first crossroads about ten miles north of the Roadhouse. The main highway went north a couple of miles to Johnston, the coal-mining town where most of the locals who drank at the Roadhouse lived. Past Johnston was the endless expanse of Wyoming. To the west was the long stretch of two-lane highway on which Wyatt had supposedly been seen hitchhiking to Utah.

Dean was supposed to have continued up north to Wyoming, so that was where Alice headed.

The night grew darker as the beginnings of fog embraced the moon and stars. The road she flew above was unpaved and overshadowed by pines and aspens. A green pickup could easily be pulled off anywhere, the cowboy sleeping across the back seats, and she wouldn't see it.

Perhaps it would be easier to go back and hunt for Tyler instead, even if he had nothing to do with Connie's pill. Alice felt a confusing pulse of excitement when she remembered Tyler's face, his smell. She hated feeling confused and hated herself for being excited by a man at this moment—a man who would never, ever be excited about her.

She grew angrier and more frantic. Imagining Connie all pumped up with drugs and breathing with the help of a machine, Alice lurched forward and paid for it by quickly losing altitude. She took a deep breath and forced herself to calm down, but this time it was much harder than usual. Her nerves were fried, her body exhausted.

And then she realized she was truly in danger. She was breathing raggedly, and her muscles were failing. The warm embrace of prana had utterly deserted her, and she was falling. As a normal human should.

Just before she plummeted below the treetops, she saw some blinking lights in the distance and registered the presence of a town ahead of her.

And then she hit the gravel road, and everything went black.

CHAPTER 10

FRIDAY, 10:00 P.M.

FORTY-ONE HOURS BEFORE THE END

"Alice."

She was dreaming, and in her dream: a voice. She was in an airplane and could hear the whine of the jet engines and the buzz of chatter among the other passengers.

"Alice."

The voice again. Was it a flight attendant? Had she been in the bathroom too long? Were they about to land? Where were they landing?

"Just try to breathe."

Wait. Why would a flight attendant know her name? Why would he need to tell her to breathe?

She tried to open her eyes and was met with a crushing pain across the whole front of her body.

"Get it off me!" she gasped, hoping the flight attendant could lift the heavy weight off her. Had the plane crashed?

"There isn't anything on you. You've been injured."

She registered now that the voice had a British accent. But she couldn't be on an airplane in a state of grievous injury. Unless she was being evacuated on a plane?

She realized she could move her hands, and she tried to remove the weight from her face.

But when she touched her face, there was nothing there but her own skin. Her hands could feel it, but her face couldn't feel her hands in return.

She felt for her eyes and found them. She was able to open her right eye with her fingers, and suddenly the feeling came back in the whole front side of her body.

And that feeling was not a happy one. It was heavy, throbbing, violent pain.

She sat bolt upright, both eyes open, ready to fight or run.

But she could do neither. She was in the back of a moving vehicle, driven by the English cowboy. He was driving very fast and had a look of desperate concern on his face.

"I have taken the liberty of peeling you off the road and placing you in the back seat. At least, most of you—I had to leave some of your blood and skin back there in the gravel. We're heading to Johnston, where they have a medical clinic. It's after ten, but I'm hoping we can wake someone up and get them to see you."

"Let me out of this vehicle right now."

He looked back at her, and his mouth dropped open in shock. "How did you heal so quickly? You were ..."

He slowed the truck down and put it in park.

"I thought you were dead, in fact. Or near death." He cleared his throat, continuing to gape. "You are welcome to leave. I was only trying to help. But you must realize you were in quite a serious accident."

Alice sat there for a second, conflicted. She remembered where she was and why. She had been looking for this very person, Dean, who had somehow found her instead.

She looked down and saw she was covered with a dirty blanket. Lifting it up, she saw that her pants were so torn, she was nearly naked, and her shirt was in a similar state. She was covered in blood, but her wounds had healed over nicely. She touched her face again and felt dried blood there too, but those wounds and bruises were also manageable. She was still in a fantastic amount of pain, but she thought she could walk if she had to.

Her phone was still in her back pocket. Although the screen was cracked like a spider's web, it seemed to work. There were about ten messages from Madison, the latest consisting of only a question mark. She desperately wished Madison were here right now. But there was no signal in this remote spot.

"Okay," Alice began. "Tell me how you found me out here. And then you can tell me how you knew something was wrong when I got that call from my dad earlier tonight. And then you can tell me everything you know about those bad people you said were out to get me. And then you can tell me about black magic, or whatever put my sister in a coma tonight, and I'll let you drive me to Johnston." She immediately realized she sounded insane.

Dean smiled, and it was that gentle smile that had warmed her in the Roadhouse. It seemed like ages ago.

"I have abilities," he said, "just like yours. Well, I take that back—nothing like yours. I've never seen anyone heal so quickly. But my skills come from the same source. You and I can both sense things. I believe we're both sensing the presence of a powerful person driven by ego and malice. He or she is operating in this area and is desperate. I don't know anything specific about black magic or about your sister. Still, I believe you are sensing the same presence I am."

"What abilities do you have, exactly?"

"I can see glimpses of the future. Or rather, I can sense the future, and if I trust my instincts, I can predict certain outcomes well enough to lend assistance. I had a feeling I would find you in a bad way on this road tonight, and I did."

"What else?"

"I'm dashingly attractive. I'm a rather good archer. And I can sense people's thoughts, but only vaguely. I know people who can see into the minds of others so clearly it's as if they're looking at a computer screen. I believe you have that skill, Ms. Brickstone."

"How would you know that?"

"I was in contact with a friend of yours, Mr. Srikrishna Rao."

Alice sat straighter. She sensed danger, or at least an egregious invasion of her privacy. Mr. Rao and his shrine on the cliff above her cabin were her secrets. Sometimes she even questioned whether he had really existed.

Then she began to suspect something about Dean. Perhaps this man with the smile and the ragged long hair and the posh British accent and the strange power that had enabled him to find her ... maybe *he* was the real source of the bad energy she had sensed earlier. She looked around and saw a toy bow and quiver of arrows on the floor of the car. They looked harmless, but she didn't care to find out if he was armed with anything more serious. She had been in bad situations with strange men before and had barely survived them.

"Okay, I need to get out now," she said.

"Alice, I am not here to hurt you. I promise from the bottom of my heart, I am only here to help."

"What help could you give me? I've met lots of men like you. They all offered to 'help.' None of them actually helped me. In fact, it's my experience that all men in positions of power say they want to help young women, but all they really want is to sleep with them or use them to prop up their own egos. And I'm warning you right now, man—reading minds and healing fast are not my only abilities. I'm also quite good at smashing people," she lied.

"I don't doubt it, Alice, and I don't intend to give you any cause to smash me."

"So what, then? Spill it. If you really knew Mr. Rao, you

would know I'm not a big fan of riddles or mansplaining, or any kind of bullshit, really. Why are you here?"

"I did know him, and Mr. Rao approved of my intention to seek you out eventually. My name, as I've already told you, is Dean. Dean MacRae. And as I explained to you in the Roadhouse, I'm a recruiter for a special university for talented young people like yourself."

"What?" This was sounding more ridiculous by the second. Alice was feeling tired again, the weight of the day and her crash descending on her quickly.

"A university. Quite secret. It is an old and deeply revered institution in London. Revered, that is, among people like you and me. It's a tightly held secret from everyone else. I have been authorized to issue you an invitation to attend."

"In exchange for what?"

"For nothing. It's free. You just need to make your way—"

"—to platform nine and three quarters," she guessed hopelessly.

He flashed his warm smile again.

"I will be more than happy to give you the full set of instructions if and when you formally accept this invitation. It is a place that will help you, Alice. A wonderful place. It exists because of and for people like you. And it's not only about developing your abilities. It is also about emotional healing, because—"

"How far is Johnston?" she interrupted.

"Of course," he said, putting the truck in gear and proceeding up the gravel road again.

"What do you know about that weird graffiti face sprayed around town?" she asked.

"Ah," he sighed.

"'Ah?' What, are you a dentist now?" Alice actually thought she might need a dentist, as a few of her teeth felt loose.

"As I mentioned to you earlier, Alice, I have the gift of sight.

My abilities are rudimentary compared to those of other siddhas at the university. But still, I can see that there is danger for you if you continue to pursue that riddle. My advice to you is to steer clear of it."

"Oh, wait; did I completely forget to tell you? You can hereby keep all your patronizing crap to yourself. Forever. I don't need some strange man telling me what I should and shouldn't do."

"The truth is, I am aware of that tag, but I have been unable to discover who is making it or what it's for. But I, like you, sense that it's the signature of the evil person of whom we are both becoming painfully aware."

Alice put her head in her hands. She felt exhausted, sick, and hopeless. She had gotten nothing from this wild goose chase except a crazy story about some Hogwarts-like place in England, which was probably a scam. If it was real, it was probably some lame club of smelly, fantasy-loving boys who met at a Village Inn Pancake House, or whatever the London equivalent was, and pretended they were wizards.

And meanwhile, Connie was on a ventilator, being fed with IVs.

Alice remained silent for the remainder of the drive, stewing in her frustration and exhaustion.

"Where would you like to be let out?"

"Just some diner, if there is one open. Do they have a Village Inn in Johnston?"

"There is a diner, but I strongly suggest you change first. There are some spare clothes in that bag by your feet. Something might fit you."

"Are you saying I'm fat?"

"I'm saying something might fit you, and you're welcome to it."

After they left the gravel road and struck pavement again, the dim, unromantic lights of Johnston came into view at last.

Alice was now wearing some smelly borrowed jeans and a flannel shirt. She was sure she would contract some kind of disease from them, but Dean was right; she couldn't walk into a diner looking like someone who had been driven over by a steamroller.

"One last piece of advice," Dean said as he pulled up in front of a diner that was attached to a cheap motel.

"No thanks," Alice said firmly, her hand on the door handle, ready to jump out.

But Dean gave it to her anyway. "I don't know how you ended up unconscious and injured on a road in the middle of nowhere. But it is common for young people with siddhis to lose them temporarily when they reach their late teens. It has something to do with losing brain plasticity; we become too fixed in our doubts and persuaded by mainstream pressure to be normal. I want you to know that you are not alone. People like us help each other. It's in all of our interest to support each other's development and celebrate our abilities. That's what the university is about."

"Thanks for the ride." Alice opened the door, trying not to listen to Dean's endless "advice."

"In the pocket of that shirt, I have left you some basic principles of meditation. They may help you prevent such injuries from occurring again. And should you ever wish to contact me, my cell number is on the back."

Alice jumped out before he could say or do anything else.

CHAPTER 11
FRIDAY, 11:00 P.M.
FORTY HOURS BEFORE THE END

She hit the ground, and her right leg gave way, but her other leg held. She limped quickly toward the diner and pushed inside. She could still hear Dean's V8 engine as his truck rumbled dejectedly away.

The place was a dark warren of poorly lit hallways. Alice walked into a small room functioning as a bar, and a row of guys nursing beers and shots stared at her. Ignoring them, she limped deeper into the place and reached a large room set up as a family restaurant. There was—remarkably for this time of night—one other table occupied. Wedged into straining chairs was a family of four, all in overalls and white T-shirts. The overalls seemed to mark them as farmers rather than miners, but they could have been anything. She felt a remote sense of kinship with them because of their apparent devotion to food. The smallest of them must have weighed three hundred pounds. They were all so busy eating giant portions of something covered in gravy that they didn't notice Alice's entrance.

A waitress, however, did notice.

"Can I help you, honey?" she asked in a friendly but tired voice.

"I'll have whatever they're having," Alice replied. Her

strained smile probably made her look like she was on drugs. She had also forgotten that she was still covered in blood. "And a coffee, please."

"Sure, but I meant, can I call the police for you? You look like you've had a bad night. Is your boyfriend still around?"

"I'm fine. I just fell over."

"Right," the waitress said, walking away as if she had heard it a hundred times before. She probably had heard it a hundred times before from local battered women and their children.

Alice put her aching head in her hands. She was beyond exhausted. But pressing her hands against her eyes gave her a moment of clarity. She saw herself as she was. A freak. Useless. Alone. She felt herself drifting off into a new kind of darkness.

She began to cry as she recognized how low she had sunk tonight, and how quickly. Was she really that different from her Mom? Maybe Alice needed some of those online medications too.

When the waitress brought Alice's coffee, she wiped her eyes and thanked her. The concerned look she got in return told her the clock was ticking, as the lady had definitely already called the police.

Alice stood painfully and hobbled to the restrooms. She took out her phone and called the first person she thought of. It surprised her that it was actually Dad she wanted, not Madison.

It was not a pleasant phone call. There was no good way of explaining to him how she came to be in Johnston. But he sounded alarmed at the despair and exhaustion in her voice and grumbled that he'd pick her up. The map on her phone told her he was about forty-five minutes away. She could only hope he would arrive before the police. Perhaps they had a backlog of domestic violence to deal with tonight.

After washing the blood off her face and body as thoroughly as she could, Alice went back to her booth and downed the cup of scalding coffee.

Moments later, some kind of roast beef was set in front of her.

It tasted amazing.

Now all she had to do was wait. Who would walk in the door first, her dad or a police officer? What could she say to either one about how she had gotten hurt? About how she had come to Johnston?

Just as the farmers left their table, Alice's phone announced the arrival of a text message.

She almost smiled when she saw it contained nothing but a smiling poo emoji from Madison. Then she saw that Madison had texted her about ten more times. She had arrived at the hospital just after Alice left, wanted to know where she was, and pleaded with her to get in touch.

Alice texted back: *I'm okay long story explain in morning*

Then another text message arrived. Dad was in the parking lot of the diner.

She paid and hurried out, a bit more nimbly this time, straight into Dad's arms, and suddenly started crying again.

After a long hug, he pulled away to look at Alice. He instantly choked up and put a hand to his mouth.

"Dad, Dad, it's not what you think," she said hurriedly. "No one molested me. I'm fine. Is Connie awake yet?"

"No. But ... what happened to you?"

"It's a ... long story," she stammered, wiping her mouth on her borrowed shirt. "But can we just head home?" Alice was losing her ability to stand and was falling into exhaustion. She sensed darkness approaching, obscuring her vision, though the streetlights had grown no dimmer.

Her dad noticed, caught her arm, and led her into the truck.

Just as their truck pulled out of the parking lot, the sheriff's

SUV pulled in. In the rearview mirror, Alice watched him lug himself out of his car and lumber into the restaurant.

On the way home, she spun a weak story for her dad about how she came to be in a diner in Johnston, all beat up and in borrowed clothes: when she left the hospital to go get food, she also had to pick up her car from the Roadhouse. But when she got there, she tripped and fell hard in the gravel parking lot, injuring herself and tearing her clothes. Someone in the bar drove her to the nearest doctor, who happened to be in Johnston.

Dad objected, saying Madison and Karan had arrived at the hospital soon after Alice left and had seemed confused about Alice's whereabouts. With no Mustang, how had Alice gotten from the Roadhouse to the hospital and back again?

All Alice could say was that she'd gotten a lift from another friend, and how dare he question her honesty at a time like this?

Dad didn't buy it, but he let the silence communicate his displeasure, a typical dad tactic.

They picked up Alice's car from the Roadhouse and drove home in a convoy. Dad made sure Alice was all cleaned up and ready for bed before returning to the hospital to resume his vigil.

After he left, Alice went back over all the insane things Dean had told her about why he was here, then pulled out the card he had told her contained meditation instructions.

In a very florid, old-fashioned hand, she read the following words:

The mind doesn't develop its own strength when it is habitually fixated on evaluating external objects. Meditation is the answer. To meditate is to focus on three things at once: relaxation, knowing, and acceptance.

On the other side of the card was a phone number, written in the same hand.

After being rescued by Dean tonight, she was feeling much less hostile toward him. She was even beginning to wonder if he might actually be who he said he was. Perhaps he really did mean well. Could there really be a university out there that catered to people like her?

She looked at the card again and thought about how her powers had indeed failed her tonight. Perhaps she really did need to develop more mental strength. She would certainly need it in the coming days.

She sat up in bed and tried to concentrate on "relaxation, knowing, and acceptance." She got as far as five seconds of attempted relaxation before slumping sideways and falling into a restless sleep.

CHAPTER 12

SATURDAY, 7:00 A.M.

THIRTY-TWO HOURS BEFORE THE END

Alice woke up sore, exhausted, and riddled with self-doubt and a feeling of impending doom.

Her nervous system was like an electric circuit gone haywire. She thought immediately of Connie, and a cascade of other images followed like rocks through glass. Tyler, Dean, the graffiti, the catlike eye. It was too much. Her adrenaline surged, then left, leaving her panicked but limp and exhausted.

She searched for her phone, found the battery dead, and plugged it in. She was desperately thirsty, so she shuffled to her bathroom and drank for a long time, straight from the faucet.

As soon as her phone charged enough to turn on, it erupted in a barrage of incoming text messages. One of them was from her mom, about twenty were from Madison, and a couple were from Dad. She read his first.

Connie stable. No major changes, but some small signs she is improving, and the doctors are cautiously hopeful.

The next one was less optimistic: *No change. I'm heading home for some sleep. Mom will stay here; they say she needs treatment for opioid withdrawal. See you at home.*

Alice looked out the window and saw Dad's truck out front.

She ignored the rest of the texts and did a few stretches to assess the damage to her body after last night's wipeout. She was not surprised to find her injuries mostly healed.

Nevertheless, she knew she was very fortunate not to have swim training today. Coach had, for no apparent reason, called off their Saturday morning session this week.

Her phone sounded the receipt of another text, and she picked it up and started to read through Madison's many messages. Most of them were simply kind notes of encouragement with appropriate emojis. She and Karan had spent most of the night sitting with Mom, Dad, and Connie.

The last text from Mad was different. *Alice. Call me when you wake up. Urgent.*

Alice looked out of the window of her garage apartment at the cabin and saw no lights or movement. She knew Dad desperately needed his sleep.

She dressed as quickly as her injuries allowed and drove straight to Bitches Brew, her regular café.

Walking in with a slight limp, she ignored the cheerful chatter coming from the small café tables and made a beeline for the ordering counter. The barista was a thirty-something woman with stick-thin, tattooed arms, who was also coincidentally named Alice.

Tattooed Alice already knew Alice's order (quad latte), so all Alice had to do was pay and wait. The sound of steaming milk, the clink of cutlery, the music playing in the background, and the smell of coffee were helping her forget about the horror of last night. When the surly barista pushed her large quad latte across the counter, Alice drank a good amount of it standing right there.

Finally feeling somewhat awake, Alice turned and looked around the café for a table. And there was Tyler the Xanax dealer in the corner, staring right back at her. Last night, she would have given anything to find him and wring answers from him. Now he was sitting calmly at her café, all dressed up in his cool urban clothes, his hair perfect, his demeanor calm, as though he had planned to meet up with her. A mixture of fury and excitement coursed through her body. The caffeine gave her the courage to stride straight over to him ,and she knew her mutism wouldn't stop her this time.

She set her coffee down hard on his table, spilling some, and blurted out, "Have you ever heard of an online pharmacy that sells people Xanax laced with fentanyl?"

His cool façade cracked. It was like a light went on, flooding the dark, unobserved parts of his face and revealing a scared young boy who couldn't speak. But the crack almost instantly resealed itself.

Befuddled by the slip of his mask and his quick recovery, the only thing Alice could think to do was press on. "Um, because my Mom was buying them, and then my six-month-old sister ate one off the ground and went into a coma."

Tyler calmly drank some coffee, took a deep breath, and put his head in his hands. Alice knew the little boy's emergence and disappearance had not been an act, but this was. It looked like he was trying to make her believe he was devastated by her news. He finally looked up and said, "I'm sorry. Do you have time to sit down?"

Alice sat down. Some instinct warned her against trying to read his mind, so she prepared to listen to what he had to say.

"I'm so, so sorry to hear about your sister." He looked so genuinely sorry, Alice had to remind herself it was an act. Or probably was.

"Website," she insisted, realizing her mutism had caught up to her.

"Look, I'm not going to try to sell you some story. No, I don't know where your mom bought her pills. But I understand why you would ask me. Because yes, I sell medication ... to kids. They aren't party drugs, but they are illegal for me to sell. I only started because I know what it is like."

She could no longer speak, so she just rolled her eyes.

"I did not have a happy childhood. I was always attracted to weird nerdy things, and my dad was always ... violently disappointed in me. No matter what I did, he was never satisfied. Antianxiety medication helped me climb out of a very dark place and do well in school. Later, when I became an IT consultant for the school district, I saw a huge number of kids suffering like I did, and no one was helping them. They just fell through the cracks. I encouraged them to see their doctors and ask about medication. Most times, they did. But sometimes they didn't, or couldn't. They didn't want anyone to know how they felt. So I started finding ways to help them. I found good clean sources of drugs like Xanax and provided them at cost to a few kids, and it helped them like it helped me."

Alice shook her head, unimpressed. Her sister was in a coma right now because her mom had bought pills without seeing a doctor.

"I get it. You're skeptical. I was too. I knew it was wrong, so I stopped. But word had gotten out, and I kept being approached by suffering, sad kids. So I started selling again. But now I see ..." He paused, apparently choked up, or pretending to be.

Alice started looking around for a way to escape this sob story. She could just stand up and leave, but she still hoped he could give her some useful information, so she reluctantly nodded for him to continue.

"I see how wrong I was to do so. I don't know what website your mom used, but if she had reached out to her doctor, she and your sister wouldn't be in this situation. It makes me wonder how many kids out there should be doing the same instead of coming to me. I'm truly, deeply sorry."

Alice was angry again. No way was she going to let this guy, attractive or not, lecture her about what her Mom should have done. Her anger helped push back against her mutism's strangle-hold on her voice. "So you're a local drug dealer, and yet you're telling me you know nothing about any pharmaceutical website selling Xanax? They're your direct competitor, but you know nothing about them? You don't know anything about Xanax laced with fentanyl?"

"I take full responsibility for my actions. I'm not trying to wriggle out of that. But as I told you, I have only sold a limited quantity of high-quality antianxiety meds to high school students in need. I have no reason to do a competitor analysis, because I'm not a businessman. And I think you know that. You and I aren't that different, I feel." At this last word—*feel*—Tyler smoldered, his eyes burning into Alice.

Alice felt herself being drawn in and tried to resist. "We're very, very different," she insisted.

"I don't mean I understand how you feel about your sister languishing in the hospital. I ... can I do anything?"

Alice couldn't respond because she had lost her voice again.

"Look," he said warmly. "I promise I'll use every resource available to me to find out what happened. Which website did your mom use? There are probably hundreds, but my suppliers might know something that would help. My ex-suppliers, that is. Because I will never, ever sell again after today. After seeing the pain in your face ..."

Alice looked down, heart beating fast. How could her stupid heart betray her like this? He was lying. She knew she should walk away right now.

As he smoldered at her again, she stood up to go.

"Wait," he said. "Let me help. Please!"

Against her better judgment, she paused, her back turned to him. She became painfully aware that he might be staring at her butt, so she turned around to face him again.

"Here's my number," he said, standing. "Please text me your mom's website and any other information about the pills she bought, and I'll do everything I can to find the person who did this to your sister." He squeezed her shoulder as he walked by.

"Please take care, Alice. You've been through a lot. You're more vulnerable than you think."

Alice sat back down at the table and stared at his cell number. She could still feel his hand on her shoulder.

After a while, she absently drank some coffee and came back to herself. Then she shuddered, a scary question forming. How did this guy know her name?

"Hey." A rough, voice woke her from her reverie. It belonged to the other Alice who worked at the café.

"Uh, did I forget to pay?"

"No, genius." The other Alice sat down where Tyler had been sitting and folded her tattooed hands. "I just didn't want my best customer to get shafted by some jerk. You know that guy is a total fake, don't you?"

"What guy?"

"Tyler Rowley. Mr. 'You're more vulnerable than you think.' He's an actor who preys on women. He may look pretty, but underneath all that hair gel is one rotten malevolent misogynist excuse for a human brain."

"What?" Alice didn't really trust Tyler, but Barista Alice seemed to really hate the guy. It sounded a bit harsh to her.

The other Alice let her head fall onto the table dramatically. Then she lifted it back up and leveled her eyes at Alice. "I work in two cafés. The other one, Apples, is more like a bar. He's there all the time, hitting on different girls, acting all smoldery and contrite, like he just was with you. Total bullshit artist. He plays the rich guy, but I doubt he has any money. I heard him tell one girl some shit like, 'I make a hundred thousand dollars a month as the director of a new start-up.' I'm telling you, that guy's full of it."

"Um, can I have another latte? Takeaway, please."

Alice, fully embarrassed about having a crush on someone who seemed to be a narcissistic drug dealer, had no idea what to do next.

CHAPTER 13

SATURDAY, 10:00 A.M.

TWENTY-NINE HOURS BEFORE THE END

Alice sat next to her mom for a while, watching Connie breathe. They had taken her off the respirator, and she was breathing on her own, which Dr. Leppan said was a very good sign. Mom also looked a touch more human than she had yesterday, though she still couldn't look Alice in the eye. Alice decided to avoid a confrontation with her; it felt good to just sit with her mom, keeping vigil.

An hour later, she gave her mom an awkward hug and told her she was going to the library for a while. Descending the main steps of the hospital, Alice called Madison, expecting to be chewed out.

"You're alive!" Madison said instead of hello.

"Sort of," Alice said.

"Alice, I'm so sorry about Connie." Madison's voice broke, and it sounded like she was crying.

"It's my fault," Alice said, surprised at Madison's display of emotion. "I shouldn't have been at a stupid bar last night with you guys. I could have been home, looking after Connie instead of ..." Her voice trailed off.

"Are you serious? You can't possibly blame yourself that Connie swallowed a random pill on the ground."

Alice didn't answer.

"It's not your fault. And you weren't just hanging out at a bar. You're not even old enough to drink. We were there to help with the search for Wyatt." Madison took a deep breath. "Alice, how did ... how did you get to the hospital last night? Did you get a ride? Was your car broken? When we left the Roadhouse, it was still sitting there."

Alice felt herself tightening up and didn't respond. There was a long silence. She felt the distance between her and Madison grow by miles every second. Alice was embarrassed that she didn't really want to talk about finding Wyatt right then. She didn't even want to be with her friends. All she could think about was finding out who ran the online pharmacy that had poisoned Connie. Tyler seemed to be a jerk, but maybe he could really help? At the thought of him, her pulse quickened, and she felt ashamed.

Madison broke the silence. "Never mind," she said in a cheerier voice, like a mom getting ready to rally the troops. "Anyway, can I pick you up? I'll bring you a quadruple latte from Bitches."

"Um, I'm at the hospital. And I've already had two coffees."

"Oh," Madison said, clearly disappointed that Alice hadn't called her right when she woke up. "Well, can you come to the rare books room?"

"Can we meet a bit later?" Alice asked.

"Oh, Alice, please come to the library right away. Asher says he has more information about where Wyatt is."

"Are you serious? I didn't tell you, but that kid was following me yesterday. Lurking around the day care."

"Are you sure it was him?"

"Yes. But why do you need me there anyway, Mad?"

"Because ... Asher says he won't divulge anything without you there."

Alice had a bad feeling about this. For some reason, the

graffiti face loomed in her imagination like a dark wizard, taunting her.

"Also, I didn't want to tell you on the phone ... but something happened last night. Besides Connie."

"What?" Alice asked, fearful of the answer.

"Crystal was attacked. After we left the Roadhouse."

"What? Is she okay?"

"She was brought to the hospital for head injuries, but she left the emergency room before they were able to run any tests. Presumably she's back home. Or up on Witchat again, searching for Wyatt."

"How do you know all that? And who attacked her?" Alice demanded.

"I'm on a text chain now with that group of Crystal's friends and family who are searching for Wyatt. The text I got this morning said a car full of guys approached her out by her house when no one else was around and beat her up. She didn't know any of them or recognize their truck. While she lay on the ground crying, they called her a whore and shouted at her to go back to China. Even though she's more American than they are."

"It must have been those incel boys from the bar," Alice said, infuriated.

"I'm sure the authorities will get them. It's a violent assault and a hate crime. Helping find Wyatt is the best way for us to help her. His absence is hurting Crystal much more than an attack by a bunch of racist, misogynist assholes. And her mom hasn't slept in days."

Alice stood there shaking her head, seething.

"Alice, it's just so vital that we find Wyatt," Madison continued. "I keep picturing him lost and hurt in the woods. It's been more than forty-eight hours since he was last seen. And his family is so desperate. I just feel like helping them is the right thing to do."

"I guess ... Okay, I'll be there soon," Alice said, and tapped off.

She paused, thinking of Tyler's face and struggling with a boiling cauldron of feelings: attraction toward him; grief over Connie's condition; anger toward her parents and the world. She quickly texted Tyler the URL for the online pharmacy with no personal note or anything. Then she stared at her phone, willing him to respond. *Please.*

On it, he wrote.

Even though it was only two words, it felt like a love letter.

As she parked near campus and walked toward the library, Alice's sense of foreboding returned. Her stomach started to hurt again. It felt the same as it had in her dream: like a gaping mouth/eye was watching, drawing her toward it, hungry to swallow her and everyone she loved.

Where she usually climbed the library steps two or three at a time in anticipation of seeing her friends, today she climbed slowly and laboriously.

Alice looked up at the windows of the rare books room. They were magnificent arched stained glass, like those in a castle or a medieval church, and had always lifted Alice's spirits. Until today.

Her windows had been vandalized.

She stopped dead in her tracks and stared. Above the windows loomed a larger-than-life size version of the face, freshly sprayed and clearly visible from the library steps. "You can't be serious," Alice said out loud in a dejected tone. Someone must have rappelled from the roof to spray it there. It would have been a huge effort.

Why would they put it *here*? Right above her private hangout? Dark magic or no, it felt like a deliberate threat to her personally. But why?

When she opened the heavy door to the rare books room,

she found Madison, Karan, Asher, and another kid all there
sitting in silence, waiting for her.

Alice looked from Karan and Madison to the kids. Asher
looked appropriately sheepish. He also had a fat lip.

Alice felt no sympathy for him. "Okay, kid," she said. "I
know I said you could have your Dumbledore watch back, but I
was lying. Unless you want me to shove it down your throat.
You better have a damn good explanation for why you were
taking videos of me."

He didn't say anything and looked to the other boy for
support. Alice noticed the other kid didn't seem afraid of her in
the slightest. He could have been the twin of the actor who
played Harry Potter. He was shorter, but he had messy black
hair and wore the same wire-rim glasses, T-shirt, and jacket as
Daniel Radcliffe wore in one of the films. He remained silent
and defiant and turned to look at Madison, as though waiting
for her to make Alice quiet and polite.

Then Alice thought of a reason this kid might look so confident in her presence. What if Asher *was* part of a preteen
surveillance program? What if he had used that forehead
camera of his to film her flying, and they were here to blackmail her? Or maybe they had already told the authorities, who
were on their way with a straitjacket?

Her anger at Asher disappeared, and she sat down in a
brooding silence.

Karan got up and moved across the table to the seat next to
Alice. She looked as nervous as Alice felt. She returned Alice's
gaze, and they shared a moment, not unlike they had yesterday
while out flyering. Some kind of wordless intimacy passed
between them. It gave her strength.

Turning toward Madison, who also looked nervous, Alice
gave a curt nod.

Madison turned to the boys. "So we're here, but we're busy,
and I need to know what information you have about Wyatt."

She looked at Alice and added, "And whatever it is, you need to explain why you won't tell his family or the authorities."

The Harry Potter look-alike nodded at Asher, who looked fearfully at Alice and then at Madison, as if he couldn't decide who scared him more. He seemed to decide they weren't going to force-feed him his Dumbledore watch—at least not right then—so he proceeded with what appeared to be a planned presentation.

He unfolded a portable whiteboard and plugged it in. It was way more high-tech than anything Alice had seen in her classrooms at the high school. It burst to life, and the screen, as clear as an expensive television, displayed the words THE CLUB in an elaborate font like on a Halloween party advertisement. The text was in front of a spooky background of mist and trees. Alice wondered if she was about to be shown a film trailer.

The Harry Potter look-alike, still sitting down, crossed his legs like a lawyer or a bored adult. Then he started to narrate Asher's presentation. "We are here as representatives of a secret society called The Club. My name is James, and you already know Asher."

Alice turned to Karan and rolled her eyes as if to say, *These kids are nuts.*

Asher, oblivious to the looks passing behind him, touched the logo, and the screen swirled into a photo of Daniel Radcliffe from one of the Harry Potter moves.

"The founders of The Club were huge Harry Potter fans. Despite their young age, they were smart, and they got together to research whether there might be real magic in the world. The friendship they formed was the beginning of our club."

Asher tapped again, obviously feeling more self-assured now. He was standing tall and had his hand on his hip. The screen split into four grainy videos, all paused, ready to be watched. James smiled at Asher. Perhaps they were winding up for the exciting part of their presentation?

"The first real lead they found had nothing to do with the Harry Potter books," James said. "What they uncovered was perhaps more interesting. It was a legend, known only to some English history buffs, of a mysterious hidden university in London. Asher?"

Asher tapped the first video, and it came to life, showing a very old lady walking down a London street.

"Excuse me?" the old lady asked, stopping and looking up and away from the camera. She held a long white cane, and Alice thought she looked blind. She was at least ninety years old and hunched over.

"Mrs. Chadwick, may I speak to you about the hidden university for magic?" This was a girl's voice, quite loud, so it was probably the person holding the camera.

"Young lady," the woman said in a very proper accent, "it is just a myth. Don't go troubling yourself about it."

"But can you just tell me what you know about the myth?"

"Who are you?" she asked, squinting hard, probably seeing nothing.

"Mrs. Chadwick, I heard about your late husband's work. I'm a great admirer. I just wanted to ask you a few questions."

The lady appeared to soften at the mention of her husband. "Young lady, my husband was a raving lunatic."

"But what about his claims of a secret university hidden in London?"

"Hogwash."

"But how did he think it was hidden? I mean, according to the legend?"

"I have never read his so-called articles, of course," the old lady said. "But my husband, rest his soul, was fascinated by dark alleys and the cellars of old pubs and churches."

"That's why I came to you, Mrs. Chadwick. I just want to know if he found anything. Maybe he didn't get around to publishing everything he found."

The woman resumed her shuffling walk, apparently done with the conversation.

"Please, did he find anything?"

She stopped, pursed her lips, and looked back at the camera. "I can't tell you that, young lady. You seem like a smart girl. Does it ring true to you?" Receiving no response, the old lady frowned and continued. "He died before his research, as it was, was complete. But ... in his final days, he claimed he had grown confident there had been a group of people—witches— who used to meet in pubs before the Great Fire of London."

"You mean the Great Fire of 1666?"

"Yes, you know your history. Did you know the fire was started in a bakery? Well, my husband believed the baker in question was secretly friendly with the Lord Mayor of London. My dear husband was under the delusion that he had finally found some proof they were both involved with this association of magical witches. He claimed the baker started the fire, and the Lord Mayor let it burn quicker than it would have other-wise. They aimed to burn a few harmless blocks and then rebuild them, in cahoots with other powerful friends, while hiding a complex of buildings within. They got more than they bargained for. Most of London burned down, as you know. According to my daft husband, the baker and the Lord Mayor took the opportunity to sculpt a magnificently large hidden campus, concealed by magic. Totally and utterly ridiculous."

"But how is that possible?" the old lady's interviewer asked. "What about all the modern archeologists who study London's history? Surely modern technology could locate such a huge campus hidden among the buildings."

"Ah, now you appear to be using your head. That's why it is total and complete hogwash. My husband never found a single shred of evidence. The only thing he told me in his last days was that he couldn't find it because he was too old. 'Conceal-ment of this kind can only be broken by a child,' he said. 'It relies on conditioning—on what we are used to seeing. Children do not have the same degree of mental conditioning, and therefore they can see what we cannot. I'm fully confident that someday, a twelve-year-old child will succeed where I failed.' Then, with those ridiculous thoughts in his mind, the poor, dear old befuddled man died. Now, I must be going, young lady."

Asher closed the old lady video.

"Our founders were twelve years old, and they were excited by the idea that children might be the only ones capable of finding this hidden university. There were no hard facts yet, like photographic evidence of a secret doorway. But they knew they were on to something. So our founders got organized. They began to carefully vet and recruit like-minded kids under twelve years old to help locate the secret university in London and to keep an eye out for real magic of any kind around the world.

"Over the years, our founders discovered many secrets. Not many of them were magical, but they were enough to give them vast material wealth."

Asher seemed uncomfortable with James' last statement. "Yeah, we sort of became a paparazzi organization for a while, selling photos of rich people doing ..."

"That is all in the past," James interrupted, angrily. "All of these funds were reinvested in The Club to make it what it is today."

Alice looked hard at the starting pictures of the three remaining videos. She assumed these would be the grand results of The Club's well-funded hunt for magic. If one of those videos showed her flying and these kids played the footage for Madison and Karan, her life as she knew it would be over.

Madison glanced at Alice and appeared to notice her mortification. "So," Madison said in a bold voice, asserting her control over the discussion, "I am hoping that one of those videos is going to help us find Wyatt. If it is, you should show us now, or I'm afraid we will need to ask Brian to show you out. We're busy."

James smiled at Madison, totally unperturbed by her interruption.

Alice noticed his confidence and realized she had probably been right. These kids must have some damning evidence about her. What was she going to say when they showed it to Mad and Karan? What was she going to do? She could try to convince Mom and Dad to move the family somewhere far, far away...

"The Club goes wherever the evidence leads," James continued. "Some of that evidence lead them here to Hardrock. In the early two thousands, one of our members, a kid named Molly, provided solid evidence that there was a magical person in the area. Over a few years, Molly secretly observed a young boy who was a master of magical concealment. Asher?" James gestured toward the whiteboard.

Asher tapped the next video, which turned out to be a collage of photographs. The first photo showed a beautiful alpine meadow full of wildflowers. It was about the size of a football field, bound by jagged rocks on one side and pine trees on the other.

"These photos were taken by a camera Molly hid in a tree on the south side of the secret meadow," James pointed at a meadow cradled by big pines on one side and a wall of jagged boulders on the other. "The camera was about thirty feet from the closest of those rocks, and it took a photo automatically every minute."

The scene was unremarkable; pretty much the same as any remote meadow Alice had visited in the wilds north of their town.

The next photograph showed a boy on the right side of the

frame, near the jagged rocks. He looked about ten years old. He was wearing gym shorts and Converse and was bending over awkwardly, as though he were injured or handicapped. He appeared to be adding a stone to a rock cairn.

The scene looked a little like Wyatt's weird parchment petroglyphs—did these kids think this boy in the video was "granted high power?" And this meadow "that place you learned to conceal?"

The next photo showed a completely different scene. The boy was gone. The meadow was gone. In its place were jagged rocks butting up against tall pine trees.

But as Alice looked closer, she noticed that the rocks were the same as those in the first two photos, and the pines appeared to be the same as well. The meadow between them had simply been removed. Probably Photoshopped out, Alice thought.

"That boy in the last photo had real magical powers. He could use them to cloak an entire physical space. Molly captured it all on film. She also believed he had other abilities, perhaps even the ability to survive a jump off a cliff. Unfortunately, not long after supplying these remarkable photos, both Molly and the boy disappeared. We never found the cloaked meadow."

"Probably because it's still cloaked," Asher added.

James looked supremely annoyed to be interrupted. "We never heard from Molly again, and we found no further evidence of magic in the Hardrock area for years. Until last year."

Alice's heart raced, and for the first time, James seemed conflicted. Then he seemed to decide something. "As you can imagine, keeping our club secret from nonmembers is one of our most sacred responsibilities. Members are not allowed to tell anyone. Not even their families. Their best friends. Anyone. Today is the first time any nonmember has ever been told about our club. It is the first time any nonmember has seen this presentation. It has only ever been shown to new members as part of the induction process."

He looked straight at Alice. "I had to get authorized to come here today to meet with you. It had to go through our board of directors. But I am good at persuading people."

"Yeah, James had to get his parents to agree to come here from New York on a vacation to see the fall colors," Asher blurted, "'cause he wasn't allowed to take a plane by himself." At a sharp glance from James, Asher shut up.

"Yes, here we are." Madison sounded fed up. "And I wish you all the luck in the world with your witch hunt. It sounds to me like you have no information for us about Wyatt, so I will—"

"Wyatt was a member of The Club," Asher interrupted. "He and I were the only members here in Hardrock."

James looked at him sternly, but Asher just shrugged.

"Yes," James continued, "Wyatt was a member. And we have information about his disappearance. We are authorized to share that with you. On one condition."

CHAPTER 14
SATURDAY, 12:00 P.M.
TWENTY-SEVEN HOURS BEFORE THE END

The room went silent again. Alice's heart started pounding so fast and hard she thought she would faint. She gripped her legs and squeezed hard, trying to distract herself with pain so she could calm down.

Karan reached over and tried to take one of Alice's hands. Alice pulled away instantly but then regretted it. She looked at Karan, who tried to smile at her.

James nodded insistently at Asher, who seemed like he wanted to run away again.

"I'm really sorry, Alice; I was recording you the other day." He tapped another video on the screen, which showed an aerial view of a distant figure skating down a tree-lined street on a skateboard. "Before that, I had another video of you flying. But it was from really far away, 'cause I didn't have this cool drone. But ... anyway, just watch. It's totally amazing."

Alice's mind raced. Why hadn't she thought of the possibility of being filmed by a drone? She had been so careful otherwise.

Alice closed her eyes and began to plead, mentally, that Madison wouldn't freak out. Her pleading turned into a kind of prayer. *God, please don't let her abandon me. Please don't let her abandon me.*

She opened her eyes but didn't dare look at Madison.

The video zoomed in a little, and though it had been shot from behind, everyone could see Alice's short-cropped brown-blond hair, her broad shoulders, and the straps of Connie's carrier. The camera followed Alice as she turned onto the paved bike path by Hardrock River. The green branches and leaves of cottonwood trees obscured the view, but flashes of Alice emerged when there were gaps in the canopy. The trees flew by beneath the drone's camera for a mile or so, until they reached the lonely part of the path where people seldom ventured and where there were no buildings or homes. Alice's takeoff spot. Then, suddenly, Alice burst through the canopy, swimming gracefully through the air. The drone followed her for another thirty seconds but could not match her speed. Soon she had disappeared into the blue.

"Our condition is this." James was speaking calmly, as though Alice's life had not just been violated and probably destroyed. As though her chance at an ordinary friendship with anyone had not been obliterated. As though her chance at a normal future, at attending the local university and remaining close to help with Connie, had not just been vandalized. Torched. By a kid with a Dumbledore watch and his nerdy Harry Potter look-alike boss.

"We're not allowed to provide any more information about Wyatt to you or any other nonmembers. But if Alice allows herself to be inducted, studied, and documented by The Club, we'll show her with all the information we have about Wyatt's disappearance and she can act on that information to find him."

It was too much for Alice. She couldn't think. She couldn't breathe. And then there was a sound, like a cow or something, the volume rising steadily. She realized it was coming from her.

The ultimate indignity—now she wasn't even human. She couldn't even make human noises.

She couldn't see or hear anything anymore. So she simply covered her eyes with her hands and let the sobs come.

After an eternity, she began to emerge, as though waking from sleep. She felt arms around her. Were they taking her away to some military base to be dissected? But the arms were not forcing her anywhere; they were just holding her. One of the hands was stroking her hair. It felt good.

Then her ears began to function. She heard Madison's voice. "It's okay, it's okay. Shhhh. Alice, we're here for you. Shhh."

Another voice joined Madison's. "We'll never let them force you to join their stupid club," Karan whispered. "We're with you no matter what."

"It's okay, it's okay," Madison repeated in a quiet but firm motherly tone.

Alice removed her hands from her eyes and tried to blink them open. She saw spots and closed them again. They began to hurt; perhaps she had pressed them with too much force. She tried to open them again.

"Take your time, sweetheart," Madison said. "We're alone."

"Yeah, we kicked those little shits out," Karan said.

"Karan almost threw them through the wall."

"I'm pretty sure I broke their whiteboard," Karan said. "Whoopsie."

Alice blinked again. She saw spots and blotches, but this time she was able to make out two empty chairs across the room, which had previously been occupied by James and Asher. One chair was upended.

She felt hands take hold of her own. She closed her eyes and let herself be held a little longer. Then she heaved a huge breath and opened her eyes again to look around.

Madison and Karan had pulled up chairs and were sitting

on either side of her. They seemed to sense that she needed some space now, and they took their arms away. Madison looked like she had been crying too, but she held herself tall.

"I'm so sorry," Alice said stupidly, looking at Madison and then Karan.

"For being miraculous?" Karan said. "Or for being an irresponsible flyer? I bet there's some law against free flying with a baby, you know. What would her day care people say?"

"Shut up, Karan." Madison looked stern. Then she softened, turning back to Alice. "I have to admit, I'm a little scared of what I just saw. And I'm having trouble fitting it into my understanding of the world. Of ... of you, and me, and how things work. How the world works. Am I ... am I supposed to believe in everything now? Like those kids do? That there's magic everywhere if you look hard enough? If people can fly?"

Alice just shrugged slowly. She hadn't dared to ask those questions herself. How could she answer them out loud? She lowered her eyes and felt herself tightening up again.

"I don't trust anyone about anything," Karan quipped. "Like, take for example—"

"Karan!" Madison shouted.

"Yes? Anyway, I'm just saying. Why can't people fly? Until there's incontrovertible evidence for or against, I'm trusting what I see. And even then ..."

As Alice lifted her hands to cover her eyes again, Madison quickly reached out and grabbed them with her own, preventing Alice from hiding. She flashed Karan a look of such searing intensity that she had to shut up.

Mad turned to Alice. "I don't need anyone to run tests on you. I believe in you completely ... in what you can do. It explains everything. About last year, especially."

Alice wanted to run away. They were talking about the most heavily guarded taboo subject in her life. It terrified her. She had thought no one would ever find out exactly what had happened to her last year or how she had survived.

Karan watched with rapt attention as Madison continued. "This is why I feel so ... why I'm such a shit friend. You actually told me last year that you could fly. Don't you remember?"

Alice shook her head. Of course she remembered, but she did not want to talk about it.

"You actually tried to show me too. I brought you a coffee at your old house. You got on a bike and pedaled as fast as you could. But then you disappeared around a bend. I ran to see what happened, but I only found the bike heaped on the side of the road. I thought it was a weird joke. But you must have used the bike to help you fly, somehow."

Alice remembered using a bike to gain enough speed to take off. Reckless, but effective.

Madison shook her head, as though frustrated with herself. "Later, I actually asked how you reached Kirsty in the middle of the Knifespur, because it was too far for you to have gone there and back on foot. And you said, 'I flew.' I'll never forget that ... But back then, my mind just wouldn't let me believe you could actually do it. It was like ... you know the legend about how some indigenous people couldn't see the colonial ships arriving because they were so far from anything they had experienced before?"

Alice didn't know that one.

"Seeing that video just now," Madison continued, "I felt an enormous sense of relief. I'm relieved that I don't have to lie to myself anymore that you're just an average girl like me. You're not. You're amazing—the most amazing person in the world. And I'm the one who should apologize. I'm so sorry to have been such a terrible friend, Alice." Madison's voice cracked, and she seemed about to cry again. "I should have listened when you tried to tell me ..."

Karan seemed ready to break into sobs as well. Instead, she got up and started reading an ancient-looking Bible.

After a pause, Madison shook her head and stared teary-eyed at Alice. "I'm here now. Ready to listen. Karan is too. All we want is to understand you."

Alice said hesitantly, "I'm sorry ... I think ..."

"No way, Alice. You are not allowed to apologize for being amazing," Madison said.

"No, I mean I'm sorry because I think I'm going to throw up." Alice furiously looked around for a trash can.

Madison's eyes widened again, and she dashed over and grabbed the can from the corner of the room.

Alice closed her eyes and tried to stem the nausea that had overtaken her. The puking might have offered some relief, she knew. But she also knew it wasn't yet time for relief, and she didn't want to vomit in a trash can. "No, I'm okay."

Karan put away her Bible and sat back down. "So besides flying, what else can you do?" she asked.

"I also get ... feelings about things."

"Like magic GPS?" Karan asked.

"There's no such thing as magic GPS," Madison scolded before creasing her brow and returning her attention to Alice. "Wait—is there?"

Alice just shrugged.

"What else?" Karan asked.

"Well ..." Alice began slowly. This was really, really hard for her to talk about. Like she was pulling out her internal organs to show them. Which organ first? Her kidneys or her liver? Either way, she would die in the process. She had to remind herself Mad and Karan were on her side. Telling them this stuff was not going to be fatal.

"There's this substance called prana ..."

"Wait, what's prana?" Karan asked. "You mean Prada, right? Like handbags?"

"Um ... no?" was all Alice could say, especially since the only kind of handbag she had ever owned was a gym bag. Prana was a complicated subject that she barely understood.

Alice suddenly felt incredibly restless, and she realized she had disclosed enough.

Sitting up straight, she said, "Mad, call those kids. See if they can come back right now."

CHAPTER 15

SATURDAY, 1:00 P.M.

TWENTY-SIX HOURS BEFORE THE END

"Are you going to throw up on them?" Karan asked giddily. "Or maybe shoot fire out of your eyeballs? Can you do that? Do you have a cape? Do you have invisible feathers? Can you lay eggs?"

"Nobody is hurting those boys," Madison said.

Alice was pleased that they had all reassumed their respective roles. Madison, the mother. Karan, the clown. Alice the ... what? If not the freak, then what?

"I'm not going to hurt them," Alice said as firmly as she could, though it wasn't necessarily true. "I just need to talk to them."

Madison remained serious. "I won't let you be bullied or blackmailed by this band of fantasy paparazzi geeks, Alice. We'll find Wyatt some other way."

"I just want to see what they know," Alice insisted. "I'm not going to join them or let them blackmail me if I can help it."

"You want to find out what they know about where Wyatt might have gone, or about something else?"

Alice paused, embarrassed. Then she looked at Madison. "Mad, you know that instinct thing I mentioned?"

"Magic GPS," Karan said. "Totally cool."

"Well, it's screaming at me. I feel like the graffiti, Wyatt, and Connie's overdose are connected and that these kids can tell us how."

Madison nodded, obediently took out her phone, and called.

While Madison was talking to one of the kids on the phone, Alice spoke as loudly as she could. "And tell them to bring us strong lattes from Bitches Brew. It's been almost two hours since my last coffee. And we need some healthy food."

Madison stuck her hand over the phone in a lame effort to prevent James from hearing, but she smiled.

Eventually, the kids returned, tails between their legs and coffees and sushi in hand.

Alice had promised to let Madison handle the negotiations. They all resumed their respective places. Both James and Asher looked more like children now and less like twelve-year-olds all puffed up with the secrets they had discovered.

Before James could reassert himself or reestablish his confidence, Madison spoke quietly but firmly. "You will not now, or ever again in the future, treat my friend Alice as an object of study. You will not threaten her. You will not offer to trade things for her. You will never again withhold information from us or the authorities when someone's life is at stake, as Wyatt's is now."

She remained sitting and let the silence oppress her audience and make them squirm. Finally, she added, "Is that perfectly understood?"

Asher nodded frantically. But James just looked down, apparently conflicted.

"James?"

He lifted his chin defiantly. "You sound like you are negotiating. You're telling us terms. So tell me, if we satisfy your terms, some of which are against our club's rules, what will you do for us? Like, Alice, will you agree to—"

James stopped speaking and shrank away as Alice started to rise from her seat, angry and menacing.

But before she could stand up and do her best to shoot flames out of her eyes, Alice felt a hand on each of her shoulders. Madison's long, thin fingers were on her left shoulder, Karan's oversized digits on her right.

"Let me handle this," Madison said quietly. Then she redirected her gaze at James. "This is not a negotiation. I am not stating terms; I'm just telling you stop all this club crap and try to be humans. We have invited you back here to extend the hand of friendship, despite your previous naive display of ill will and attempt at extortion. None of us has anything else to say to you until you have agreed."

Again, Asher began nodding frantically as he looked from Alice to Karan, then back to his boss, James.

"No. I won't agree," James said, turning his face away, a child hiding his tears.

Even Asher looked embarrassed at James's sudden loss of control. He turned to James and slouched down. "Um, but we still want them to help us find Wyatt, right?"

"Shut up!" James shouted, in what seemed a last attempt to assert authority over Asher and the world in general. And then something inside of him seemed to break. He covered his face with his hands and started to cry in earnest.

After a moment of quiet except for James's sobs, Asher spoke up. "Look, I think we already got approval to tell you guys stuff about Wyatt. So I'm sure that's okay. We didn't mean any harm, you know."

James stopped crying but didn't take his hands away from his face or contradict Asher.

Madison let Asher talk. Alice thought that was smart. Asher seemed to be taking over as chief negotiator for The Club.

"Is it okay, James?" Asher placed a hand on James's shoulder.

James nodded but kept his hands over his face.

"Okay, so you guys already know Wyatt is a member of The Club. And yesterday I showed you that parchment about the god of Witchat Mountain and how he would grant you healing powers if you jumped off a cliff or something."

Glaring, Karan quipped, "Yeah, the Mr. Potato Head god."

"Yeah, haha," Asher said nervously. "Well, what I didn't tell you was that wasn't Wyatt's parchment. It belonged to the magical boy in Molly's photos, the boy who could make an entire meadow disappear and reappear. His name was Nathaniel. And not only did the parchment belong to Nathaniel, we think he was also the kid *in* the parchment drawing." Asher paused for effect, but seeing the glares from the girls, he quickly continued. "It's easier just to show you this article we have about Nathaniel," Asher said quickly. "Good thing I have a hard copy, since somebody broke our whiteboard ..."

Karan put her hands on the table as if she was going to get up and attack the boys again, but Madison put a hand on her shoulder.

Asher placed an old newspaper clipping on the table in front of the girls. It was dated ten years earlier.

JOHNSTON BOY MISSING, PRESUMED DEAD

By Melba Goldberg

FOLLOWING *an exhaustive two-week search of the area around John- ston, authorities have called off the search for missing ten-year-old boy, Nathaniel Narrow. County Sheriff Brian Wilkinson made the announcement during his daily press conference, called to brief media on the search. Nathaniel's father, well-known local mining magnate Henry Narrow, also made a rare public appearance and told assem-*

bled media, "My heart is broken." Mr. Narrow recently resigned from his position as CEO of Johnston Mining Corp., though he retains ownership of mineral rights to the mines.

Nathaniel disappeared while on a hike under the supervision of a babysitter. According to Mr. Narrow, he had instructed the babysitter to allow Nathaniel some time to explore the woods on his own. Tragically, the boy never returned from his sojourn.

Authorities have, however, cleared the babysitter of any wrongdoing. "He and every single one of the childcare specialists from Johnston Care is well trained and highly responsible," a friend of the family said recently. Johnston Care is a local charity established to support single parents who work for the mine.

Nathaniel's disappearance is the latest in a string of tragedies suffered by the Narrow family, once considered the most powerful and celebrated local dynasty in northern Colorado. After losing his wife to complications from childbirth, Mr. Narrow has been raising his mentally disabled son, Nathaniel, by himself. The two were inseparable and were fixtures around the town of Johnston. "This is going to kill him," a family friend told the Gazette. "First his wife, now this. It's unthinkable. Nathaniel was the happiest kid in the world. He loved his dad so much. And Henry was like Super Dad. They were best friends, fishing buddies. Besides school, the only time they were apart was when a local boy took Nathaniel out for afternoon hikes. Henry would always be waiting at home with dinner on the table. It sure was something. Henry was waiting with dinner that night, and Nathaniel just didn't come home. It's so incredibly sad."

While Mr. Narrow was widely admired for the effort he put into caring for his disabled son, executives at the mine have been increasingly critical of his leadership. When coal prices fell dramatically throughout the 1990s, Mr. Narrow laid off 50 percent of his workforce, and yet the mine is still rumored to have been losing money for years. It is unknown who will succeed Mr. Narrow as CEO at this troubled but essential company that is such a staple of Johnston's culture and economy.

Mr. Narrow will not hold a memorial service for his son, but flowers and messages of condolence are being accepted at the Johnston Mine offices by Ed Toomes, head of Human Resources.

"What kind of crazy name is Melba Goldberg?" Alice asked. Then she heard a sob. She looked up from the article and saw that Karan was in tears. "Oh, for god's sake," Alice said, impatient that Karan was losing it again.

"I told you," Karan sobbed, "I can't help it!"

As Madison tended to Karan, Asher tried to answer Alice's question. "Melba Goldberg was a local journalist until she moved to New York City," he said. "She's like a famous food blogger now."

"There *is* a parallel between Wyatt and Nathaniel," Madison said in a clinical voice, still holding on to Karan's shoulders. "They were both close to their fathers, and both disappeared into the wilds on Witchat."

"Yeah," Asher continued. "So, Wyatt was really interested in Nathaniel. Obsessed, especially about his cloaking ability. And Wyatt's a good kid, and his own dad just died. Cancer, just like Nathaniel's dad."

"Yes, I'm familiar with the Narrow story," Madison said.

Alice threw her a quizzical look, as she had never heard of Nathaniel Narrow or his family.

Asher, encouraged, asked Madison, "Did you guys know that Nathaniel's dad got diagnosed just before Nathaniel disappeared? It was really, really sad, my dad said. There were tons of articles about it besides this one. You can look it up. My dad even said Mr. Narrow was a good man, and my dad is not a big fan of coal. He drives a Prius. Anyway, Wyatt really wanted to find out what really happened. He thought the parchment was a clue; you know, the part about healing people by jumping off a cliff. Besides, I guess Wyatt sympathized with Nathaniel. And also, Nathaniel was, like, the only real magical person we had solid evidence on. Before you, Alice, that is."

Alice looked down, refusing to meet Asher's eyes. Was that what everyone would think of her now? That she was a "magical person"? It sounded like something out of a cartoon.

Asher continued. "So, it would have been a huge deal for Wyatt if he'd found Nathaniel's hidden meadow. And our club had collected the parchment years ago. Wyatt figured out the picture in it was of Witchat Mountain, 'cause he lives right by there and recognized the shape. It was the first major new clue. So, for the last month, he'd been riding his horse up into the mountains every day after school, looking for that meadow. It was really cool. He's really good with horses, and—"

"But Asher, for those of us who don't care about legends of magical meadows," Madison said, "can you at least tell us and the authorities exactly where on Witchat Wyatt was searching?"

"Only that he thought the meadow would be near some cliffs or an abyss or something. Like in the parchment. Other than that, I don't know anything. But I can tell you this: the day before he disappeared, Wyatt told us he'd found it. He *actually* found the meadow. Isn't that amazing?"

"The board of directors thought he didn't have enough evidence," James said, apparently trying to pull himself together.

Asher ignored James's interruption. "Yeah, anyway, the next day, he skipped school—"

"You're talking about the day he disappeared, right?" Madison asked. "Thursday morning?"

"Yeah. He even called us from up there to say he'd found it."

"Wow," Madison said skeptically. "Then what happened?"

"So, that's the sad part. We didn't hear from him again."

"You have to tell the police!" Madison said insistently. "They can try to triangulate that last call he made!"

"No, they can't," Asher said calmly. "There's only one cell tower repeater up there. They can't use it to find him. We tried. We have lots of tech too, you know. Not in Hardrock, but in our other—"

"You're absolutely sure Wyatt gave you no other clues about where the meadow is?" Madison interrupted.

"No. I mean, yes, I'm sure. I know Wyatt. He wanted to wait until he had some serious evidence before filing a report. Because he wanted to prove himself to The Club."

"So we have nothing." Madison looked like someone had stolen her cat.

"Maybe that meadow thing is like in those Irish tales," Karan offered randomly. "You know, you get taken by a pookie down into a secret hole and have a giant party with fairies, and they give you gold that turns into a pile of leaves when you return home."

"Right," Asher said. "But fairies are make-believe. Nathaniel isn't. Or wasn't." He glanced at Alice. "Can't you find him by using magic or something? And flying?"

James guffawed at that before wilting again under Madison's stern gaze. Then he cleared his throat. "Um, actually, we have one more clue."

It was time for Asher to raise his eyebrows in surprise.

"The Club always thought the meadow would be up where there were no trails. Because Nathaniel had cloaked the entire area. Nobody could see it, not even animals. If it's still cloaked and not near any trails, and if Wyatt's inside, it could explain why the search teams still haven't found him."

They were silent for a moment, and then Alice asked the question she had brought them back to ask. She knew it was connected to all this somehow. "Do you guys know anything about that tag around town? The graffiti with the face with weird eyes?"

Both Asher and James sat up straight when Alice finally started to participate in the conversation. "Yeah, of course," Asher said.

Alice's heart leaped.

"We know about it because it's a drawing of Nathaniel, based on a picture of him taken before he disappeared. Wyatt recognized it immediately and did some research."

"Really?" Madison asked distractedly. She probably wanted the kids out of the room so they could discuss what they had learned and make plans to find Wyatt, but Alice knew the tag was far more important somehow.

"Wyatt looked into it because they're using Nathaniel's face. He said he couldn't find out who's spray painting them, but we know how it works. One of the eyes in the graffiti looks weird because it is actually a QR code. You hold your phone up to it, and it calls up a website for a pharmacy in India. They sell everything: painkillers, Xanax, whatever. They just ship it to you."

"But surely you told the authorities about the QR code?" Madison said derisively.

"Nah, we didn't tell anyone, because it's not our thing. It's not magic or anything. It's just some weird advertisement for drugs. Nothing to do with us, right?"

"Wrong!" Madison exclaimed. "With all the news about the opioid epidemic? You don't think the DEA would be interested?" Madison looked like she was finally warming up to Alice's cause. "You do realize that Alice's baby sister is in a coma right now because of some pill she found on the ground and swallowed? You realize that pill could've come from that Indian pharmacy? If you had tipped off the police, even anonymously, or even written a letter to the local paper to warn people about it, maybe that pill wouldn't have been lying on the floor of Alice's house the other day."

It was Alice's turn to put a hand on Madison's shoulder to keep her from jumping all over Asher.

"I'm fine," Madison said before continuing her prosecution. "Asher, are you telling me nobody even notices illegal prescription drugs coming through the mail from India?"

"Wyatt researched it. He read somewhere that UPS doesn't have the technology to scan every single package."

Madison just stared at the boys in astonishment.

"Sorry," Asher said. It was probably all he could say.

Just then, Alice's phone chimed, and she glanced down. It looked like a long message from Tyler, but she did not want to read it in front of everyone. Madison would not understand her ... relationship with him.

"Thanks, Asher," Madison said in a tone that indicated they were done. "We'll need you to text us a photo of Nathaniel's secret meadow, please."

James sat up and puffed himself up. But before he could say anything, Asher elbowed him in the shoulder pretty hard.

"Sure, Madison. Let's go, James," he said.

"We'll be in touch when we have more information on Wyatt," Madison said as Asher practically dragged a disconsolate James out of the room and closed the door behind them, leaving the girls to the heavy, living silence of the rare books room.

CHAPTER 16

SATURDAY, 2:00 P.M.

TWENTY-FIVE HOURS BEFORE THE END

Karan broke the silence. "This is so cool. We can be just like Harry, Hermione, and Ron. I got dibs on Ron. Mad, you're Hermione. So, Hermione, what do we do first?"

Madison didn't smile and took a long sip of her coffee, which she hadn't yet touched, before responding. "I think we should show Alice some respect."

"Right," Karan said, shifting to face Alice. "Alice, you're the best." Then she looked back at Madison. "What's the plan?"

"No, Karan," Madison reprimanded. Then she turned to Alice. "You've had a major shock. If you want to take the day off, I respect that. Spend some time with your family at the hospital. Or if you just want to hang out here. Catch up on homework. Study for SAT. Hit the pool. Whatever. You just tell us what you need, and we'll support that." Madison folded her hands in a gesture of infinite patience. But Alice watched her eyes flick to her phone, which was shining brightly with the time, two p.m.

That meant it had been over two days since Wyatt was last seen. Alice knew Madison was exerting a massive amount of self-control to resist launching off with all of their resources to follow up on the Harry Potter club's new information. But she had to break the news to her: she couldn't fly. At least not at the moment.

But before she could find the words, her phone vibrated again, and she remembered Tyler's text message.

"Um, I think I just need to take a short walk by myself," Alice said. "To clear my head. Can I meet you back here in ten minutes so we can make a plan?"

Madison readily agreed. "Whatever you need." Karan nodded.

Alice stood up and left the heavy air of the rare books room, where she had been for ... she didn't even know how long. It felt like days. She was exhausted. Her world had changed fundamentally, and she had already grieved her loss and started on a path that might allow her to welcome the future.

But before she could fully embrace that future, she had to indulge this ridiculous, stupid, ill-advised game she was playing with Tyler.

Emerging into the Saturday afternoon sunshine, she sat down on the library steps and took her phone out. She felt a surge of excitement as she read: *Can u meet me on the college campus somewhere? Like the library steps? Have some info for u.*

Another bolt of electricity pulsed in her stomach as she scanned the lawn in front of the library for him.

She screwed up her eyebrows as the smothered little rational voice in her head screamed at her to be cautious. Why was Tyler on campus? Did he know she was there? How? Could he be following her? She turned around and again caught sight of the tag above the rare books room that had upset her earlier. Now that she knew it was an advertisement, she opened her camera app and pointed it in the right direction. Unsurprisingly, her browser called up the same website her mom had used.

Could it have something to do with Tyler?

Because when she'd met Tyler yesterday while they were

out hanging flyers, he had warned them about this tag. Said he'd "heard" bad things happened when you defaced them. Why would he say that kind of thing unless he had a stake in keeping it functional as an advertisement for his drugs? Could the online pharmacy be his?

But that didn't make sense. Those kids had said the online pharmacy sent things from India. How they knew *that*, she had no idea. But she thought Tyler sold drugs to people face-to-face, handed them out in little packages in school bathrooms. That was the rumor, anyway, though she had never witnessed such an exchange herself.

"I thought I'd find you here," Tyler's smooth voice said from behind her. As she turned, she caught a whiff of his cologne, and her anger cooled a fraction. But only a fraction. "How is your sister?" He looked genuinely concerned.

Not knowing if her mutism would let her get any words out, Alice did her best to calm down, take a few deep breaths, and asked, "Are you making those tags?" She pointed at the one above the windows.

"What?" he asked, a confused look on his face. When he saw it, he raised his eyebrows. "That graffiti artist is a daring person, isn't he? That must be a hundred feet up!"

"It's not you?"

"Me? I'm not into graffiti. An admirer of the athlete who figured out how to get up there, but ..."

He seemed genuinely ignorant. Alice began to doubt herself. She bored into his eyes with her own, trying to read him, but she sensed nothing. Perhaps she had lost her ability to read minds too.

"Anyway," he continued, unfazed by Alice's deep stare, "if you are talking about the website you texted me, I have some info for you. I asked around, and it seems if you order something from those guys, it gets sent to you from India by UPS."

Alice stared bullets at him. "You have nothing to do with that website yourself?"

He held up his hands. "I swore to you I would never sell another pill, Alice. I wasn't lying. You and Connie have had a huge effect on me. I'm not selling anymore."

Alice didn't buy it. She tried to yell at him for being a hypocrite, but her words were gone. She walked away and paced up and down in front of the library steps, like a madwoman, trying to get her mutism to subside.

Finally, she just gave up. She walked back to a bemused Tyler, pointed her phone at the tag above the rare books room windows, and showed him how it called up the website.

"Oh," he said. "I didn't know it did that."

Something about his feigned ignorance helped Alice find her voice again. "If you didn't know about this, why did you tell us that crap about these tags having black magic?"

"Honestly, Alice, it's just something silly people are saying."

Alice stared at him.

"And I ... needed an excuse to ... come say hello. To you. I'd seen you around town and wanted to get to know you."

Completely disarmed, Alice blurted, "Dude, I'm a high school student."

"Yes, I know. I'm sorry. I'll just go. I ... I had to give you that info. For your sister."

"Wait." Alice knew she would regret this.

He stood there looking hurt, but was even more attractive for his vulnerability.

"Can you find out for me who is spraying the tag around town?"

He smiled so big his hair moved. "I'll do everything I can."

Alice stood there, full of conflict, as Tyler turned and walked away.

In a daze, Alice walked back into the library. All she knew was that she was not going to mention any of this to Madison.

Back in the rare books room, Mad and Karan were waiting politely, empty coffee cups still where they were before.

"I'm sorry, guys, but I have to tell you something." Alice sat down, lifted her empty cup to her lips, and shook some long-cold drops into her mouth. "So, you know all these things I'm supposed to be able to do?"

Both girls nodded, giving Alice their undivided attention.

"I can't do any of them right now."

"But," Madison started, "you—"

Alice's anger flashed, and she interrupted Madison. "Sorry to disappoint you, Mad. Something happened, and I'm broken. All right?"

"Hey, I'm not disappointed, Alice. I was going to say that we don't care what you can or can't do. I mean, we do care, but ... I think what I'm trying to say is that you're not broken. You're as whole as Karan or me."

Alice glanced at Karan's scars and regretted her use of the word *broken*. Madison had also banned her from using the word *weird*. So what words was she allowed?

"Do you want to talk about it?" Madison probed.

"Okay, sure. So, you know that guy—the weird dark cowboy in the Roadhouse last night?"

Madison raised her formidable eyebrows. Karan almost looked like she was going to wink at Alice, but she held back at the last minute.

"His name is Dean," Alice continued. "After I went to the hospital last night, I kind of flew off the hospital roof to chase him down."

"But why, Alice?" Madison sighed.

Alice shifted in her seat, then continued haltingly. "I don't have a thing for him, okay? I had this feeling he had something to do with Connie and that weird tag. Obviously I didn't know anything about the QR code in the eye; I just had a feeling about it. As I told you, my feelings about these things are usually right. I chased him up north but couldn't find him. Then something happened. I fell ..." Alice looked around restlessly. "This isn't coming out right. It sounds too weird."

"It's okay, Alice," Madison said. "Stop using the word *weird*. You have a gift. Yes, it is going to take us some time to understand it, but you may as well just tell us what happened. We're here for you."

"Yeah," Karan said pointlessly.

"So, tell us how you fell," Madison said. It almost sounded like a demand, but Alice didn't mind. She was relieved to be telling them all these things, previously her deepest secrets and proof she was abnormal and doomed to be alone forever.

"Okay. So, do you remember Mr. Rao? That old Indian guy?"

"Of course—the mysterious old guy who lived in your family's cabin before you. He was an old friend of your family, right?"

"More than that. He was helping me with my ... supernatural stuff."

"You mean like Obi-Wan Kenobi?" Karan asked.

"I guess. Mr. Rao knew about people like me. Actually, he could do some of the things I could do, like reading thoughts. He—"

"Wait. You can frickin' read minds? What the hell is that about?" Previously impressed, now Karan looked genuinely alarmed.

"Sometimes. But I don't do it with you guys. So don't worry, Karan."

Karan sighed and rubbed her head, which was apparently chock-full of embarrassing thoughts.

"So, Mr. Rao said people like me could read minds and do the stuff I can do because we can use something called prana. It's a kind of energy. I can see prana when people are thinking, and it kind of speaks to me. It sometimes tells me things that are happening far away, too. I think that's how I get my instincts about things. That's how I got the bad feeling about that graffiti. I can also see prana in the air. That's not a very common ability, according to Mr. Rao. He said people meditated in the Himalayas for years and years to be able to see prana like I can. And I guess it's unusual to be able to feel it and ... swim through it. That's how I fly."

"Well, la-di-da," Karan said before getting a backhanded slap on the shoulder from Madison. "So prana is like The Force in Star Wars. Very cool."

"Yeah," Madison agreed. "So you were flying to find this cowboy, and you fell. What does that mean?"

"Usually, prana supports me like water. But it does more than water. Prana responds to my, like, intentions. It's like instant communication. But yesterday as I was flying, I kind of panicked, and it simply disappeared. I fell out of the sky and landed on a dirt road near Johnston. When I woke up, I was in that guy's truck."

"Whoa, Johnston? Seriously? How fast can you fly?" Karan asked. She didn't get punched this time, probably because Madison also wanted to know.

"About a hundred miles an hour," Alice responded.

"And you hit the ground at a hundred miles an hour?" Madison asked incredulously.

"That's just my horizontal speed. I looked up terminal velocity for a skydiver, and it's about a hundred and twenty-five miles per hour."

"So you hit the ground at one twenty-five?" Karan said, scratching her face. "How are you still alive? Did the little prana guys catch you?"

"Sort of. No, not really. They're not guys. I told you, prana is like an energy."

"So you fell on the road. Then what happened?" Madison asked gently.

"I woke up in that cowboy's truck. I think prana helps me heal faster than other people. Otherwise, you're right, Karan—I would not be sitting here. So, yeah, I guess prana hasn't completely abandoned me. I still can heal fast, and I still get those instincts and feelings. Maybe I've only lost the flying part."

"But the British cowboy ... you couldn't find him, but he found you." Madison lowered her voice. "Did he ... want something?"

"He just wanted to help, I think. He is like me. He has some siddhis too. *Siddhis* are the abilities that come from prana. He said he had a feeling I would be there on that stretch of road."

"And did he ... help?" Madison asked quietly.

"He didn't rape me, Madison," Alice responded.

Madison breathed a sigh of relief. "That's good. He just looked scary last night. So then what happened?"

"You know the hidden school those boys were just telling us about? The one they couldn't find in London?"

"Yeah?" Madison asked.

"Dean represents it. Or one like it. He says it's a university for people like us. He wants me to attend. So I guess it's real. At least his school is."

"Awesome!" Karan said, perking up again. "Can we come too? When do we leave? Do we need owls?"

"I didn't say I was going, Karan."

"Are you out of your mind?" Karan said. "You said no to an invitation to a real school of magic? Was it because you hit your head on the road? Wait—if someone hits you in the head with, like, a steel bar or something, it wouldn't hurt?"

"It would hurt." Alice smiled. "Same as you. It's just that I might heal quickly after. But please don't hit me with a bar."

"No worries," Karan said, her hand fussing with the scars on her face.

"What about the tags? I'm guessing Dean is part of the reason you're so obsessed with them?"

"Sort of. I did ask him about the tags. He said he didn't make them. But he said he had the sense someone evil was behind them. And he warned me not to look into it."

"Sounds like he was hiding something," Madison said.

"I don't think so."

"Alice, with all due respect, have you considered the possibility that this Dean guy is behind the tags *and* the Indian pharmacy?"

"I don't trust him either, but I don't think he's a bad guy who would do something like that. I think he's for real. The university, the siddhis, everything."

Madison looked uncomfortable. She was politely giving Alice space to tell her story but would obviously prefer to burst out of the room and search for Wyatt.

"So, what I'm trying to tell you guys is this," Alice said, leaning forward. "I don't think I can fly right now. Something is wrong with me."

"There's nothing wrong—"

"Madison. I appreciate all the kindness. But I mean it. I used to be able to fly, and now I can't. Or at least, I'm a bit scared to try it in case I crash again. What if I don't heal from the next crash?"

"So, how do we fix you?" Karan asked.

"I assume my ... abilities will come back if I can figure out how to reconnect with prana. That guy Dean said it might help if I start meditating."

"Meditating? That's it?" Karan asked. "That's how you get superpowers? Frickin' meditation? Why isn't everyone meditating?"

"I tried last night, but I just fell asleep."

"Does he know you can fly?" Madison asked.

"No. I think he just heard from Mr. Rao that I can read

minds. And he figured out I can heal fast because he saw me do it."

"I still don't think you should trust that British cowboy," Madison said.

"Okay. But the fact remains that I can't fly. At least, I don't think I can. So I can't search for Wyatt from the air."

Madison looked relieved. They were back on the subject of Wyatt. "Okay. So let's make a plan. We have quite a bit more information than we did this morning."

"Just one more thing before we focus on Wyatt," Alice said, to supportive nods from the girls. "Okay, I want to help find him. I really do. It's just that I ... I have to do something about those stupid tags."

"Sure. Of course," Madison said quickly.

"It's not just because of what happened to Connie. I know the tags have something to do with Wyatt's disappearance too. I feel it. It's no coincidence that they're pictures of Nathaniel." Alice wanted to tell them her suspicions about Tyler—that he probably knew damn well who had sprayed them, perhaps even on his orders. But she was so confused about him and ashamed by her confusion that she kept it to herself. What if she was wrong? Alice would be slandering an innocent man. Someone who was under a lot of stress and felt real regret about selling illegal meds. Wait, did she believe he was innocent?

As this turmoil boiled in Alice's mind, Madison was running her fingers through her thin black hair and thinking hard.

"Okay, Alice," she finally said. "What do you have in mind?"

"Well, firstly, the authorities might not know about the QR code in the tag. So let's tell Nancy, my friend who works at the sheriff's department. I trust her. She can help."

"Good idea," Madison said with no enthusiasm, obviously frustrated they weren't talking about Wyatt. She likely wanted to go straight up to Witchat Mountain and search for that so-called cloaked meadow.

"No, seriously, Mad, it's important. And while we're at it, I want to ask Nancy why the sheriff's office believed that tip about Wyatt hitchhiking to Utah."

"Yeah, who would even want to go to Utah?"

Madison rolled her eyes. "Karan, Utah is nice."

Alice was thinking hard. "I think we can also tell Nancy about Wyatt's obsession with Nathaniel and that parchment thing."

"Yes, I bet Asher didn't tell the police anything about it because it's a club secret."

"But let's not say anything about Asher's club. Or about Dean and his secret university."

"Or about how you can fly," Karan added helpfully. "Hey, by the way, do you need goggles to fly? Don't you get cold? Do you hit birds? Do you eat like pounds and pounds of flies every time? Do you get sunburned? Chapped lips? Vertigo? Are you scared of hitting airplanes? Do you wear your shoes? Does your belly fat blob around?"

"Right. Yeah. Let's not tell Nancy I can fly," Alice said, ignoring Karan's questions. "And I want to buy some spray paint, and every time we see one of those tags, I want to paint over it. From now on."

"And we should put it out on social media what those tags are and what the tainted drugs did to your sister," Karan added.

"Um," Alice said hesitantly, "can we leave Connie and Mom out of this? Maybe we can just tell people to spray over any tags they see."

"By the way," Karan added, "I'm not speaking to Nancy. Last time you took me to her gym, I was sore for two weeks. I'm still sore. She's a total ogre."

"Anything else?" Madison asked patiently.

Alice shook her head, relieved not to be the focus of attention anymore.

"Okay. After we go see Nancy—"

"And spray over all the tags on the way," Karan added.

"Yes, after that, we'll focus on finding Wyatt. He believed he'd found Nathaniel's hidden meadow and that it was somewhere on or near Witchat Mountain." Madison looked at Karan. "Can you look up exactly where Nathaniel and his dad lived? I'm sure that information is online."

Karan opened her laptop, and after a moment, she replied, "Nathaniel and his dad lived in Johnston." Karan punched more keys. "Their place was ten miles northeast of the Roadhouse. Right on the other side of Witchat Mountain."

"Okay," Madison said. "Witchat Mountain stands between Wyatt's house and Nathaniel's house. Nathaniel was on foot. So the hidden valley must be walking distance from his place, probably up the north side of Witchat somewhere. All we have to do is look on the maps and find somewhere where there are no trails. It may look weird on the map, like somewhere the topographic lines don't make sense."

"But I can't fly, so how do we—"

"You and I will just hike in, Alice. Whatever it takes."

Karan gave them an abandoned puppy look.

Madison put her hand on Karan's. "While we're out searching, Karan, I need you to stay here and do some serious research to help Alice regain her ... what did you call it?"

"Siddhis," Alice said. "Yogic siddhis."

"Oh," Karan said with a disappointed tone. "Yoga. I'm not that into yoga. Wait, if you're some kind of yogi or whatever, why are you so angry? No offense—I would be too."

"Karan ..." Madison intoned.

"I'm just trying to get my head around this. You don't go to yoga classes, right?"

"Correct," Alice said.

"And you don't shop at Lululemon. You don't say stuff like *namaste*."

"It's not that kind of yoga, Karan. I don't know how to describe it. All I know is that terms like *prana* and *siddhi* are supposed to be related to yoga. At least the ancient Indian kind."

"Maybe you can start by researching where the terms *siddhi* and *prana* come from and see if there are any ancient Indian legends about how people get these kinds of abilities?" Madison suggested.

"If I'm the researcher, I guess that makes me more like Hermione, not Ron. Cool, cool."

Madison smiled for the first time this morning. "Good luck. Actually, I think we studied something about this in religion class. Didn't the Indian monkey god, Hanuman, fly around?"

"Oh, great," Alice said sardonically. "Now I'm a flying monkey."

"Anyway," Madison said, "let's go see Nancy. Wyatt's been lost for more than two days."

CHAPTER 17

SATURDAY, 3:00 P.M.

TWENTY-FOUR HOURS BEFORE THE END

Standing outside of Nancy's gym—an old whitewashed brick warehouse—Alice looked up. She remembered flying through the liquid blue sky, Connie squealing with delight against her chest. It had been just yesterday, Alice had to remind herself. She remembered seeing the earth, deep green with endless pine trees, curving away on all sides, the air sparkling with currents of prana, supporting her like a mother. She longed to be able to be up there again. But she had to go sling iron around with Nancy and Madison, while trying to tactfully ask her for helpful info. Alice was not good at tact, so this was a doomed mission, she feared.

She and Madison pushed open the doors of Nancy's gym, paid ten dollars each, and walked in, confronted by a cacophony of pumping house music, big steel plates clanging together, and aggressive shouts and grunts from all directions. Men wore tight T-shirts that highlighted the muscles in their tattooed arms, while most of the women wore leggings that highlighted their butt muscles. Alice knew from her rare forays into the gym's locker room that more than one of those butt cheeks had needle marks from the steroids they injected.

Nancy was altogether different. No tattoos, no leggings, no needles.

"Today is push day. She'll be on the bench." Alice knew Nancy's workout schedule because she had to. Alice had been caught up in multiple felonies last year, and Nancy had shielded her from the most uncomfortable and unanswerable lines of questioning. In exchange, Nancy had made Alice submit to an unofficial parole: lifting weights with her twice a week.

They saw her across the gym, lying on a flat bench, pushing a rusty Olympic bar loaded with two steel plates on either side. Two hundred and twenty-five pounds: a ridiculous amount of weight for a female lifter.

There were three identical benches on either side of Nancy's. All were occupied by large guys. A few of them were on Alice's high school football team.

None of them had as much weight stacked on his barbells as Nancy did.

As they walked over, Alice saw one of the football players take photos of Nancy's last few reps. It was often like this; she was a legend in the gym.

Despite the fact that she was a legend, Nancy didn't posture in front of mirrors or act like she was superior. She was well liked, said hi to everyone, not just the regulars, and she was friendly and open, always prepared to help newcomers and seasoned gym rats alike.

Outside the gym, however, she was a very different person. Quiet and introverted, she was not at all confident in her daily duties as a deputy sheriff. In her uniform, Nancy looked solid but was shorter than most women officers and was often disrespected by male colleagues and male perpetrators alike. And her coworkers harassed her ruthlessly for dating an Indian-American journalist named Rama. She often told Alice it was because her choice of a dark-skinned man threatened their white masculinity. Alice just wished Nancy would up and smash them all and be done with it.

But Alice knew also there were problems in this world that couldn't be solved with a good smashing from Nancy or anyone else. Nancy never spoke of it, but judging from the local police blotter, she was kept busy dealing with all the problems endemic to modern society that Karan often complained about —domestic violence, sexual assault, drugs, and so on. Alice respected Nancy, almost like a mentor, but wouldn't want her job for the world.

"You're late," Nancy said with a smile, standing up from her bench. She was a head shorter than Alice or Madison. Her bare shoulders rippled with muscle, and her cheeks were rosy. "How's Connie?"

"In a coma. Do you remember Madison?" Alice asked her.

"Of course. Nice to see you." Nancy smiled serenely, unperturbed by Alice's comment. "Are you working in with us today, Madison?"

"Um, okay ..." Madison said, glancing back at Alice for guidance.

"Don't worry, Mad. We won't make you go heavy."

"Let's pull off the plates so you can warm up," Nancy said congenially. "Jump on there and get to work." Before Alice could lie down on the bench, Nancy took her arm gently. "Alice," she said softly, "I visited Connie and your mom last night. I'm really sorry about what happened."

Alice pulled away and lay down on the bench. She pushed out twenty very fast, very angry reps, doing her best to replace emotional pain with its simpleton cousin, physical pain.

Nancy responded to Alice's willingness to work hard and put them all through a crushing workout. Madison would probably be sore for a week.

After the last set, they were pulling Nancy's plates off the bar one last time, and Alice decided to take advantage of the emotional high Nancy was probably feeling. It was time to talk.

"Hey, Nancy. We've been out hanging more lost boy flyers for Wyatt."

"Oh yeah?" Nancy said, still breathing hard. "That's nice of you."

Madison took her cue. "We know Wyatt's sister Crystal. She told us there's no way he hitchhiked to Utah. He's still up there in the mountains somewhere."

A cloud darkened Nancy's face. Alice knew that look. It meant she was angry Alice was meddling in something she shouldn't.

Madison didn't seem to notice. "Nancy, do you know why the sheriff's office doesn't believe Crystal? Why did you guys call off the search?"

Nancy turned to Madison and softened. "Madison, I'd tell you if I could. It's above my pay grade. I can assure you both, however, that search and rescue is still up there looking. Not as many resources as I would like, but they are still up there."

"We also met with Wyatt's friend Asher. He said Wyatt was obsessed with Nathaniel Narrow's disappearance ten years ago, and on the day Wyatt disappeared, he was searching for a place Nathaniel used to go. It was up on Witchat Mountain, somewhere near a cliff."

"Nathaniel who?" Nancy asked. Her face was threatening, but it was encouraging that she was at least asking questions.

Alice suddenly got the feeling she was being watched. She wheeled around and saw it. On the white-painted brick walls near the toilets, about head high: the damned tag, staring at her with its evil eye.

Alice forced herself to look away from the tag. "Nancy, did my dad tell you exactly why Connie is in a coma?"

"Alice, your mom is not under investigation. She's a victim, not—"

"That's not what I mean. I know it's not directly Mom's fault. I understand how hard depression is. Sort of. What I mean is ..."

Nancy narrowed her eyes at Alice, suspicion starting to creep back in.

"Oh, come on, give me a break," Alice said. "Look, Nancy. Come over here. I need to show you something."

Alice pulled out her phone and strode over to the evil face. Nancy and Madison finished stacking their weights and then followed her.

"See that ugly face up there?" Alice pointed her phone at it.

"It's not my job to police graffiti, Alice."

"Just watch." Right on cue, her phone called up the website for the online pharmacy that had almost killed Connie.

"Wait, how does that work?" Nancy asked, interested now.

"The eye has a QR code in it," Madison explained. "This particular one encodes the web address for an online drugstore. You place an order, and they send it to you from India by UPS. It's where Alice's mom got her pills. Those things were laced with the strongest and most addictive opioid ever made, so she got instantly addicted."

"She's got postpartum depression," Alice said, in her mom's defense.

"Hey," Nancy soothed, "I don't blame your mom for trying to help herself. I'll tell you what: if I didn't have this place"— Nancy gestured around them—"I'd probably be in jail or worse. But I know your mom realizes she doesn't need those pills because she has you. You're better than all the heroin in India. She'll get through this.

"I didn't know about the graffiti," Nancy continued, "but I knew that Victoria got her drugs from an online pharmacy in India. I passed all that information on to the DEA. I'll pass this on to them too. I'm sure they'll handle it."

"Really?" Madison asked, eyes wide. "Federal drug enforcement? Wow, that's great. Isn't it, Alice?"

"No," Alice replied.

Nancy had regained her composure and looked up at Alice.

"We can't fix the opioid epidemic overnight, Alice. And I can't personally do anything about some rogue pharmacy in India. The feds will do what they can. But I promise we will at least prevent them from advertising their shit in my county."

Unimpressed, Alice played her last card, the one she had come to play. "I bet Rama could help find those guys in India. He's a genius. And you told me he's in Delhi right now, researching something for a story."

Anger flashed across Nancy's face again. She paused, as though choosing her words carefully. "Alice, I know you. You're getting in over your head. I know your mom and Connie are in the hospital because of these bastards. But you need to listen to me." She paused again and looked Alice right in the eye. "Put all your energy into helping Connie heal and supporting your mom and dad during this hard time. Leave the sleuthing to the authorities. I'm serious. I don't want to see you get in trouble again."

"But—"

"Enough gabbing. This is supposed to be a workout. Time for triceps." Nancy led them over to the cables and away from any further questions.

As they walked under the ominous, watchful eye of the tag, Madison's phone chimed, and she stopped to read it. "I'll be with you in a sec."

Alice was ten feet away already when she heard Madison gasp. She spun around and saw Madison staring in horror at her phone. Then she noticed Madison was standing right under the graffiti face. Had it dark-magicked her somehow?

Alice ran over, assuming something had happened to Connie and she just hadn't received the text yet.

Madison showed her phone to Alice and looked away in disgust.

It was a message from Karan. She had forwarded a social media post featuring a cartoon version of Karan's face, all the scars highlighted in black. It made her look like a zombie. Below the image was the caption, "Alert: promiscuous new girl at Hardrock High. Killed her dad last year and suffered no consequences. Now she is hunting new victims. Who knows what she is capable of? Watch out. #blackwidowofhardrock"

The text from Karan was one word: *Help*.

CHAPTER 18

SATURDAY, 4:00 P.M.

TWENTY-THREE HOURS BEFORE THE END

The girls charged toward the library in a panic. Alice drove furiously, imagining Karan hanging by a noose from the rafters, while Madison continuously called and texted her to no response.

They both were acutely aware of Karan's emotional fragility. Madison and her parents had been briefed by social workers and told to expect substantial mood swings. Karan's accident had left her in a state of trauma made worse by her acute amnesia. Her doctors from the town in Arizona where she used to live had said she'd been extremely anxious and susceptible to bouts of depression even *before* the accident that killed her father and left her severely injured.

Karan had already been mistreated on and off social media in the short time she had been in Hardrock. Most of it was just the usual arrogant kids in school making insensitive comments, showing off to each other. As far as Madison and Alice knew, it had all been nipped in the bud. But this was in another league. They had never expected Karan to get bullied this ruthlessly and openly on social media or for so many of their classmates to repost it without question.

"I know it was those pool-playing idiots from the Road-house. First they beat up Crystal, and now they're attacking Karan online because she was sitting with Crystal," Madison said through clenched teeth as Alice ran another red light.

"How do you know it was them?" Alice asked.

"Just a feeling," Madison said. "I'm allowed those too, aren't I?"

"Oh. Actually, I agree because of something Dean said. He warned me those two boys playing pool that night were into scary chat rooms. Something about being involuntarily celibate. Incel or whatever. This 'black widow of Hardrock' garbage is something boys like that would come up with."

"Incel? Isn't that the ideology behind a ton of recent mass murders? And how the hell would some college recruiter know those guys were incels?"

"Madison, I thought I told you Dean has siddhis."

"Even if that was true, how can he know what two guys post on some dark corner of the internet? Because they're sure not doing it under their own names. I'm telling you, Alice; that British cowboy is suspicious."

Alice considered this. She hadn't seen any computer equipment in his truck. Not even a laptop. It could have been locked away, she supposed. It was more likely Dean had help. From whom? Did his magic school in London have a team of wizard hacker geniuses that fed him intel?

But she had no time to ponder Dean. She threw the Mustang into an illegal parking spot near the library. Leaving the car unlocked, they ran together up the front steps, through the atrium, and past Brian's office.

Karan was not in the rare books room.

Alice barged into Brian's office and demanded, "Have you seen Karan?"

Brian didn't seem ruffled. He rarely did. His unflappable sarcasm matched his perfect grooming and expensive clothes.

As he smoothed an imaginary wrinkle in his skinny jeans, he looked casually at Alice. "Ah, so pleased to see you looking so well on this lovely autumn day in our fair town."

"Cut it out. Where is she?"

"She left just after you did, about two hours ago. I do not have ESP, and therefore I do not know where she is."

As Alice turned to leave, Brian added, "I do, however, know that some boys were just here looking for you three. And it didn't seem like they wanted to invite you to study for the SAT, if you know what I mean."

"What did they look like?" Madison demanded, now glaring at Brian more fiercely than Alice had.

"Young, five-ten, T-shirts bearing names of ski brands, poor teeth, sneaky. Not your type, nor mine, for that matter. Not that I would ever presume to know what your type is."

Alice and Madison looked at each other. It sounded like Brian was indeed describing the incel boys from the Roadhouse.

"Have you ever seen them before?" Madison pressed. "Did they ask you anything?"

"No and no. Is something wrong?" Brian finally seemed concerned, perhaps remembering how close Alice and Madison had been to grievous injury last year.

Madison said, "Hey, Brian, if you see them again, please take a picture and text it to me. Okay?"

"I am not a dating service."

"Those guys are not interested in asking us out, trust me. We think they may have started an online campaign to bully and threaten Karan. She sent us an SOS, which is why we're here."

"Oh, Jesus. Of course I'll photograph them, should they come by again."

"Thanks, Brian. And if Karan comes back, text us immediately. Try to keep her here. We'll search for her in the rest of the library, and then around town. It's vital that we find her. Okay?"

"Absolutely," he said firmly, with only a trace of his usual sarcasm.

Madison and Alice rushed out into the stacks of the vast library. There were six floors of books, each the size of a football field.

"Stay with me, Alice," Madison said as they stormed toward the East Asian books. "If I run into those incel boys, I don't want to be alone."

"Let's just hope we find Karan before they do."

Alice's and Madison's very long legs propelled them through the giant library at top speed.

Not finding Karan in the East Asian or South Asian sections, Madison checked her phone and immediately cringed. She held it up to Alice.

There were already hundreds of comments on the black widow post. Most of them were just variations on "Ew" or vomit emojis. There were a few mildly supportive posts, but there were also more than a few that were personal and vicious:

Oh, it's human? I thought it was an orc.

I've heard she has a plan to shoot everyone at school.

My mom wrote to the school to get her removed. She's a threat to our safety.

Doesn't she live with Madison Percival? I wonder what they do together at night.

After a frantic search of two more floors of the library, Alice shouted, "There!"

Karan's now-messy ponytail was the only visible part of her. She was in a section where the books on depression in teenagers were shelved. It was dark, as the lights in her section had timed out, and Karan was on the floor, surrounded by books. But she wasn't reading any of them. It looked more like the books had fallen on her in a kind of landslide. When she turned her head to look at them with swollen red eyes, it was apparent she had had been crying.

"Karan! Oh, sweetheart, I'm so sorry," Madison said, dashing to her side.

Alice clicked on the fluorescent light and remained at the end of the aisle as a guard, watching both ends of the hallway in case the incel boys showed up.

Karan didn't respond at first. It seemed like she couldn't speak. Then her face crumpled, and she covered her eyes.

Alice's heart broke for her, knowing what it was like to be the outcast. "Karan, I've gotta tell you something about that post you forwarded."

Karan looked up, responding to Alice's serious tone, as Madison patted her back.

"We think we know who did it and why," Alice continued. "They weren't just bullying you. Well, they were. But it wasn't because of you or your accident. Well, it was. Oh, crap. Madison, can you please explain? It's not coming out right."

"We think it was those idiots from the Roadhouse—the guys you confronted last night when they were playing pool. Alice thinks they are online trolls or, like, computer geniuses."

"I wouldn't go that far. I actually have no idea if they're smart or dumb. I can't imagine they're computer geniuses, but they could be. You never know. But Dean said they were into incel things online, and I believe him. And if that's true, it means they have some serious mental health issues, and they like to take them out on young women. Like you."

"And they must have been the ones who beat up Crystal and called her racist things last night," Madison said.

"Yeah. So please don't take it personally."

Karan sniffed and rubbed her eyes. "What, it's not personal? When someone says all that personal stuff about me, and everyone else forwards it to all their contacts? You don't call that personal?"

"If it helps," Alice said firmly, "we are going to destroy them for it."

"Yes. That might help. A bit." Karan's spirits seemed to lift at the thought of revenge.

"I think we need to get outside," Madison said. "This place is stifling."

"I'll tell you what is stifling," Karan said. "Being new in a town, embarrassed about my disfigured face, totally alone in the world because both my parents are dead, and having someone spread lies about me all over the school."

"You're not alone in the world," Alice and Madison said at once. It was like a harmony. Like they had practiced.

They looked at each other and smiled. Their smile seemed to infect Karan, who cracked a very faint smile too. It seemed her crisis had passed for the moment.

"So," Karan said, sighing, "do you guys want to hear what I found out?"

"About what?" Alice asked, looking at the untidy piles of books about depression.

"About you. Your siddhis."

"Oh, those."

Karan dug out a pile of old hardbacks, presumably not about depression. "These are great, but the best stuff was from a PhD dissertation I read. A lady in Australia wrote it thirty years ago. She summarizes all of these other old books in her literature survey, and she went around the world, interviewing people about siddhis. She even spent a year living in caves in the Himalayas."

Madison and Alice were looking at Karan in awe. "You did all that while we were gone just now?" Madison asked. "We were away, like, two hours tops. And you were ..."

"Crying my eyes out. Yeah. I would have read a lot more if it wasn't for that nasty post. Oh," she exclaimed, holding her hand out defensively. "By the way, I turned off my phone. You guys haven't been calling, have you?"

"Only about a hundred times," Alice said.

"Oh. Sorry. Anyway, this is the serendipitous part. Get this, Alice. The author of the dissertation spent a whole chapter talking about some old guy called Ramakrishna Rao. She met him in a cave. That couldn't be the same guy as your Mr. Rao, could it?"

"Uh, yeah, that *was* his name ..."

"I thought so. That was the most amazing chapter of the whole dissertation. The Aussie lady said Mr. Rao was considered the most knowledgeable and gifted scholar on siddhis in all of India. She hunted him down and spent six months learning from him. Then he simply disappeared. The legend was he had turned into an immortal being of light and floated off deeper into the mountains to support other seekers in their meditation. I guess he didn't. He must have just come to America to be your Obi-Wan."

"No, I wasn't even born then. He came here much later."

"So, is there anything in there that can help us find Wyatt?" Madison seemed suddenly nervous. It was like she had finally reached her limit with learning about siddhis. She was okay talking about it when Alice was vulnerable and she could help. But now her brain seemed to be struggling with the enormity of the idea that her friend could be a kind of yogic superhero.

"Well, the Aussie lady quotes Mr. Rao saying siddhis are *developed*," Karan said. "They're not bestowed or innate. They come from hard work and personal discipline."

They all looked at each other while the fluorescent light sizzled angrily above their heads. Then it flicked off, and Alice didn't bother turning it on again.

"Let's go back to rare books," she suggested.

They helped Karan off the ground and started gathering all the books she wanted.

Madison's phone rang. "Brian," she said to Alice, declining the call quickly so she could give Karan her full attention.

Then her phone pinged with a text from Brian: *ANSWER!*

Then Alice's phone rang. They looked at each other. "What?" Alice said brusquely, putting Brian on speakerphone. "What have you done?!"

CHAPTER 19

SATURDAY, 5:00 P.M.

TWENTY-TWO HOURS BEFORE THE END

"Why?" Alice asked Brian. "What's the matter?"

"Well," Brian said in a shaken voice, "just after you left to look for Karan, I was visited by two irate detectives from the sheriff's department. It was terrifying. I hate guns."

"Were they here to arrest you?" Alice asked. "For being a dick?"

"They were searching for you."

"Why?" Alice asked.

"They claimed someone put an anonymous tip in your high school's see something, say something app about you."

"What tip?" Madison asked, her face turning ashen. Mad was not used to being in trouble. For Alice, it was second nature.

"Evidently, you three are planning a school shooting, which is against the law these days. You're supposedly targeting all the kids and teachers associated with the Young Republicans club because they oppose action on climate change."

"Oh, that," Karan said casually. "Yes, we're also planning to shoot everyone dumb enough to be at school on a Saturday."

"Karan!" Madison shrieked. "Someone might hear you!"

She turned to the phone and shouted, "We are *not* planning a school shooting, Brian!"

"I *know* that," he said. "I told them. But they say they have to take these things seriously. So I told them I had no idea where you were."

After a moment of silence, Brian said, more earnestly than before, "Girls, you should go turn yourselves in. It would look better. You can explain how much you love Republicans and how scared you are of guns and violence."

"Okay, Brian," Alice said, rolling her eyes. "We'll talk to Nancy about it first."

"Good idea."

"Are they gone?"

"Yes, thank god."

Pocketing her phone, Alice looked at Madison and was about to make a joke, but instead she had to steady her friend. "Mad, relax! It's nothing!" When her admonishment only made Madison look worse, she shouted, "Madison, breathe! You have to breathe!"

Finally, Madison took a deep breath and closed her eyes.

"That's it, breathe, Mad, breathe," Alice said, patting her roughly on the back. "It's going to be okay. Or not."

Karan laughed.

"Is that supposed to be reassuring?" Mad responded.

"Not really. Just being honest. At least you didn't faint."

"But the police are after us!"

"Yes, maybe. Story of my life. Sure, it feels scary to be on the wrong side of somebody in the sheriff's office. But you have to ask yourself one thing."

"What? Like, why did we ever think we could help find Wyatt?"

"No, Mad. This is my question: Why haven't our parents called us? If we were in genuine trouble, surely the police would have gone to them first, at least to ask where we were?

And if that were the case, I know for a fact you'd have at least five hundred missed calls from your mom by now. I'd probably have a couple dozen from Dad."

Madison and Karan grabbed their phones and confirmed they had not received any calls from Madison's parents, who were also Karan's foster parents.

"You're right. But why? Why haven't they gone to our parents?" Madison asked.

"The only reason I can think of is that there is someone in the sheriff's office who is just trying to scare us. They don't want to involve our parents, who would ask them uncomfortable questions about where they got this stupid fake information about us wanting to shoot up the school."

"That makes sense, actually," Karan said, pocketing her phone.

"If that's the case, we need Nancy's help. Like, now," Madison said, fear still written all over her features.

Agreeing, Alice dialed Nancy's number.

"Is Karan okay?" Nancy asked.

"Yes. A little shaken up, but okay. I think."

"Good."

"Hey, Nancy—have you heard anything around work about us wanting to shoot up our high school?"

"I didn't hear what you just said," Nancy said in a tired voice. "I'm hanging up the phone right now."

Before she could, Alice said quickly, "Because it's a lie, but there are still some officers looking for the three of us."

"I'm really hanging up the phone."

"Nancy, seriously. We need your help. We're being set up."

"Well, even if I might have overlooked your massive betrayal of my trust yesterday, or even an hour ago, I can't help you now. I've been put on administrative leave."

"What? Since when?"

"Since five minutes ago, when I questioned the sheriff about the rationale for calling off the search for Wyatt Zhang on Witchat."

"Isn't that a little extreme?"

"No."

There was silence on the line, but at least Nancy didn't hang up.

"Okay, look," Nancy finally said, "I'll meet you at your house in twenty minutes. We'll talk over your options. Okay?"

"Absolutely. Okay. Twenty minutes."

Alice reported the news to Madison and Karan.

"Great," Karan said. "I don't want to hang out here in these dusty stacks anymore."

"Karan, can I ask you a big, huge favor?" Madison asked.

"No. I know what you're going to say."

"Please?"

"No."

Alice realized Madison was going to ask Karan to stay behind; she thought their friend might be too fragile to meet with a friendly police officer, much less get interrogated by some very unfriendly ones.

"This is going to sound strange," Alice said, "but I have this feeling that we're going to need you. Like, here in the library. You could hang out in the rare books room."

"No."

"Come on," Alice urged. "It would be cool to be the 'guy in the chair.' You know, the person with the headphones who tells the other superheroes what to do."

Madison nodded in agreement.

Karan seemed less convinced. "What?"

"Haven't you seen *Spider-Man, Homecoming*?" Alice asked.

"Yeah ... but ... that means I'm the overweight kid, and you guys are Spider-men?"

"Number one, that kid was awesome. And number two, you're not overweight, Karan," Madison reassured. "And Alice is right. This is getting intense. We need someone smart looking stuff up while we're running around out there."

Madison began to walk stiffly away, and Alice grabbed her shoulder. "Let's keep our eyes open, just in case. We don't want to run into those deputies before we speak to Nancy."

"Yeah," Karan said. "And I'd also like to avoid those incel boys. At least until we have time to go pick up the weapons we were going to use to shoot up our school."

"Karan!" Madison shouted, then put her hand over her mouth.

"Come on," Alice said, emerging from the section they had found Karan in. She poked her head out, looked right and left, and guided them carefully back toward the rare books room.

Before leaving Karan there alone, Alice took hold of her arm. "Karan, you're going to be okay. Because I think you have siddhis like me. Mad does too."

They both rolled their eyes.

Alice didn't really believe they had siddhis like hers, but she did feel they were both amazing people, and she had never told them that before. "No, seriously. Madison, you're uncommonly smart. You're top of the class. And you still find time to be the best swimmer too. And to help people, like helping Crystal find Wyatt. And you're pretty much a single mom to your little sister. How do you even do that? She's only three. It's like ... you have this cosmic mother thing going on. Like you're channeling some divine power that makes people feel safe. In that sense, being around you is like being around prana itself."

Madison's eyes widened.

"Karan," Alice said, taking a deep breath, "you're, like, some kind of information magnet. It's like you sucked all those books about siddhis straight out of thin air. It's not normal. I've only known you for, like, four months, but it seems like you do that all the time. And another siddhi—you have survived a lot of damage."

"Maybe I'm indestructible, like Karna," Karan scoffed.

"Who's Karna?" Madison asked, incredulous at the direction this was taking.

"It's a he. Karna is a figure in Hindu mythology from one of those books I found. He was super strong and immortal as long as he wore his gold breastplate and earrings. I think they were given to him by the sun god, who was his father."

"What?" Madison exclaimed. "Alice, neither of us can do anything like you can. This is ridiculous."

"It's not that weird," Karan quipped. "You just change one letter, and Karan becomes Karna. Maybe I'll be known as Captain Anagram. Well, won't the Harry Potter club kids be happy."

Alice smiled, pleased Karan had finally recovered enough to joke. "So, I was just thinking, for your first assignment as guy in the chair, can you try to find out why the hell Nancy got put on leave for asking why the sheriff believes the hitching story? There must be something weird about it. Like, maybe the sheriff has a history of hating Asian people. Maybe his dad got killed in Vietnam. Maybe he's a neo-Nazi."

"Good idea," Madison said. "And keep looking for information that might help Alice get her ... powers back. Her siddhis."

CHAPTER 20

SATURDAY, 6:00 P.M.

TWENTY-ONE HOURS BEFORE THE END

I n an attempt to stay under the radar, Madison made Alice drive very conservatively—way under the speed limit, to Alice's desperate annoyance—but they still managed to arrive at the Brickstone cabin before Nancy.

The place was dark and extremely quiet. Mom was still at the hospital, and Mr. Responsible Father was looking after her and Connie.

"It feels weird here," Alice observed. "Like my parents have moved away and taken Connie with them."

"Oh, Alice. Everything will be okay, you'll see."

"It still feels like they are on the verge of going away. Or like I am. It's like twilight. Neither day nor night." She wanted to say it felt like a transition, but the only word that came into her head was *transmission*, because Dad had been telling her to watch her transmission fluid levels.

Where was Nancy? Had she been sucked into the evil suck-hole of Alice's vision?

"Let's check in with Karan," Madison said. "I'm still worried about her."

Alice nodded as Madison dialed on speakerphone.

"You guys with Nancy?" Karan asked when she picked up. "'Cause I'm still kind of freaking out here."

"Not yet. Have you seen those boys or the guys from the sheriff's department?"

"Nope. Brian let me lock the door. He said he'll tell anyone who comes that he closed early. I just wish he knew kung fu or something."

"That sounds good," Mad said, "but call us if anything happens or if you need us."

"And stay off social media, Black Widow," Alice added.

"You'll refer to me as Captain Anagram, not Black Widow, thank you very much. And don't you want to hear my first report as the guy in the chair?"

"What, already?" Madison asked in astonishment.

"Sure. You've been gone for ten minutes. So I've figured it all out."

"Figured all *what* out?" Alice gave Mad a worried look, like maybe Karan had taken the guy in the chair siddhi thing a bit too seriously.

"Okay, first of all, that story about Nathaniel doesn't make sense. 'Cause why would that kid's sitter not be totally guilty of negligence? He or she took a disabled kid on a hike and lost him. I'm calling bullshit on that. Somebody is hiding something. It just looks like a cover-up. Don't you think?"

"A cover-up? Of what? You think Nathaniel's babysitter murdered him?"

"Nope. I'm guessing it's one of two things. One: the sitter was negligent but had connections high up, and those connections bought him some protection from blame. Or two: the sitter was not negligent, but he lost Nathaniel in a terrible accident, which happened in a way that could not be allowed to go public. Like, someone had to cover it up for reasons so good, even the kid's father kept quiet."

"Karan, these sound like conspiracy theories."

"You think I'm crazy? Crazier than those kids from this afternoon?"

"No, Karan—"

"Anyway, there's more. I just texted some photos to you."

Alice pulled out her phone and saw an old high school football photo with the caption HARDROCK HIGH VARSITY, 1988. Underneath the picture were the names of all the players.

"This solves the sheriff thing," Karan said. "I think you were right, Alice. Nancy's boss is that guy in the middle, number eighty-five. The big guy next to him, number eighty-one, is the current CEO of the coal mine in Johnston. You know, the mine on the other side of Witchat Mountain. The same guys who are drilling a new vent near Wyatt's house. His name is Ed Toomes."

"Yeah, he was mentioned in that newspaper article about Nathaniel. He was the mine spokesman or something. Anyway, we have an old photo of two men standing together. So what?"

"So, everything."

Alice and Madison looked at each other warily.

Madison said tentatively, "Karan, you think Toomes told Nancy's boss to make up the hitchhiking story and to stop searching for Wyatt?"

"Duh."

"But why?"

Thinking of the video James and Asher had shown them, Alice asked, "And what about the cloaked meadow thing?"

"Just humor me for a second here. Forget about the magic stuff and just look at the facts. A kid goes missing near a mine, and then there's a cover-up about the circumstances. Ten years later, another kid goes looking for the place the first kid disappeared, and he goes missing too, and there's another cover-up. And now we see that the mine boss guy was buddies with the sheriff. It's not that hard to imagine what is going on here. It must have something to do with the mine. Like, maybe both kids fell in a mine shaft, and the company doesn't want any bad publicity about it."

"No way," Madison said. "That would be the biggest scandal in the history of the county. Toomes would go to jail, and the sheriff would be recalled."

"Right," Karan scoffed. "Like the two most powerful men in the county won't get away with whatever they want."

"Karan, stuff like that happens in the movies, but I'm guessing not so often in the real world. But ..." Madison squinted at the picture. "It does seem like there could be a strong link between those two guys."

"Look," Karan said impatiently, "we're athletes, and we know sports, right? I haven't been involved with your swim team here, but my amnesia is slowing lifting, and I remember a little bit about where I used to swim. All the girls knew everything about each other—way more than we even wanted to know. We were more than friends. So if high school football is anything like swimming, these guys were all pretty close. Look at the picture of the sheriff and Ed Toomes. They're the two biggest boys on the team. They look huge. And I looked it up; both were starting linemen. That means they would have spent even more time together, because they were in the same position group. I bet if you gave me more time, I'd find out they were best men at each other's weddings."

Alice looked at Madison and smiled. "See?" she said. "Our guy in the chair is a magical genius."

"Maybe."

"Anyway," Karan continued, unfazed, "it gives us a different way to search for Wyatt. A way that Crystal and her friends haven't tried. We should look for him wherever the mining guys don't want us to search."

"Where is that, exactly?" Madison asked. "The mine owns a huge expanse of land. Do we go search for him on the mine lease? That's near Johnston, right? But it would be, like, underground? Or do we look near their new drilling site?"

"I'm guessing the place Wyatt and Nathaniel disappeared is in some sensitive area the mine boss guy doesn't want exposed to the public," Alice mused.

"Well, I can't find any public records saying which parts of the mine property are more sensitive than other parts. I guess they would have all that information hidden in their office. I did find out their offices aren't anything fancy, though. They are just a couple of trailers set up on the highway outside of town. It would be easy to—"

"I'm guessing," Madison interrupted, "that breaking and entry will not look good on top of the other trouble we're in, Karan."

"Maybe you can find records about federal cleanup sites?" Alice asked.

"Duh. Of course I checked. There are no Superfund things associated with Johnston mine."

"So," Alice mused, "maybe they're hiding a mining waste spill of some kind? Maybe it's an illegal toxic pond that is poisoning the town's groundwater."

"Yeah, and we're all slowly turning into mutants with superpowers." Karan sounded giddy with excitement.

"And," Alice continued, ignoring Karan's quip, "maybe it wasn't cloaked by Nathaniel ten years ago. Maybe the mine boss hid it using normal stuff like trees and camouflaged tarps. And Wyatt found it and fell in or something."

"Yeah, and now he's the world's first superpowered mutant, Weapon X! And he's being held in a secret underground laboratory while they experiment on his superpowers!"

"Karan, you are making me feel a bit uncomfortable with that theory."

"Oh, Alice, quit being dramatic. You can still be the older, more pathetic weapon that always defeats the newer weapon by being more streetwise and wily."

Alice rolled her eyes at Madison. "Hang up on her. Now."

Madison smiled. "Karan, it sounds like you maybe need to get some food in your stomach."

"Right. Good idea. Good luck with Nancy. Tell her I'm putting together a letter to the editor about the corrupt sheriff. Hopefully, it will help her get her job back."

Alice didn't think Nancy would like that idea much, but Karan had already hung up before Alice could warn her.

Just then, Alice heard the distinct rumble of Nancy's huge Ford Raptor truck and the crunch of gravel under her tires. She turned to face the truck as it emerged from the trees.

Nancy's face was expressionless as she climbed out of her car. At least she wasn't pointing a gun at them, Alice thought. And she didn't seem to be pulling out handcuffs.

"Ladies," she finally said.

"Hi, Nancy," Madison gushed. "Thank you, thank you, thank you so, so much for coming."

"You girls okay?" Nancy's voice had no warmth in it.

"Of course," Alice said, pretending to be tough. But she felt like she was about to get one of the world's biggest "I'm disappointed in you" speeches, and she wasn't feeling very tough at all.

"I'm disappointed in you," Nancy said. "In both of you."

Phew, Alice thought. *That could have been worse.*

"We're sorry?" she offered.

They looked at each other in silence. Or rather, Nancy, her leg muscles bulging through her jeans and her arm muscles twitching under her T-shirt, looked up at Alice, and Alice looked down at Nancy while wearing her best puppy dog look.

After a short stare-down, Nancy asked, "So if I told you to just do your homework and drop this whole thing, you'd ignore me and keep sleuthing. Right?"

"I'm done with my homework," Alice said.

"And if it gets you killed or gets me fired, so be it. Right?"

"Nancy," Alice interrupted, "your sheriff might be corrupt. We think he and his buddy Ed Toomes, Mr. Mine Boss, are hiding the way those kids really disappeared."

"Wait a minute. There's more than one kid lost now?"

"Wyatt and Nathaniel. Wyatt was searching for the place Nathaniel Narrow disappeared ten years ago," Madison said.

"And it's probably a toxic spill or something," Alice added. "So Mr. Mine Boss has to cover it up. And he needs his best friend, the sheriff, to help him do that."

"It's a theory, at least," Madison said. "It might explain why you got your wrist slapped as soon as you asked any questions."

Nancy shook her head and let the silence settle, her ticking truck the only sound.

"But don't worry," Madison said haltingly. "Karan is preparing to write a letter to the local paper. Maybe it will help you get reinstated."

Nancy's eyes widened, and two big blood vessels began to bulge in her forehead.

Alice and Madison shuffled their feet.

"It's ... *funny*," Nancy spat, as though she was having great difficulty speaking at all. "I thought I was here because you two were in trouble for threatening Young Republicans at your school and you wanted my advice on how to proceed." The pitch and volume of her voice were getting higher and higher. "I never dreamed you would dump ... an *absurd* "—Nancy's voice cracked at the word *absurd*, and she had to close her eyes briefly—"conspiracy theory on me!"

Highly alarmed, Alice tried to get Madison's attention but failed.

Unaware of how close Nancy was to exploding, Madison said, "I know it sounds absurd. But why else would someone submit a false tip about us planning a shooting? We are being slandered because we're helping Crystal search on Witchat Mountain! It just makes sense that someone like Toomes organized the school tip to scare us. And as Alice says, they didn't even call our parents, so—"

Madison finally glanced at Alice, who desperately shook her head to get her to shut up.

"Oh," Madison said.

"Enough!" Nancy shouted. "I have had enough of this crap!"

The force of Nancy's anger made Alice and Madison take a step back.

"I will not be lectured by two teenagers about a conspiracy in the sheriff's department! Of course the sheriff knows Ed Toomes. Everyone knows everyone around here. But there is no conspiracy! You two are in such deep shit, you'll be washing it out of your hair for years! You come at me with this crap ... I can't even believe I came here to try to help you. You're beyond help."

Nancy began walking back to her truck, shaking her head. After only two steps, she stopped and turned around. "It is no secret in the sheriff's office that I have taken responsibility for keeping you out of trouble, Alice. I have stuck my neck waaaaay out for you. Have any of you considered what may happen if our local paper prints a letter from one of your close friends, falsely claiming there's a massive illegal conspiracy in the department?"

Nancy clenched her fists, looked from Alice to Madison, and got in her truck.

As she drove away, Alice raised her eyebrows. "That went well. Don't you think?"

"Now what do we do?" Madison looked desperate.

Alice took out her phone and dialed Karan again.

"Pizza is not here yet," she said instead of hello.

"Whatever you do, don't send that letter to the editor."

"What?"

"Nancy is pissed off that we're questioning the sheriff's decision to call off the search for Wyatt. It will look bad for her if you send that letter, because she's kind of my unofficial parole officer, and they all know we hang out."

"Right," Karan said. "I thought of that too. Especially since we're now coconspirators to shoot up the school."

"Karan!" Madison squealed.

"Um, I hate to be the bearer of bad news, or maybe badder news ... quite a bit badder, actually ... maybe the badderest."

"Spit it out, Karan," Alice said.

"Just check your email."

Alice and Madison both checked their email, eyebrows furrowed. Alice couldn't believe there could be worse news at the moment.

"I can't believe it," Madison said.

Alice read her email aloud:

Dear Ms. Brickstone,

I regret to inform you I have been forced to cancel my visit this coming Tuesday. An assistant brought an article to my attention. You are quoted admitting to the use of performance-enhancing drugs and defending this poor choice with the claim that "it's the only way we can keep up with those chucky ching chongs in China, who are fed steroids like there's no tomorrow."

I called your coach, who defended you and your two friends, suggesting there must be some kind of mistake regarding the drugs and the racist remarks. I'm prepared to believe him. This sort of slander of athletes occurs regularly and is often authored by other athletes hoping to secure scholarships for themselves.

Even if that turns out to be the case in this situation, I wish to postpone my trip to Colorado until the dust settles. In the meantime, I am forwarding to you a list of reputable social media consultants who work with young athletes. High-caliber athletes live in a fishbowl, and everyone is watching what we say and do. I strongly urge you to make contact. They are well worth the investment.

ALICE RAISED her eyes and saw that Madison looked like she was about to collapse.

"Um ... whoever slandered us did a pretty good job," Karan said ominously. "Google your names and see what happens."

Alice did so, and the top ten hits were links to very official-looking news articles about three swimming prospects from Hardrock. Clicking one of the mainstream media links, Alice read an article that featured the damning quote about doping "to keep up with the chucky ching chongs."

"It was written by Melba Goldberg," Madison said. "That name sounds familiar ..."

"It should," Karan said distractedly, hammering on her keyboard, obviously researching something else. "She wrote that article about Nathaniel ten years ago."

"So wait," Alice said to Karan. "Do we still think the incel boys are behind all this online stuff and Toomes is directing them? And Toomes can also get Melba Goldberg to write whatever he tells her? Or what?"

"No idea. But there are dozens of posts quoting us calling people chucky ching chongs all over Snapchat, Insta, everywhere. Melba Goldberg could have just seen it there."

"Or the incel boys forwarded it to her," Alice suggested.

"Alice," Karan said, "please fly off and kill those kids right now."

Alice knew they needed a rational plan right now. Madison was falling apart. Karan was locked in the rare books room by herself after being slandered left and right all day long.

"Karan, I need you to find Nancy's boyfriend Rama's cell phone number. He's in India, but I'm sure he keeps his U.S. cell phone switched on because he's a journalist and might need to receive calls."

"Okay. Hold on."

In a voice quiet enough Karan wouldn't be able to hear through the phone, Alice said, "Madison, I need to you come with me."

"Where?" Madison said meekly.

"To look into something Karan said earlier."

"What?"

"You know that thing about how siddhis are developed, not given? Through hard work and personal discipline or whatever?"

"Yeah?" Madison looked very skeptical.

"Well, I have an idea. But I'd like your help."

"If it involves me throwing you off a cliff, I'm out," Madison said, looking up at the cliff towering over the Brickstone property.

Alice smiled. At least Madison was still making jokes.

Karan's voice sounded over the speakerphone again. "You guys still there?"

"Yes, Karan."

"I'm texting you Rama's phone number. It was on his Facebook business page."

As soon as it came through, Alice thanked Karan and hung up. Then she immediately called Rama in India without any consideration for the time difference. She put it on speakerphone so Mad could hear too.

"Hello?" an alert-sounding male voice rang out.

Rama's voice was so warm and reassuring. He and Alice had shared a lot of hard moments last year, and she regretted that she hadn't seen him much since then. "Hey, Rama. Nice to hear your voice."

"Is that Alice?"

"Yep. How's it going over there in India?"

"I'm about to go out and do something foolish, thank you. How are you?"

"Not good. I need some help."

"What's wrong?"

"Connie swallowed a pill laced with fentanyl yesterday, and she's in a coma. Mom bought it from a website that sends this stuff from India. Can you to find out who runs the business and who owns the factory that supplies the drugs?"

"Oh my god, Alice. I'm so sorry."

"Yeah. You can write an article about it. About the Indian website, I mean. It would be a big deal."

"If it is true, and if I can find them, it would indeed be a big deal. It could also get me very killed."

"Life's a bitch."

"Thanks for caring. Does Nancy know you're calling me about this?"

"Cool," Alice said, pretending she hadn't heard him. "I'll text you the website. Call me back with the info on the drug guys."

"So you're going behind Nancy's back. That's not good, Alice."

"Okay. Call me as soon as you know something."

"It might take days."

"Or I might read in the paper that you've been killed, right?"

"Right."

"Talk to you soon, Rama. Take care doing whatever stupid stuff you're about to do."

"You too. I mean, take care. Because I know you would *never* do anything stupid. And hug Connie for me when she wakes up."

Alice hung up. "Come on, Madison," she said, and took off walking ... straight toward the cliff.

CHAPTER 21

SATURDAY, 7:00 P.M.

TWENTY HOURS BEFORE THE END

"U m ... seriously, Alice, where are we going?"

"Don't worry. I promise I won't ask you to push me off a cliff."

Alice turned right at the base of the cliff, glancing briefly at the spot where only last year she had landed hard after a failed flight.

She led Madison along a trail that traced the base of the cliff, and then into the woods, where they followed a break in the cliff face up a steep slope encumbered by granite scree. They climbed steadily until the scree slope leveled out, revealing a drainage ravine with steep walls rising twenty or thirty feet on either side. Alice led Madison up a trail on one side, then along the edge of the ravine for about a half a mile.

As they walked, Alice tried hard to remember the exact circumstances that had led her to make her first successful flight last year. She had been running through these woods, pursued by a strange man with bad intentions.

Alice looked up at the sky. Today it was a brilliant deep blue. On that day a year ago, it had been full of ominous black storm clouds marching toward her from the north. Her pursuer had been just across the ravine; all he'd had to do to get to her was find the trail across.

As she had prepared to run in a new direction, a bolt of lightning had shattered the air and struck a tree she stood next to, pulverizing it and throwing her to the ground, burned and concussed.

"There it is," Alice said to Madison, having arrived at the spot where it had all happened.

Madison circled the tree. The severed crown was still lying where it had landed after the blast. The burned stump stood about waist high.

"Wow, a burned-up tree. Looks like a lightning strike." She turned to Alice. "But are you going to tell me why we are up here?"

Alice gave Madison a bare-bones version of the story of her chase and then held her hand above the burned stump. "This was just gushing prana that day. It looked like a geyser of crystalline air. Now there's nothing."

"But how did you escape from that guy?"

"I walked over here." Alice demonstrated, standing at the edge of the ravine. "The prana from the lightning tree was flowing out over the ravine. I could see it as clearly as I can see you. I felt it pushing against my body like water. It felt warm, healing. I trusted it. So I jumped and let it carry me across. I had to swim a little, like in water. And then I landed on the other side. It gave me enough of a head start."

"Is that how you fly? Like, usually, before you lost the ability ..."

"Yep. Except most of the time, prana is much less dense. That's why I need a lot of speed for it to support me."

"Wow." Madison looked around and up, obviously trying to imagine what prana looked like. "Alice," she said hesitantly, "I just can't imagine ..."

"Yes, you can, Mad. You can. It's not so different from swimming. Or like flying in a dream. Haven't you ever done that?"

"No."

Alice set her jaw.

"But I can kind of imagine swimming in the air, if there were something like water up there. It sounds amazing." Turning to the lightning tree, Mad ran her hand through the air gracefully where the prana had once flowed. "I wish I could see you just ... dive up into this."

Alice paced around the burned tree. "I have never been back here since that day. But now, after what Karan said about how these abilities are developed, not given, I guess I wanted to see if I ... if *we* could figure it out. How did I develop that siddhi to see and feel prana? Why here? Was it the chase that did something to me? Or the lightning? Or something else? And how can I get it back?"

"You can't see any prana at all now?"

"Just glimpses. And I see nothing coming out of this tree. But I guess it could have just been a temporary phenomenon."

"You can see it even in the dark?"

"Yep. It's luminescent."

"But Alice, what *is* prana, anyway? Why would lightning make it come out of a tree?"

"No idea."

"Well ... what else is different about you now, compared to last year?"

"You mean besides Connie being in a coma, some weird kids filming me flying, the online slander, and everything else?"

"Maybe that's just it, Alice. It's been too much stress."

"You think stress blocks siddhis?"

"I don't know. We could always go back to the idea of pushing you off the cliff to see if that helps."

Alice smiled. "I thought you were against that idea."

Closing her eyes, she took a deep breath and tried to relax. She held her hands out over the tree to feel for any changes.

"Anything?" Mad asked.

"A little," Alice lied. As she stood there with closed eyes, she found herself thinking about how stupid her mom was for buying pills on the internet, and this train of thought led her straight to Tyler. And then Alice went through the same series of feelings she did every other time she'd thought about him. Her heart leaped, and she could remember his smell like he was standing next to her. How could she feel anything for that idiot?

"Let's go back," Alice said, deeply ashamed of her thoughts.

"Sure," Madison said, taking one last look at the lightning tree with what seemed like trepidation. Turning to Alice, she burst out, "Oh, Alice; what are we going to do? This whole thing just gets worse and worse. Wyatt is up there, maybe stuck in a mine shaft or worse, and we're in trouble with the police, and our whole future as college athletes seems to be ruined."

"We could always go to that magic school in London," Alice joked.

"Right," Madison snorted. "Good idea. I'll tell my mom."

They walked back to the cabin in silence, Alice occupied by thoughts of Tyler, which she tried and failed to ignore.

Alice decided she needed to spend some time with Connie and her parents at the hospital, while Madison wanted to pick up Karan and head back to her house to try to explain the police situation to her parents.

At the hospital, a place of timeless medical panic, Alice found everything the same with Connie. Puffy eyes closed, small feet and hands invaded by IV lines and wires. Her mom was doing a little better in the methadone treatment program and was starting to look like herself again. But she had a long, long way to go before she recovered from the guilt and shock of what had happened to her baby daughter.

Alice found her dad a very altered man—exhausted, stressed, and wracked with guilt for not noticing his wife's addiction in time and not being there for her when it mattered. Alice could relate to his guilt. Yet in the noisy silence of the hospital, Dad seemed to have done some deep thinking. He had formally decided he was not cut out to be a "mountain man." He was going to stop trying to fix everything in their lives by himself. If a car broke, he'd take it to the mechanic instead of poring over videos on the internet. He wasn't going to continue trying to cut and split the seven cords of wood they had to put up for the winter; he had already called someone to deliver what they needed. He also said he intended to unplug from his other moneymaking schemes. He was going to ask for more hours at the university. When he was at home, he was going to relax and focus on being present for the family.

Then he surprised Alice with a gift. "I saw your phone was destroyed last night, so I got you this. Isn't it cool?"

As she stared at the brand-new phone, the package advertising a very long battery life and water-resistance, she asked, "Dad, how can we afford a new phone, with all this—"

"Don't worry about money," he interrupted.

Alice was too tired to argue and just hugged him and left.

She drove herself home in the Mustang to eat something and go to bed early.

The next thing she knew, her new waterproof phone was screaming at her in an unfamiliar ringtone, startling her out of a deep sleep.

CHAPTER 22

SATURDAY, 11:00 P.M.

SIXTEEN HOURS BEFORE THE END

She sat up with a jolt, certain the phone call meant Connie was dead.

"What, what?" she whispered, full of panic.

"Alice, it's Rama. Sorry to wake you."

"Right. Hi," she said, trying to pull herself together.

"I was hoping you'd still be up, actually. It's 11:00 p.m., right?"

"Ummm ..."

"It doesn't matter. I'm in a taxi in rural Rajasthan, and the signal is getting less and less reliable as I get farther away from Delhi. I know you wanted this information urgently, and I have a good signal at the moment, so I thought ..."

Rama sounded nervous, and Alice guessed it was because of the "foolish" thing he had said he was in India to do.

"Yep," she said briskly. "What have you got?"

"The online pharmacy you asked me about gets their products from a pharmaceutical company here owned by the Akani Group. It's a family-owned corporation that also has significant mining interests in India and overseas."

"Okay." Alice was only barely making sense of what he was saying.

"Interestingly, there are rumors that they've signed a secret memorandum with the owners of the Johnston Mine near Hardrock. It's secret because of the extreme political sensitivity about coal in America right now. There were also some technical problems with the mine that needed rectifying before Akani could invest."

"Wow."

"Yeah, wow. And here's another thing they told me. The American who came to negotiate on the mining company's behalf was interested in hearing what Akani thought about traditional magical powers in Indian myth and religion. He wanted to go to the Himalayas to find superpowered sages or something."

"Weird," Alice said, confused. Ed Toomes, the football lineman, the conservative mining boss, would hardly be interested in something like siddhis.

"Yeah. So they sent him to Varanasi, thinking that's where all foreigners go to smoke hash and have their spiritual trips. My source had a cousin who ran one of the nicer hotels there. He said the American turned up and scared all the local gurus and teachers. Apparently, he pushed some poor sadhu off a building."

"And this was an older American man from Johnston who supposedly did all that?"

"They didn't say his age. But yeah, from Johnston."

"Wow. How did he get out of that one?"

"Bribes. Now, Alice, I know I cannot forbid you to follow up on this, because I'm not your parent or anything. And I know from experience that you'll do whatever you want no matter what I say. But I have to say it anyway: stay away from these guys. I've already told Nancy everything. She'll pass it on to the right people who can follow up."

"It's not *your* sister in a coma, Rama."

"I thought you'd say that. Alice. Anyway, I have to go. Just remember, these guys are very powerful and dangerous. Let the authorities handle it. They have all the info they need to take them down."

"Blah, blah, blah, thanks for the advice. Coming from a guy who admitted he was doing something dangerous and foolish. See you in a day or two."

After hanging up, Alice looked around at her dark room. As usual, she could smell a slight hint of gas from the garage below. Her Mustang was a perfect warrior, waiting for her to lead it into battle.

She threw on some clothes, grabbed a water bottle and an energy bar, and descended the stairs to the garage, opening the barn doors to let in the moonlight.

She turned the keys, and her car roared to life, with no one around for miles and miles who would be able to hear its ferocious V8 engine.

While the car warmed up, she threw some bolt cutters into the passenger seat, then got in and roared out into the night. Half asleep, alone, but angry and determined. As she chewed through her energy bar, she began to feel almost like herself again. Like she could fly if she wanted to.

With a start, she wondered if perhaps she *could* fly again. She searched for the usual signs of prana around her—in the dark sky, in patches on the ground, flowing around a pine tree. Nothing. Just ordinary, run-of-the-mill, damp night air.

Pushing the car to its formidable limit, she drove the now-familiar road north past the Roadhouse and around Witchat Mountain.

Up ahead, before the declining town of Johnston itself, lay the fenced-off entrance to the mine offices Karan had described. It was where all the paperwork would be. In addition to documents about sensitive sites that might have swallowed a small boy or two, somewhere in there would be a memorandum from the Akani Group. Alice would grab it before they had time to destroy or hide it. She didn't doubt Rama's inquiries had already sounded the alarms and that the higher-ups at the mine were already taking steps to cover their asses. Burning papers, bribing officials, and whatever else rich guys did to make sure they kept getting richer and never got in trouble.

Alice eased off on the thundering car and rolled to a stop in a grove of pine trees about a hundred yards from the fenced compound.

Carrying her bolt cutters, she walked boldly up to the front gate and cut the padlock. One part of her hoped there would be a security guard on night duty. Or perhaps that there were video cameras. She wanted these bastards to know they were sprung. By a teenage girl. The older sister of the girl they almost killed.

But there were no lights on anywhere and no signs of cameras. It was just a couple of single-wide mobile homes with power running to them. The grounds were tidy, and there was an empty paved parking lot between the two trailers.

She went first to the one on the right and kicked open the feeble door. It was just a kitchen and a few unoccupied beds, so she backed out and walked to the other trailer. Kicking that door down revealed precisely what she was looking for: an office. But there were no papers anywhere, nor any filing cabinets. How completely stupid of her. She had thought that an old football lineman like Ed Toomes would keep an old-fashioned paper-based office. She had half expected typewriters and fax machines and paperweights shaped like footballs. But there were only a few discarded sandwich bags and a single laptop, closed and charging. She looked around, but there was simply nothing else. Had they already been here to cover their tracks? Had they destroyed reams of paper and removed all their incriminating computers?

Or perhaps this laptop was all they had. Maybe it just

wasn't that big of an operation. Or maybe the main office was somewhere else? Alice sat down with her back to the door and reached for the laptop.

And that was when all hell broke loose.

"Hands behind your head!! Where I can see them! Move slowly!"

She was shocked to be caught, but was doubly disturbed that her captor's voice was so familiar ... She dropped the bolt cutters and froze.

Just then, she heard the man grunt and fall to the ground in a heap. Her heart racing and body surging with adrenaline, Alice screamed, spun, and grabbed the heavy bolt cutters again, ready to swing. But to her relief, she saw only a familiar person on the ground near the doorway, holding his leg. Then her shock returned as she spotted a gun next to him.

"You okay, Tyler?" she asked, lowering her bolt cutters, swallowing hard against the tension of her shock.

"Somebody shot my leg," he said, apparently as shocked to see Alice as she was to see him.

She looked out into the night and saw nothing. Then she looked down again, and beside Tyler's leg, she saw a little plastic arrow with a suction cup on its end.

Taking a deep breath to calm herself, she pointed and said, "You got shot with a kid's arrow. Look at it." At first, she thought he was just being a big baby. Then she realized this arrow might belong to Dean. He said he was an archer, and she had seen a bow with arrows like this in his truck. But could he really hurt someone with this thing?

Tyler looked down, squinted, and picked it up. "What the hell?"

"Tyler, what is the gun for? What are you doing here?"

"It's a part-time job," he said, trying to sit up straight, though clearly in great pain. "How about you?"

"Same," Alice said.

He looked at his gun, and then at the arrow, and then back to Alice. Leaving the gun where it lay, he used the door frame to help him stand. "Um, I think my job is more ... *legal* than yours. Judging from outside appearances, that is. No offense."

"None taken," Alice said, looking down at the gun.

Tyler looked back over his shoulder warily and decided to get out of the line of fire. He took a step to the side. Now he and Alice were only four or five feet apart, the gun on the floor in front of them.

"You know the jerks who run this place?" she asked, taking two steps away from Tyler toward the door. The gun remained on the ground between them.

"I just work for them," he said. "Security."

"Are you going to let me go?"

He looked at the arrow in his hand and glanced back toward the door. Suddenly, he squinted, and a strange look dawned on his face—something like excitement.

"Alice, do you know who is out there?"

"No idea. Maybe a local six-year-old up past his bedtime?"

He scrutinized Alice for a moment and seemed like he was thinking fast.

"Of course you can go. But first, can you just tell me why you broke in here?"

Alice didn't like the look on Tyler's face.

"There's nothing I can do to prevent them from coming now. They're on their way."

"Who is?" she asked.

"The mine has an arrangement with an unofficial local militia."

Alice looked wildly toward the door, longing to make a dash for it.

"Alice, I'll erase the video footage and tell them a bear broke in. I'm just saying, if you tell me why you're here, maybe I can help you."

She looked him up and down, trying to see if the man she had a crush on was still in there, underneath the security guard outfit. His hair was untidy, his uniform cheap, and his expression that of a man who was just as likely to grab his gun and shoot her as he was to let her walk away.

But still, her rational self was overcome by something else. "It's about Connie. I told you, I'm determined to find out who runs that website so I'll know who poisoned her. A friend told me the mine had something to do with it. So here I am. I was looking for documents or something, but obviously, I have nothing."

His eyes flickered with surprise, but only for a millisecond before his expression hardened. "Bastards," he said unconvincingly. "I can't believe I work for them."

He paused and looked down at the gun again, then warily back at Alice. "You sure you didn't see anyone out there?" He glanced out again with that look of excitement. "Because it may not be safe for you. Maybe I should walk you to your car."

Alice took a step toward the door. "Looks like you're in no condition to walk anyone anywhere."

"No, seriously," he said, taking a step toward the gun.

Alice made up her mind and walked toward the door.

In her peripheral vision, she saw Tyler go for the gun.

She heard a whistling noise and a metallic thud. She spun back around and saw the gun hit the wall opposite the laptop so hard it sounded like it had gone off. Another little toy arrow rolled off in the other direction. Obviously, Dean had impeccable aim.

Tyler was still bent over, reaching for where it had just been.

Alice turned and ran.

By the time she reached her car, she was beginning to feel scared. What the hell had happened back there? What was

Tyler doing there? How close had she been to getting shot? Where was Dean?

She threw the bolt cutters onto the passenger seat and fired up the engine. She hit the gas so hard, however, that she shot forward toward a tree. As she spun the wheel wildly to avoid a crash, she ran over a stump, which struck something on her car's undercarriage so hard she almost came to a complete grinding stop. But she kept her foot on the gas and somehow ground over it.

As she U-turned on the paved road, she glanced back at the mining office and saw Tyler standing out front. The light inside the building framed his silhouette.

Alice gunned it and burst down the road with incredible acceleration, her whole body pressed against the seat.

And then the engine sputtered and simply quit.

She had only made it about a quarter mile from the mining offices. Tyler could be on the phone to those militia guys at that very moment. He'd also probably heard her car die and was going to hobble over to his vehicle, perhaps hidden behind one of the buildings, and come shoot her.

She turned the key and tried to get the engine to turn over, but it just chugged and wouldn't catch.

She sat there, listening for sirens. Stunned.

Then she heard a vehicle approaching from behind her. Her heart leaped when she recognized the distinct sound of her dad's pickup truck, and she looked into her rearview mirror, expecting to see him pull up. How could he possibly have known she was here in the middle of the night?

As the truck pulled in behind her, she saw that it was not her dad.

CHAPTER 23

SUNDAY, 1:00 A.M.

FOURTEEN HOURS BEFORE THE END

I t was Dean's truck. She knew she should have expected him. He did, as he'd told her, have the ability to anticipate when she was in trouble. And she was definitely in trouble now.

Alice watched in her rearview mirror as Dean stepped down and strode toward her. His presence made her relax, and she felt all would be well. She didn't know where these feelings came from, as he hadn't done that much to earn it. Rolling down her window, she got a mouthful of dust.

"What the hell were you doing in there, Alice?" Dean whispered, his voice full of suppressed anger.

Ignoring his reprimand, she asked, "Were those your toy arrows?"

"Yes. Now, answer my question."

Thinking of Tyler, she asked insistently, "Can we just get out of here? My car broke."

Dean smelled the air and nodded. "Petrol. I mean gas. You must have hit a fuel line."

"Whatever."

Dean ran back to his truck and grabbed a tool kit, a jack, and some jack stands. "Pull the emergency brake hard and throw it into neutral," he said, sounding calmer than he had a moment ago. If he was anything like Dad, Alice thought, Dean probably relaxed as soon as he saw he could try to do something practical like fix a car. It meant he didn't have to deal with a complicated female human, at least for a few minutes. Alice hoped Dean was, however, a better mechanic than her dad.

She stayed in the driver's seat while he quickly jacked up the rear of the car and disappeared underneath.

As he worked, Alice listened hard for the sound of sirens. But as the minutes wore on, the silence only deepened. All she could hear were Dean's metallic scrapings.

Then Dean slid out, carrying a massive steel cylinder.

Startled and feeling protective, Alice finally got out of her car. "Why are you taking my car apart?"

"Driveshaft," he mumbled.

"What? That whole huge metal thing broke?"

"No. You smashed the electric fuel pump. I just removed the driveshaft so I can tow you home without damaging your car even more." Dean ran over and threw her driveshaft into the back of his truck. He put all his tools away, then pulled his truck around in front of her driveshaft-less, fuel-pump-less Mustang. He got out again carrying a tow cable and connected it underneath Alice's car. Then he got into her Mustang, straightened the steering wheel, and tied something to it so it wouldn't move.

Alice stood there, admiring his work. Who knew it was so complicated to tow a car?

"Um, perhaps we should go?" he suggested.

With many backward glances, Alice stepped into his truck. Dean put it in gear and pulled onto the highway.

Still hearing no sirens, Alice let herself take a deep breath. Before Dean could tear into her, she took stock of the situation. She had failed to find a single thing in that office. A little boy was lost in the woods, and Alice had failed to find him. A little girl was in a coma in intensive care, and all Alice could do was fail at random acts of revenge and retribution. It was one thirty a.m., and she had nothing.

She searched the air outside the truck for glimpses of prana. Nothing. Only the haunting glow of Dean's headlights shining on the corridor of pine trees.

Dean gave her a sideways look. "You seem lost," he commented.

"What were those toy arrows all about?" she asked accusingly.

"I told you—"

"Siddhis."

"Yes. I had a premonition you'd be in trouble near Johnston. I raced over and found you just in time. But why, Alice? Why did you break into that mine office?"

She didn't answer. There wasn't any point, and she didn't have the energy or desire to defend herself from Dean, whoever he was. Her anxieties were slowly taking over again and would soon prevent her from being able to speak. Even so, what would she say? Was he being honest? Did he really have these premonitions, or was he just following her around, stalking her?

A feeling of deep suspicion arose in her mind, and with it, some anger. She glanced over at him, then checked to make sure her door was unlocked. "So, what's the range on your premonitions? Do you sense all the problems in the whole world?"

"Of course not. I just—"

"Let's say you predict a car accident somewhere, some domestic violence somewhere else, a drive-by shooting of a toddler, and me doing something stupid in Johnston. How do you choose where to go?"

"I've learned to focus on the premonitions about which I can do something. It's taken me many years to be able to achieve that focus. Before that, my life was a living nightmare."

"How nice that you've chosen to focus on me."

"Alice, saving you from yourself is not my only function in the world right now."

She hated him for presuming he could save her from herself. How disrespectful.

He drove on, concentrating on not hitting any deer or cattle that may have roamed onto the road. But she knew he was thinking about her. Probably not good things. She didn't care. She almost wished she were one of the cows, asleep in the grass somewhere.

"Alice," he finally said, breaking the silence, "I can see we have a trust problem. I don't blame you. I know you haven't had a lot of trustworthy adults in your life. So I'm going to tell you a few things that I usually wouldn't tell a prospective student at our university."

"You can start by telling me what the hell you did to that security guard."

"He's okay. Don't worry."

"Yeah, but what did you do to him?"

Dean blew out a long exhalation. "It's another of my abilities. I can coax prana to carry an arrow wherever I wish it to go. And more importantly, I can control how hard it hits. I find it's easier to use toy arrows because any investigator who finds them will think them harmless."

"You shoot toy arrows using prana. Prana, like the wavy stuff I can see."

"Yes, Alice. Remember, you're talking to someone who knows what you know. Who feels the kinds of things you feel."

She looked directly at him with fire in her eyes. "You have no idea what I feel." But the fire went out immediately, and she sank deeper into the seat.

"Sorry," Dean said. "I just mean I understand about prana." Alice sighed profoundly. "I also know you're struggling with your connection to prana," he added softly.

"How? How do you know?"

"It's part of my job to keep a very close eye on prospects like you, Alice. You have to understand that we take our recruitment very seriously."

Alice looked down at her pants and thought of Madison's warnings about Dean. "Have you been taking videos of me getting dressed?"

"No, no, no, of course not. Nothing like that."

"Seriously, how do you know?"

"Deduction."

"Jerk."

Now it was Dean's turn to sigh. He drove on through the darkness for a while, then said, "Hey, I almost forgot. I brought you something."

He reached behind Alice's seat. Alice sat up straight, instantly alert for some kind of attack.

"Relax. It's just chai. Spiced tea." He held out an old, dented metal thermos. "It's not as good as Mr. Rao's chai, but I thought it would be welcome at a time like this."

Alice resisted for a second. But her craving for caffeine and sugar won out, and she took the thermos.

When she opened it and the sweet, spicy smells emerged, with strong overtones of cardamom and cloves, she closed her eyes. She hadn't drunk chai since Mr. Rao had died, and the smells from the thermos summoned up memories. She pictured scenes from Mr. Rao's kitchen, the old man bustling about, grinding spices with mortar and pestle, yammering on in his unique and endearing way.

Then the invading army of smells broached her defenses. She broke through to a memory from when she was five. She was in India, sitting in an outdoor courtyard on dusty marble tiles near a mango tree. It was early morning and already blisteringly hot, but of course, everyone still expected hot chai. The ashram kitchen used to serve it with hard Indian cookies to everyone emerging from their morning meditation. Mom and Dad were still in the meditation hall, a five-minute walk away along a dusty path, while Alice and her twin brother, Thomas, watched the ashram kitchen volunteers through a doorway. Above the sound of the large mortar and pestle grinding away at the spices, Alice could hear Indian spiritual music playing on a small radio and the distant sound of peacocks. As she became more immersed in the memory, a deep longing shook her physically. A longing for that closeness with her twin, of being inseparable from another person, like two souls merged ...

She squeezed her eyes shut tighter against the memory, and against something even worse. Tears.

Then she thought of Connie, and the longing for Thomas was replaced by terror for Connie. It was too much. Alice shook herself out of her memories.

Thomas was long dead. All was gone. Lost.

She tried to imagine what Mr. Rao would say at a time like this. As she thought of him, it was like he was there with her, and his voice, almost audible amidst the curling chai vapors, preached, "No loss, no love. No love, no sadness over loss. Same, same."

She wanted to shout back at it. "No-one knows what loss is until you lose a twin!"

But she knew Mr. Rao was right. She needed to hold on to her love for Thomas even though he was gone. The loss was simply there, like her breath. Part of her. And she knew her anger over Thomas's death was good fuel. She needed that fuel too. Could she have one without the other?

She poured a cup of the chai and sipped. It was perfect, just like Mr. Rao's.

She couldn't lose Connie. She couldn't. Not like she'd lost Thomas. Alice would simply cease to exist. Done. Over and out.

Or would she? Maybe Alice would just continue to blunder on sadly through life.

She drank the rest of the chai and felt her body start to respond to the sugar and caffeine. She poured another cup. And then another one.

Love and loss. Loss and love.

She closed her eyes and could no longer conjure memories of Thomas or the ashram. But something was different now.

She opened her eyes with a start and looked around her. Prana was shimmering and flowing from the open thermos. It was glistening outside the car in the black night. She could see it ebbing and gliding above the road. Among the dark, secretive pine trees. Within her breath. In her hands.

She thought of Connie on life support.

The prana disappeared, leaving her bereft.

But she knew what she had to do now.

She tried to play it cool. "You know that bullshit about meditation you tried to force on me before?"

Dean smiled. "Relaxation. Knowing. Letting it be. If you can simultaneously hold those things in your heart, you'll be on your way to developing strength of mind. The mind doesn't develop when it's habitually fixated on evaluating external objects."

"Right. And you think that crap will help me with my prana problem?"

"It will be a start. It's also the key to helping others with your abilities." Dean turned to look at her. "Someday, Alice, you will have the power to change the world. You'll be a beacon of light."

Alice laughed. She thought she was more bacon than beacon.

"But with great power like yours comes massive risk. I have seen far too many young people with siddhis take their own lives or get lost in mental illness. This is no joke. The very best way to ensure you have the support you need is by coming to our university. There, everyone is like you. Everyone has been through enormous trials and emerged on the other side. Everyone once thought he or she was alone on the planet. Everyone helps one another through it all. It's a wonderful, magical place."

"I notice you haven't sworn me to secrecy about that university of yours. What happens if I post it all over the internet?"

"Not much," he said, smiling. "The internet is full of stuff like that. But all the same, I would appreciate it if you'd please refrain from posting it all over the internet. Or telling anybody else." He looked over at her and added. *"Anybody."*

"My mom and dad?"

"There's a process for explaining things to loved ones. We've been doing this for a long time. The process works."

"I'm supposed to lie to them?"

"Never. But parent-student day at our university is not the same as the one at your local university."

Alice thought about that. "I want the offer in writing."

"I can do something better than a letter, Alice. I've been authorized to fly you out to London to tour the campus."

"Fly?"

"In an airplane," Dean said, laughing.

"I can't go. My sister is in a coma."

"I know. And I pray she will get better. I'm sure she will, Alice. If she has anything like your fighting spirit, she'll be fine." Dean paused and added, "You can come whenever it suits you. No rush."

Alice thought about what was, in fact, urgent in her life right now. Going to London with some English cowboy was at the bottom of the list.

"Do you know anything about Ed Toomes?" she asked, suddenly serious.

"Alice, I warned you about this yesterday. It's dangerous for you to keep chasing these leads."

"Haven't you figured out that I don't like being lectured to?"

Dean sighed and nodded. "I'm sorry. What do you want to know about Ed Toomes?"

"The reason I was at the mine office was to find proof that they're selling out to an Indian company. It's the same company that owns the pharmaceutical factory that almost killed Connie. They've also somehow gotten Toomes to convince the sheriff's office to halt the search for Wyatt, that little boy who's lost somewhere near their mine."

"Interesting," Dean said. "Do you have any proof?"

"Yeah, well, I didn't find the proof I was after. That security guard showed up, and then you shot him with little plastic suction cups. But I still think Ed Toomes is the key. He's the link to this online pharmacy that so many people around Hardrock seem to be using. We also think he ordered those incel boys you warned me about at the Roadhouse the other night to slander us all over the freaking internet. He's also probably behind the graffiti around town that advertises the online pharmacy in India. He's connected to everything."

"Um ..." Dean stammered.

"So can you tell me anything useful? Anything that'll help put him behind bars?"

"*The* Ed Toomes? Are you serious?" When Alice did not laugh, he continued, "That bloke is like John Wayne. Like everyone's favorite grandpa. He may be many things, Alice, but I know he can't have anything to do with drug dealing. Trust me."

"Why can't he have anything to do with drug dealing?"

"Because, as everyone knows, his family has been through hell because of drugs. Heroin, actually—his son struggled with heroin addiction for years. It was terrible for the Toomes family. Ed is a very public figure, a perfect character, a true red-blooded American, a mining champion, a working man's hero. It didn't fit with Ed's image or his values to have an addict in the family. He set up a Christian foundation for recovering heroin addicts and funded it lavishly. His son was successfully treated. The foundation has been a huge success in this county, and now it's a major national interest. Ed Toomes is one of the most anti-drug public figures in the entire state."

"What about his wife?"

"She's a private figure. I don't know much about her."

"His son? Is he still clean?"

"Well, I don't know, exactly. Tyler is his name. I don't know much about him except that he joined the army after he was treated. People now think of him as some kind of war hero, but I can only imagine that's wishful thinking."

Alice's heart almost stopped. When she had enough air to breathe, she asked, "Where is this Tyler Toomes now?"

"Alice. I just have this feeling something bad will happen to you if you keep pursuing this puzzle."

"Don't you dare—"

"But I have learned," Dean interrupted, "not to lecture you. So if you are indeed determined to hunt down Tyler Toomes, please accept my humble assistance."

As they pulled up to her cabin, he added, "But please, can we start tomorrow? I need a few hours of sleep."

CHAPTER 24
SUNDAY, 8:00 A.M.
SEVEN HOURS BEFORE THE END

After a few hours of fragile sleep, shattered several times by nightmarish scenes of Connie alternately drowning, slipping from her chest pouch and plummeting to the ground, being kidnapped by a pedophile, and disappearing forever in a supermarket, Alice woke up to the sound of a text message. Assuming it was to inform her of Connie's death, she jolted out of bed.

No change in Connie, her dad's text informed her. *Doctors keep encouraging patience. But Mom is out of bed! Due to be released today. Let's have lunch as a family to celebrate?*

Alice responded yes, chucked her phone onto the bed, and took a deep breath, trying to calm the adrenaline that was pumping through her body. She felt terrible. Her phone said it was eight a.m.

She ran her hand through her tangled hair and realized she hadn't washed it in days, so she showered and dressed, which made her feel a little bit more human. She stumbled down the stairs, intending to charge away in her Mustang. It was, of course, not there, since she had broken it in the middle of the night. Dean had towed it off somewhere with a vague promise to fix it. She didn't know where. She didn't even know where he lived.

She stood there, wondering what to do next. She needed coffee. She also needed to tell Madison and Karan about Rama's new information linking the mining company to the Indian pharmaceutical manufacturer. She needed to confess to them that she'd raided the mine office and almost gotten shot. And was rescued by Dean and his toy arrows. And most importantly, she needed to tell them about the guy who seemed to tie everything together. Not Ed Toomes, but his son, Tyler. They needed to sit down and make sense of it all and come up with a plan.

She felt like they were nearing some kind of endgame. Something was coming. It was like the gaping suck-hole eye of her dream was real and was fully intending to swallow her.

Alice grabbed her bike and cycled up to Mr. Rao's steering wheel. She dismounted and stepped to the cliff edge. How many times had she jumped off this little cliff, connected with the prana and swum up into the morning mist?

She looked down, hoping for telltale swirls of liquid air. Nothing. Perhaps the prana was just teasing her? Maybe she needed to take a leap of faith?

But a failed leap of faith could leave Connie without a big sister, and she simply couldn't risk it.

She grabbed her mountain bike and began the twenty-minute ride to the library.

When Alice stepped into the rare books room, she saw Madison and Karan sitting in big leather chairs, bathed in morning sunlight from the stained glass window. They had giant, welcoming smiles on their faces despite all they had been through, in spite of what they had discovered about their freakish friend.

Alice suddenly became aware of a strange noise in the room. It sounded like laughter, but her friends were silent. She searched the room pointlessly, then closed her eyes, listening. And just like in her nightmare a few days ago, her inner vision telescoped in on the eye on Witchat Mountain. It was making a hollow howling noise that faded in and out like laughter.

"You look like shit," Karan said, startling Alice out of her vision.

Madison, more observant, noticed Alice's sudden change. "What is it?"

"Nothing," Alice lied.

But when she saw the looks on their faces, Alice changed her mind about lying and decided to try to describe what she had felt and seen. "It's just that bad feeling I've been getting. It's like ... you know the Lord of the Rings?"

Karan nodded enthusiastically. Madison still wore a concerned look.

"It's like Sauron's dark tower is somewhere on Witchat Mountain, and it's been taunting me."

"Yeah?" Karan encouraged.

"Yeah, and now I can even hear it. It's like it's laughing at me or something."

"Cool!" Karan said. "Like a vision? Or an omen? Or a hallucination? A portent? A chimera?"

"Karan!" Madison exclaimed, exasperated.

"I've always thought of this kind of thing as a message."

"Maybe you're possessed?" Karan asked excitedly.

"I don't think that's a thing, Karan."

"When did you start getting visions of this Witchat thing?" Madison asked.

"First on Thursday afternoon. I thought it was just a nightmare. Then it came again when I saw that graffiti for the first time when we were putting up flyers. And a couple more times when I saw the graffiti. And just now, for some reason."

"But what does it mean?" Madison asked.

"I guess there's a connection between the eye in the mountain and the eye in the graffiti."

"So Nathaniel is still alive and is a supervillain hiding in a cave in the mountains while he builds up armies of zombies to take over the world?"

"These messages usually aren't literal. Like, I doubt Nathaniel is actually involved. These visions are like mash-ups. Combinations of feelings and places and people."

"Mash-ups?"

"Look, it's easier to explain with an example. You know that bouldering site called Bottle Rock?"

"Yes," Madison said. "It's that tall thin boulder near town that kind of looks like a Coke bottle. People fall off it all the time."

"Right. I once had a vision that the rock was cracked, and tears were coming out of the crack. It was also wearing a torn necktie."

"Oh, let me guess!" Karan bubbled. "You went straight to the mayor's house and helped him pull a Coke bottle out of his—"

"Karan!" Madison shouted.

Laughing, Alice shook her head. "Nope. After I got that message, I went to Bottle Rock and found a guy there, unconscious and with a broken arm. I called 911, and they came and got him in an ambulance."

"So ..." Madison said, pinching her chin, "this time, it could be something like ... the eye you are seeing *does* represent a cave in a mountain somewhere? And the eye matches Nathaniel's face because Wyatt is in the cave after getting lost looking for Nathaniel's hidden meadow?"

"That's such a boring interpretation, Madison," Karan said. "How do you explain the evil part? Can't there be a supervillain in there somewhere?"

"The problem is, when I get these visions, usually they point very clearly to where I should go. But this time, I have no idea. I've never seen any caves on Witchat. Or anywhere near there. Have you?"

Madison thought and said, "Well, there must be some up there in those cliffs."

"And Wyatt is an evil mastermind who found a ring in that cave that made him invincible?" added Karan.

"I just don't know if the vision has anything to do with Wyatt. Maybe it's not just a combination of a place and a person. Maybe it's a new kind of vision for me. I don't know."

Madison smiled and said, "We'll try to figure it out together. But you know, Alice, Karan's right. You do look terrible. Are you okay?"

Alice plopped down in a chair. "I don't know. But I think I know who made Wyatt disappear and slandered us online and almost killed Connie."

"Cool," Karan said casually. "Who is it, then?"

"Tyler Toomes," Alice replied, sighing.

Karan and Madison both sat up straighter. "Wait, you're serious? What the holy hell are you talking about?" Karan asked. "Is this another vision thing? Or have you got a new power that makes you all-knowing?"

"Don't you mean *Ed* Toomes, Alice?" Madison asked gently, gesturing at Karan to tone it down.

"No." Alice pulled out another energy bar. "I'm sorry I didn't bring you guys one," she added as Karan and Madison stared.

After a few dry bites, she leveled her gaze at her friends. "Okay, here's what I found out," she began. "Ed Toomes, the mining boss, has a son named Tyler. We already know him, because he also goes by the name Tyler Rowley, the IT guy at school who sells kids Xanax."

Madison and Karan still had looks on their faces that indicated deep concern for Alice's sanity.

"I ran into him last night. He also works as a security guard at his dad's mine."

"You did what?!" Madison exclaimed.

Alice explained what had happened to her last night: the call from Rama; the break-in; the failure to find documents about an Indian company; the success of finding Tyler and his gun; the rescue by Dean and his toy arrows.

She left out the heartache she felt about Tyler turning out to be a lying jerk, as everyone else had already suspected, and also the slight excitement she felt about him regardless. She also left out her secret meetings and texts with Tyler and his pledges to help her identify the online pharmacy owners. How stupid was she to have trusted him?

"But ... Alice," Madison pleaded, as though to a confused child, "you're saying our school IT guy is moonlighting as a Xanax dealer, and also as a security guard?"

"That's a lot of moonlighting," Karan added. "I hope he applies enough moonscreen to his skin. Get it? Moonscreen?"

"Oh," Alice said, ignoring Karan's crappy joke. "I guess it does *sound* unlikely when you put it that way. But I still think it's true. And Rama said he heard some weird stuff about the guy who negotiated the deal for his dad's mine, like he pushed some sadhu off a roof. It doesn't sound like something big Ed would do. So either Ed has some other weird guy working for him, or he sent Tyler to India to negotiate the deal. Which means Tyler sounds like some kind of ..."

"Supervillian! Exactly!" Karan pounded the table.

"Alice, that's so unlikely. For so many reasons. Like, why would a mine executive have his own son working as a security guard, and not in some more senior role? He's an IT guy at our school, so why wouldn't he at least be the IT guy at the mine? And why would an IT guy get sent to India to negotiate an important deal? Wouldn't that require someone with business skills? And Tyler the IT guy just doesn't sound like someone who would go around pushing monks off buildings. None of this makes sense."

"You know what makes less sense than that?" Karan asked. "Alice, you said you got saved from the supervillain by a guy who shoots toy arrows at people," Karan repeated. "Like, the little suction cup ones from Kmart. That makes no sense."

"Dean says he does it by using prana," Alice said. "Like, the same way I fly, or used to. The prana helps him guide any projectile so it'll hit whatever he wants as hard as he wants. And he uses plastic toys so that if they're discovered, nobody believes they could be lethal weapons."

"Oh. Cool, I guess," Karan said. "But not as cool as your thing."

Madison was still silent, grappling with her thoughts.

"Well," Karan chirped, "I believe the whole thing, lock, stock, and barrel. So let's call Nancy and tell her so she can go arrest the jerk and be done with it."

Just thinking about making that phone call made Alice's head hurt. Nancy might literally kill her. She couldn't actually go make an arrest anyway, as she had been put on leave. "I need coffee," Alice grumbled, and the room grew silent.

Just then, a knock on the door startled them all out of their thoughts.

CHAPTER 25

SUNDAY, 9:00 A.M.

SIX HOURS BEFORE THE END

It was, thankfully, a gentle, tentative knock rather than impatient pounding.

After raising her eyebrows at Mad and Karan, Alice rose, unlocked the door, and opened it just enough for a terrified face to peer through. It was Asher.

Karan stood up and approached the door menacingly.

Asher's head made a hasty retreat. "Hey, I come in peace!"

"Easy, Karan," Madison said, holding a hand up. She turned to the door. "Nobody is going to hurt you, Asher. Come on in."

Alice let him slink into the room, carrying a briefcase in front of him like a shield. It looked like another high-tech whiteboard like the one Karan had broken.

"I just want to help you guys. Okay?"

"Sure, Asher," Madison said.

"This is for you. A present," he said, setting the briefcase on the table. Then he ran back out the door.

"That was a short visit," Karan joked.

He returned a second later, carrying a tray holding three large coffees. "These are from your favorite café—Bitches Brew." He set them down next to the briefcase and waited for them to comment.

"You didn't have to do that, Asher," Madison said.

"Oh, yes, he did," Alice said, grabbing a coffee greedily. "Did you bring some food too?"

Downcast, he said, "I didn't know you were hungry …"

"She's just giving you a hard time," Madison said, taking a coffee for herself and passing one to Karan. "Thanks for the coffees. And we can't accept that whiteboard, if that's what's in the briefcase."

"No, no, no, it's okay. Really. Please take it. No strings attached. We have loads of them." Asher flipped open the latch and started setting it up.

Alice didn't care what he did. She was too busy sucking coffee into her body. She felt none of the terror that had burned through her veins yesterday when this same boy had revealed her secret to Madison and Karan.

"No, seriously. We don't want anything from your club," Madison said firmly.

Asher stopped what he was doing. "Look, guys. I'm really sorry about yesterday. I straightened it out with The Club. They agreed that James was taking the wrong approach. We just want to be friends with you guys. No research, no nothing. We're not the CIA or whatever. We can't do anything mean to you anyway. It's against our charter. For real."

Madison pursed her lips like a schoolmarm. "Where is James?"

"He's taking a break. I promise he won't bother you again, Alice."

"What, you killed him?" Karan asked.

"Killed? No!" Asher said. "The guys in charge just told him not to talk to you anymore. They're the ones who supply all the money and stuff. What they say goes. Except for Wyatt, I guess. He did what he wanted."

"So, what exactly would it mean to be friends with you and your club, Asher?" Madison asked.

"Well, can we start by working together to find Wyatt? I mean, he's just a kid. He's ten. The more time goes by, the more I just feel like …" Asher started to cry.

Alice thought he looked like a vulnerable little boy. He was probably not much older than Wyatt.

Nobody got up to comfort him. Probably nobody knew how, after what had happened yesterday. It was all too weird.

"Asher, sit down. Here, have some water." Madison passed over a water bottle, which he took gratefully. "Of course we're trying to help Wyatt," she said. "There's just a lot going on."

Asher sniffed loudly and wiped his nose with his sleeve. "I have some new information for you about Wyatt." He gestured at the whiteboard. "May I?"

Madison nodded, and Asher, now visibly refreshed and in his element, booted up the whiteboard, narrating how to use it at each step.

"And once you turn on the whiteboard, this little icon here is something else I got The Club to give you. It gives you access to our network. So it's just like you're members now! Isn't that cool?"

"No," Alice said casually.

"What information do you have for us about Wyatt?" Madison said in a motherly tone.

"I need to show you a message that just got posted on our network. It's one reason I had to push for you to get access." He tapped the icon and opened up what looked like a Harry-Potter-movie-themed chat room. "Here. See, isn't this amazing? Molly is back! *The* Molly, who first reported on Nathaniel. She's been silent for ten years, and now she's back!"

Alice read what "Molly" had posted in the chat room.

Since Nathaniel's disappearance ten years ago, I have remained silent and broken. There has been nothing of note for me to report on this forum in all that time, until now. I have been watching and carefully charting the movements of a powerful drug lord who is abusing Nathaniel's image to sell illegal, tainted narcotics in Hardrock. This man, the son of an Indian cartel boss, is dangerous, and I cannot handle him by myself, nor can I go to the authorities, because they are infiltrated by his spies and allies. All the way to the top.

This powerful cartel is heavily armed and responsible for countless deaths in India and the rest the world. Our friend and Club member Wyatt discovered the drug lord's identity and was then discovered in turn. That is why the drug lord kidnapped Wyatt, has been torturing him for information about The Club, and is very likely going to kill him soon.

I tried to free him but failed, and I am now severely injured. I taught the people holding him that The Club deserves respect, however. As a result of my efforts, they are nervous, and so they're moving Wyatt today at ten a.m.

They have been holding him in the woods near the new drilling site by the Roadhouse. Somehow, the drug lord also knows about Alice Brickstone and her powerful archer ally. He is afraid these two are now after him, and he is scared, perhaps for the first time in his life. He seems to think she is allied with The Club.

As soon as Wyatt is moved, this drug kingpin plans to bring the hammer down on Alice. He wants to kill all of her friends and family and allies.

So I implore you to reach out to Alice and warn her. She may be able to save herself, and she may even be able to save Wyatt. She is his only hope. She must act quickly. The enemy has not had time to fully organize, and Wyatt is relatively poorly guarded. They only have local muscle right now and plan to move him in a convoy of four-wheel-drive vehicles. The cartel's armed crews from Denver and beyond have yet to arrive.

And tell Alice she must bring her archer friend, as she will need the support of this powerful, magical person. Only together do they have a chance of succeeding. And warn her not to trust the county sheriff's office. I don't know when I will be able to post again. Godspeed.

"SEE? WYATT'S STILL ALIVE!" Asher enthused.

"Asher," Madison said firmly, "can you step outside for a moment?"

He looked wounded but stood up and left.

As soon as the heavy wooden door closed, Madison turned to Alice and Karan. "We have a huge problem, and it is not an Indian drug lord."

"What? You think Molly kidnapped Wyatt?" Alice asked skeptically.

"Alice," Madison said, "the only way Molly would know you have an 'archer friend' is if 'she' were there last night when Dean rescued you with his toy arrows. So Molly is either Tyler Toomes or Dean McRae."

"Or someone they know," Karan said. "Or someone who was hiding in a corner and watching. Or someone watching a video feed. Or—"

"In any case," Madison interrupted, "you are in real danger, Alice. Whoever is posing as Molly knows way too much about you. They know you've been talking to Asher and his club, and they know you were at the mine office last night. If Molly is Dean, he's a real nutcase, and there's no telling what he is capable of doing to you. If it's Tyler ... I don't even want to think about that."

"Duh." Karan rolled her eyes. "It means he's a supervillain."

"We have to call Nancy and show this to her."

"Maybe," Alice said, the threat dawning on her.

"I hope it's not Dean," Karan said. "I would much rather put my trust in a sexy cowboy guy who looks like Strider than a metrosexual drug dealer." She looked at the screen, where Molly's message was still staring at them. "Yeah, and this message was posted this morning at 2:06 a.m." Looking at Alice, she asked, "What time did Dean drop you back home?"

"I guess about two a.m.," Alice responded weakly. "But I just feel like Dean wouldn't hurt Wyatt. He wouldn't hurt anyone."

"What if Dean just kidnapped Wyatt as a kind of test for you, Alice?" Madison asked. "You know, for that magical university of his."

"No way," Alice said, more insistent now. "He has saved me twice, and both times, he totally could have hurt me instead. He would not kidnap a little kid. No way. I just feel it."

"So it's Tyler, then," Madison said.

"A supervillain of many disguises." Karan looked like she was calculating something, then said, "So, Tyler Rowley, our school IT guy who moonlights as a Xanax dealer, is actually Tyler Toomes, the security guard who moonlights as an international executive negotiating multimillion-dollar mining deals in India? *And* he used to be Molly, a founding member of a culty international club of kids obsessed with magic? It would explain why he was running around India pushing people off buildings. He probably wanted to see if they could fly. But could one supervillain play all those roles? Dude's like a shapeshifter. Wait, is that one of those siddhis?"

Alice smiled at Karan. "I don't think that's a thing. I can't do it, anyway."

"But it's more than shapeshifting, even. It means Tyler was obsessed with Nathaniel, and now he uses Nathaniel's picture for his tag. It's like he is begging to be discovered."

"The main question is," Madison interjected, "what does Tyler want right now? Why write this message?" She scrunched her brows and exclaimed, "Wait a minute. He used to be in The Club. What does that say about his motives?"

Karan held her finger up. "Maybe he wants to catch Alice and Dean on film to share with his buddies? So he can get back in their good graces? Or maybe ... maybe he's just totally lost it, and he doesn't give a shit about anything and is just in it for the LOLs?"

Madison took a deep breath. "Regardless, this is a matter for the sheriff's office. Because if it is true, he has broken about a million laws. And if they get him soon enough, maybe he'll just tell them where Wyatt is."

"I don't think so," Alice said. "I get the feeling he'd weasel out of being questioned. His dad has money and contacts, and his football pal is the sheriff. These kinds of guys always win. At least in the movies. I guess we could tell Nancy, but ...."

"But we *can't* tell her *everything*," Karan continued. "Like, we can't tell her about this Molly character or Asher's club, or about Alice breaking into the mine office, or about her being able to fly. Alice would be in such trouble if we did. And we can't really tell her about any of that magic siddhi stuff like Dean's ability to shoot toy arrows at people. How much is left we could actually tell her?"

"Enough is left," Madison said. "She's a trained officer of the law; she'll be able to gather evidence and put a case together. This isn't the movies."

Karan rubbed her scars. "But what do they have? There's no evidence Tyler sprayed that graffiti or has anything to do with the online pharmacy. There's no evidence Johnston Mine is working with any Indian company either; Rama said he just heard about it. And there's no evidence they're hiding Wyatt's final resting spot from anyone, because nobody has found it. I bet if Nancy starts asking questions again, or gets her partner to, Tyler will know she's friends with me, and will keep twisting all this around so it looks like our fault. Or at least, Alice's fault. she'll end up in juvenile detention for sure."

"Don't you think Nancy is smart enough to figure out how to ask questions quietly, so the sheriff doesn't find out?" Madison insisted. "She is on leave, after all."

"I guess," Alice said. Her real fear was Nancy's wrath, rather than juvenile detention. "I guess we have to tell her what we know eventually. Except for the siddhis stuff. But can't we wait a while? Because if we tell her now, she'll kill us for getting involved. And she'll make damn sure we get uninvolved."

"No way, Alice."

"Wait. I'm just saying, what if there were a completely safe way to go out to the place this Molly says they're hiding Wyatt and check it out? Then we go and tell Nancy? That way we know we've really done all we could for Wyatt."

"No. Way." Madison looked like she was ready to explode.

"But Mad," Karan continued, "there is just so much on the line here. Not just Wyatt. Think about it—what if Nancy arrests Tyler, Wyatt dies in the meantime because nobody found him, Tyler tells them everything about Asher's club and Alice, and it comes out that she is some weirdo who thinks she can fly? It wouldn't just be Wyatt's life that was over. Hers would basically be over too."

Alice looked with Karan, admiring her logic and feeling gratitude for her protectiveness.

As Madison struggled with her thoughts, they interrupted by another tentative knock on the door.

"Well," Karan said eagerly, "lets at least let Asher back in." She jumped up to open the door.

But rather than Asher, Brian was standing there. He had a newspaper under his arm.

"Ladies," he said formally.

"Hi, Brian," Karan said. "What brings you to work on a Sunday? Golf courses all closed?"

"This," he said, handing the newspaper to Madison, who took it back to the table. The three girls huddled around it to read.

CHAPTER 26

SUNDAY, 10:00 A.M.

FIVE HOURS BEFORE THE END

L OCAL KIDS SHOW THEIR TRUE COLORS
   By Melba Goldberg

I LEFT Johnston ten years ago, but my heart remained behind. Recent events in my hometown have inspired me to return.

Johnston is a coal town in danger of extinction.

This much is not news.

What has inspired me to return and put pen to paper now is a photograph emailed to me by a friend. I have asked the publishers of this paper to withhold the picture, as I don't want to encourage acts of revenge.

I can tell you, however, that it shows three girls hanging flyers around Hardrock, Johnston's wealthy big sister. The girls are well known within the Hardrock community. They are infamous celebrities at their high school. And yet, they have clearly not received an education about common decency, nor have they been taught to respect the history of our humble corner of the world.

The flyers they were hanging read: COAL CREATES IDIOTS. IDIOTS RUIN THE PLANET.

This alone would be false and insulting. But even worse, below the inflammatory words is an image of Henry Narrow and his late son, Nathaniel.

The Narrow family was legendary in Johnston. Henry's father bought the mineral rights to the land and opened a mine that created the town out of nothing. Henry followed his father's footsteps and brought the mine great prosperity during the 1980s, fueling America's great wealth under President Reagan.

And when multiple tragedies struck Henry's family, his town stuck by him every time. When Henry's wife died in childbirth, the town stepped up and helped him look after his new motherless baby. I remember my mother bringing him casseroles almost every day. When it became apparent that Henry's son had a severe disability that affected his speech and development, the town created a kind of neighborhood watch so that Nathaniel was always looked after. Henry could rest easy, knowing that if his boy went wandering, as he often did, a neighbor would bring him back home safely. And when Nathaniel disappeared for the last time, the whole town—each and every one of us—helped look for him. Months after the official search was called off, we were all up there in the woods above Johnston, calling his name. I am told that some people still call out his name when hiking on Witchat.

When Henry battled cancer, we all supported him in his time of need. "It was kindness," he wrote in his goodbye letter, "of the kind I could never repay." This is why he went away to die alone in a hospital or palliative care facility in Denver. At the time, no one knew where he had gone, and the whole town searched for him, but we searched in vain. Even today, his name is still spoken with reverence, even though his family has been gone for years.

But now, a new generation of rich white kids has emerged in Hardrock. These kids never met Henry or Nathaniel. Their wealth is built upon the foundation he and people like him built for them. And this is how our young people repay him: by calling his son an "idiot." By implying that Henry helped ruin the planet.

I returned to Johnston and found not only those disgusting posters but also graffiti of Nathaniel's face sprayed all over town.

I, for one, am disgusted. The parents of these kids should be too, as should all self-respecting citizens of Johnston and Hardrock. I can only hope the community will join me in condemning acts of hate such as this and hit the streets to tear down the offending flyers and paint over the graffiti.

"More lies!" Alice said, louder than she meant to.

Madison and Karan, who had been reading over Alice's shoulders, seemed about to explode.

"But why would they let her print this stuff? It's like there has been an orchestrated campaign against us from the beginning."

"This is just … infuriating!!" Karan shouted, and slammed a fist down on the newspaper. Then she got up, took a random PhD dissertation off a shelf, and stood there leafing through it. Alice saw it was something about the ecology of a river basin.

Alice looked at Madison. "Now do you see what we're up against? We just have to do what we can. Right away. Please!"

Brian cleared his throat and said, "I thought you should know about this. Also, there's a boy out here who looks very nervous and lost. Is he yours?"

"Yes, he can come in, Brian," Alice said, hoping Madison was now angry enough to go along with her plan. Which was not yet so much a plan as it was a random string of ideas. But it would have to do.

Brian turned to leave. "I'll be in my office if you need me."

After a moment, Asher walked in tentatively.

Madison, her voice urgent, asked, "What can you tell us about this Molly person?"

"Nothing. She joined The Club before they had many

requirements for entry. Nobody has ever met her in person. We don't even have any biographical details on her."

"But she is clearly local," Karan observed. "She claims to know a lot about the local sheriff's office and has an interest in Nathaniel and Alice."

"Yeah, and she's probably good at finding things on the dark web. That's how she found our club in the first place. But she only has the lowest security clearance. She can only see the basic stuff on our site."

Karan raised her eyebrows. "Like the video of Alice you showed us?"

"No. That one requires higher clearance. Molly can only see an earlier one I posted. It's really sketchy and hardly shows anything. Everyone in The Club thought it was fake."

Alice finished her coffee, sucking noisily at the last few drops.

"So ... which one of you is the archer she's talking about?" Asher asked.

Alice knew this was coming and was prepared. "Nobody, Asher. I think this Molly of yours is misinformed. About a lot of things."

"Like, there is no Indian drug lord in town," Karan added.

"Asher," Alice said, "I sort of have an idea. But we're seriously going to need your help with this."

CHAPTER 27
SUNDAY, 1:00 P.M.
TWO HOURS BEFORE THE END

"Okay, all the drones are in position." Asher's voice was in Alice's earpiece. He sounded distant but very confident. "They're too high for him to see or hear, but I can see anything that moves down there."

"What do you see, Asher?" Alice asked.

"I can just see you, Alice. Nobody else is nearby. Madison and Karan, you're clear too. No vehicles or anything anywhere. Just those two trucks parked at the drilling site. They've been there all morning. No people."

Karan's voice responded, "Can you guys really hear me on this thing?"

"*Yes*, Karan," Madison said for the fourth time.

Two hours earlier, Alice had set out from the Roadhouse on foot, painstakingly bushwhacked through the trees to avoid the road, and hidden in the forest above and behind the drilling site, binoculars in hand. From this vantage point, she could see the clump of trees about half a mile away behind which, according to Asher, Madison and Karan had just parked the Subaru.

She knew Madison and Karan planned to walk for only forty seconds, then stop and just stand there. That put them a twenty-second sprint from their car. The drilling site was half a mile away, and even the fastest vehicle would take twenty seconds to drive that distance.

While they had no idea what Tyler had in store for them, they guessed it was not benign, and they had no intention of getting close enough to be in harm's way. All they wanted was to draw him out, trigger a response, catch it on film with Asher's drones, and maybe discover some new piece of information that would lead them to Wyatt. If that happened, they would call Nancy and tell her. If the plan went poorly, they would retreat and call Nancy anyway.

"Awesome," Karan said. "Hey, Asher, you make a much better guy in the chair than I did."

"What's a guy in the chair?" he asked.

"Superheroes often have a guy back at a computer somewhere helping them out."

"Cool," Asher said earnestly.

"But the problem is ... now I'm either a sidekick, or I'm expendable. Like, the friend who has to die to make the movie more exciting."

"Can we focus please, Karan?" Madison said.

"I'm just saying I'd prefer to be a sidekick. But I think I'm actually the other thing."

Alice cringed when Asher said, "You should put that bow on your shoulder, Karan. You know, so he can see it clearly."

"Oh, so that settles it," Karan sighed. "I'm totally the expendable friend."

The autumn sun warmed Alice and gave her a false sense of security. She forced herself to sharpen up. Everything depended on her eyes and the cameras on Asher's drones. They couldn't let the slightest movement escape their notice, or they could be in great danger.

Through the binoculars, she scanned the valley on both

sides of the gravel road on which Madison and Karan were walking. She saw nothing but dry grass swaying in the wind.

"Oh," Asher said. "This is not good."

"What, Asher?" Madison demanded.

"You know those two trucks I told you about? Parked at the drilling site?"

"Yeah?"

"Now there are fifty."

"What, did they have truck babies?" Karan asked.

"Some guys just appeared out of nowhere and pulled tarps off the rest. I'm really sorry. They were totally hidden. The tarps were the same color as the dirt road. I think they must know we have drones."

There was silence on the line. Everyone was stunned. They had expected some kind of reception, but not an army.

"We're coming back, Asher," Madison responded. "We're aborting. Alice? You head back too. We'll meet at the Roadhouse."

"Weird," Asher said. "There are two more trucks coming toward you from the other direction. Like, really fast. But I think you can still make it to your car. They're more than twenty seconds away."

"Asher, call Nancy," Madison said. "Right now."

A heavy ache in her stomach suddenly overcame Alice, and the image of her Dad appeared in her head at the same time.

"Wait," Asher said. "One of them is Alice's dad."

"How do you know it's my dad?" Alice demanded angrily. She couldn't see anything past the clump of trees where Mad and Karan had parked.

"We've been watching you for months, remember?"

Alice dialed her dad's phone, but it just rang. "He's not picking up. Asher, you're seeing a green Ford F150? Crew cab?"

"Yes. And another truck behind it. I don't know what the other one is. It's silver and kind of looks like a racing truck.

Keeps flicking its lights on and off, like it's chasing the first one."

"That does sound like Dad, and it sounds like Nancy is following him," Alice said. But then she wondered if it could be Dean, not her dad, in the first truck.

There was a pause. Madison and Karan seemed to be frozen in their tracks.

"Okay, now we really have a problem." Asher had dropped his official-sounding guy-in-the-chair voice and reverted to a scared eleven-year-old–kid voice. "A car just left the drilling site parking lot and is heading toward you, Madison and Karan. Fast."

"Guys, just get off the road!" Alice shouted into her mic. "You won't make it back to the Subaru!"

"Now, that's weird," Asher's voice added nervously. "Alice, the car driving from the drilling site is yours. It's your Mustang."

"What?" Alice sounded angrier than ever. She looked down and saw it emerge from the trees below her, engine as loud as she had ever heard it. "Asher, fly a drone lower and see who's driving."

"But they'll see the drone. We agreed—"

"Now!" Alice demanded.

"It looks like two teenagers in your car, Alice," Asher reported. "Boys. They're wearing trucker caps or something."

"Must be those incel boys," Karan growled.

"Little shits probably stole my car in the middle of the night," Alice exclaimed. "Dean took it so he could fix it for me."

"Yeah, or maybe Dean is on their side, Alice," Madison said ominously.

"Karan, where are you going?" Madison cried, her voice full of alarm.

Alice saw Karan begin striding toward the speeding cloud

of dust that was Alice's Mustang. It looked like a classic David vs. Goliath scene.

"Karan!" Madison shouted. "Get off the road!"

"What's she doing?!" Alice demanded.

Karan started running.

The driver must have been confused by Karan's insane challenge and taken a foot off the accelerator. The engine grew quiet.

Karan just kept running.

Would the incel boys balk? Would they turn around and drive back to the drilling site?

Apparently emboldened rather than frightened by her insane game of chicken, the driver revved the engine again, accelerating hard toward Karan. They were only two hundred yards from her now.

In response, Karan also picked up her speed. She looked like she was sprinting all out now. What the hell was she trying to do?

The rest happened so fast, Alice found herself questioning what she had just seen. Just as the collision was inevitable, Karan dove up into the air and simply jumped over the Mustang. Then the Mustang skidded sideways and was T-boned by Alice's dad's truck, which had just arrived at the crazy scene from the other direction.

Alice blinked and looked again, and Karan was still standing there, hands on her hips, staring at the smoking collision.

How had Karan even done that? Alice found herself wondering if her siddhis had rubbed off on her friend. The thought gave her a surge of excitement. Maybe she wasn't alone in the world after all?

Alice followed Karan's line of sight and scoured the crash site. Thankfully, her dad immediately got out of the car, apparently unharmed.

"Wow!" Asher chimed. "That was cooler than the high jump at the Olympics!"

Maybe in Olympic terms, Karan's feat wasn't that big of a deal? Olympic high jumpers cleared over six feet. Her Mustang was probably less than five feet tall. But still, Karan had no track and field experience, no soft cushion to land on, and instead of a bouncy pole, she had jumped over a two-ton missile. Karan might well have had some help from prana. Perhaps she did have the beginnings of the ability to fly. But that would be too good to be true.

Alice watched her Dad help the incel boys out of the Mustang. They looked dazed but otherwise fine.

As Nancy dashed over to the scene of the accident, her voice rang out over the radio, steady and calm. "You okay, Karan?"

"I'm fine," Karan responded. "Those are the boys, Nancy—the incel boys who've been spreading nasty rumors about us. They just tried to kill me with a stolen car."

The incel boys—docile until then—appeared to wake up. They had just been seen in a stolen car, trying to run over a pedestrian and then smashing into an approaching vehicle.

They made the only logical move available to dumb people: they ran.

"Stop!" Nancy shouted as the boys jumped over the ditch. "I'm with the sheriff's department!" Then she ran back to her truck and took out a shotgun. "Stop, police!" she shouted again, though the boys appeared wholly uninterested in stopping.

Then she fired the shotgun into the air. The sound of the blast took a second to reach Alice, then echoed up the mountain forever.

Karan ducked, along with Alice's dad.

But the incel boys kept running.

Nancy walked calmly back to her truck and got on the radio.

"Oh my god, why did you do that?!" Madison had emerged

from her crouch on the side of the road and was hugging Karan. Alice could hear heavy breathing in the earpiece.

"I just knew they would keep coming," Karan's voice replied.

"Where is Alice?" Mr. Brickstone seemed to have pulled himself together and was facing Madison and Karan with a stern look on his face. "Why did those two boys have her car?"

"She's fine," Madison said. "She's nearby."

"Mad, tell him I'll meet him at the Roadhouse in a while," Alice said.

After Madison told him, he asked, "Are you speaking to her on that earpiece? I need to talk to her. Like, right now."

"Fair enough." There was some static as Madison took the earpiece out of her ear and the receiver unit from her shirt. "Here," she said, handing it to Alice's dad.

"Alice?"

"Hi, Dad."

"Darling, are you okay?"

"I'm fine. Dad, what are you doing here?"

"Connie woke up!" he said, his voice shaking with emotion.

"What? Is she ... okay? Like, all there and everything?"

"Seems like it. She's babbling away. We think she's looking for you, though. Can you believe it?"

"Dad, that's amazing!"

He grew suddenly serious. "Exactly where are you? Why weren't you answering your phone?"

"Why weren't you answering *your* phone?"

"I asked first."

"I'm kind of ... doing something to help find that lost kid. Wyatt Zhang. I'm sorry I didn't tell you."

"Ah. But where are you?"

"I'm in the woods nearby. I can see you. I'm safe. How did you find us?"

Alice saw her dad looking around, scanning the woods for

her. "Brian told me you might be up here. He wouldn't say why. I couldn't reach you, so I drove up to tell you the news. Kinda too fast, I guess. I'm sorry to tell you I just … ran into your car."

"That's okay, Dad. I saw the whole thing. It wasn't your fault."

"Honey, why the radios?"

Before Alice could attempt an answer, Asher's voice broke in. "Hey, Karan, one of those trucks from the drilling site is coming toward you now. Maybe you should go tell Madison and Nancy."

"Thanks, Asher," Karan said.

"Please don't mention The Club," Asher pleaded. "Just say I'm a kid you met."

"How many people are on this channel?" Alice's dad demanded.

"Dad, I'm sorry, but can you put Madison back on? I need to know what Nancy wants us to do."

"Okay, but you need to make your way back here right now. I don't feel comfortable with the way this situation is developing."

Alice watched as a large, shiny new truck pulled up and stopped right in front of the wrecked Brickstone cars.

An older man in cowboy boots, jeans, and a flannel shirt stepped out and addressed Nancy, Madison, and Dad. "Everybody okay?" his deep voice rang out.

"Mr. Toomes," Nancy's voice replied. "What brings you out here?"

Alice couldn't believe she was finally looking at Ed Toomes. She didn't know what to think. She wanted to scream questions at him through the radio, reach through the binoculars, and shake him until he answered each of them.

"This is quite a scene here," she heard him drawl in what sounded like a mixed-up Southern accent. He walked up to the T-boned Mustang. "Where's the driver?"

"Those little shits ran away," Karan told him.

"And who are you, missy?" Toomes asked.

There was a little scuffle as Nancy appeared to restrain Karan. Then Nancy walked up to Toomes. "Good morning, Ed," Nancy said, shaking his hand. She did not sound like she wanted Ed to have a good morning.

"How'd you happen to be on the scene, Ms. Oakland? I thought you were on leave."

"How would you know I was on leave, Mr. Toomes?"

Alice thought she heard a hawk call in the distance, like in an Old West showdown. "Madison, ask the idiot if he knows where his son is," she chimed in on the earpiece.

Madison walked up next to Nancy and was about to address Ed Toomes when Alice's earpiece went all crackly. She set down her binoculars and reached inside her shirt to see if anything had happened to her radio. She punched the channel button a few times and heard some strange voices. When she heard her name, she paused.

"... tall, fat teenager is a domestic terrorist. Your mission is to hunt her down and disable her before she has a chance to activate the explosives she planted in the mine."

Alice's jaw dropped. It was the voice of Tyler Toomes. He was on another frequency, commanding somebody else to hunt her down.

"Yes, sir," she heard a string of voices bark, one at a time. There were at least ten of them.

When the channel went quiet, Alice quickly looked around her, then desperately flicked back to the channel the girls were on.

She heard Ed say, "That is absolutely none of your business, missy."

Just then, Asher's voice broke in on the earpiece. "Got him," he announced. "Tyler Toomes."

"Where is he?" Alice demanded.

"Alone on the Gold Creek Trail, about ten minutes ahead of you. But you'll never catch him. He's practically sprinting straight uphill."

"I'll do my best," Alice promised, already running in the direction of the trail. "Asher, keep a drone over him and tell me his movements."

"Will do," he answered. "But ..."

"Madison?" Alice interrupted.

"Alice, you should come back," Mad responded. "This is all getting out of control. Let Nancy handle it."

"Madison, I'm sorry, but I have to do this. Maybe I can get him to confess what happened to Wyatt and where he is. Maybe he's still okay."

"But Alice—"

"Tell Nancy that Tyler is on another radio channel with a bunch of guys. I just heard him tell them to hunt me down because I'm a terrorist trying to blow up their stupid mine."

"What?!" Madison cried.

"Oh," Karan interjected, "that totally explains why you feel the need to chase Tyler through the woods. Because there are hunters all around the woods trying to kill you. Makes total sense."

"You guys try to convince Nancy to come up here to arrest Tyler. Gold Creek Trail goes to the top of the mountain. Maybe she can get an ATV from the Roadhouse and meet us up there."

"No way! Alice, come back! It's too dangerous!"

"Asher, please keep a drone on me, okay?" Alice asked. "Let me know if you see anyone nearby."

"On it," he answered.

CHAPTER 28

SUNDAY, 2:30 P.M.

THIRTY MINUTES BEFORE THE END

Alice was starting to catch glimpses of Tyler through the thinning trees uphill. Her legs were burning so badly she thought they were simply going to melt. But even if they did, she was determined to keep running on her molten stumps.

Her dad's words echoed in her head. *Connie is awake!* Every time she replayed that simple sentence, the relief she felt poured more energy into her legs while at the same time making them burn hotter.

As long as this guy was still running around up here, she, her friends, her parents, and Connie were all in danger.

Tyler's hunters had not shown themselves, but she felt they were close. Hopefully they were on foot and their fitness level was not up to this kind of chase. Then again, they could appear any second from behind any tree, hunting rifles in hand. She would feel the bullet strike her before she heard the explosion of the gun.

She wished she could fly again. Everything would be so simple. The hunters would never know to aim their weapons toward the sky. She could fly ahead of Tyler and wait for him. Knock him on the head with a big stick or something when he arrived. Get him to confess everything and record it with her phone. Sit on him until Nancy showed up.

Unfortunately, she couldn't fly. Her ability to see prana had left her again.

Her legs were seriously melting. She was already slowing. It wouldn't be long now before she would have to stop running and risk losing Tyler.

Her desperate chase had led her above the timberline, and she could finally see the top of Witchat Mountain up ahead. She could also see Tyler clearly now. A tall, agile-looking man, he had slowed but was still running uphill with a controlled gait. Despite a slight limp, presumably from Dean's arrow last night, he looked as if he could run like that all day, while Alice knew she was already way past her body's limits.

To make matters worse, she had lost radio contact with Asher. The last thing she had heard was the news that Madison, Karan, and Nancy had found an ATV, but then there was nothing but static. She knew Asher was still watching her via the drone. It was a little bit reassuring to see it up there from time to time. Twice, a new drone had replaced the original one, presumably because their battery life was limited.

When Tyler reached the summit of the mountain, about a hundred yards ahead of Alice, he finally stopped, turned, and stared down at her.

She stopped too, concerned he was about to aim some kind of weapon. She gasped for air. Her heart rate was so far beyond sustainable that she knew she was going to puke any second. But she stood tall and swore not to show Tyler her pain.

She glared up at him.

Tyler stood there like a statue, his hands hanging loose and relaxed by his sides. He didn't even seem to be breathing hard. He didn't look up at the drone. He just stared at Alice, looking commanding, confident, and curious.

Alice concentrated on him as hard as she could, trying to

sense his thoughts. All she could pick up was a vague feeling that he had a screw loose. Or maybe a whole jar full of loose screws. Trying to get a rise out of him, she flipped him off.

Tyler didn't even smile. He seemed to be waiting for her to do something more than fling ineffectual vulgarities. Then, with a slightly disappointed look on his face, he turned and jogged away, down the other side of the slope and out of view.

Okay, Alice thought. *Let's run some more.*

Her legs were almost too heavy to function, but she willed them back into action.

But by the time she crested the mountaintop and looked down, Tyler was, impossibly, gone. Everything was whisper quiet, except for the sound of her heaving breath.

Desperately scanning the vast mountainside below her, she searched for hiding spots. She could see a very long way. The cliffs were at least a mile off; there was no way he could have run that far in thirty seconds. A little closer, there was a tall grove of pines. It was a couple hundred yards away, but he could have reached it at a mad sprint. He was either in there, waiting to attack Alice with a stick or a gun, or he had disappeared somewhere else. Perhaps into Nathaniel's secret meadow.

She jogged down the trail, scanning both sides carefully, hoping to see a thin path or footprints leading off somewhere. But there were only patches of tiny alpine flowers and scree, and she was no tracker.

She looked up at the drone and held up her hands in an appeal for help. It appeared to dip precariously, as though it was falling out of the sky, and then recover. She wondered if Asher was trying to tell her something.

Then the drone simply flew off toward the Roadhouse. Alice guessed it had reached the limit of its range.

She was alone. As usual.

Up ahead, the trail struck the timberline again and veered

right, rather than through the first grove of tiny white pines. She felt something there. A hint, a tingling that told her something was in those trees. Was it Tyler? Or was Wyatt in there?

Walking carefully, she scanned for the tiniest sign of Tyler's presence, but she found nothing. And yet the feeling was growing stronger. Something was in here. The trees were taller and thicker ahead, with odd droplets of mist hanging from some of the pine needles. The moisture made no sense. It had not rained in days. As she brushed against the unlikely cold dew, she began to feel thirsty.

The grove was dark, even though the day was bright above the canopy. The vegetation was all wrong. Mossy, soft earth, swarms of mosquitos, and the smell of a bog.

Slapping ineffectively at the mosquitos covering her sweaty back, Alice suddenly sensed something behind her. She swiveled and ducked.

"Hey … Alice …" Karan gasped, bending over double.

Madison was right behind her, skidding to a halt just inside the pine grove. "You're okay! You idiot!"

Alice straightened and tried, once again, to pretend she wasn't winded. Karan also tried to stand up, failed, and stumbled over to hug Alice awkwardly around the waist. She seemed to be sobbing.

"Oh, for god's sake, Karan," Alice said, patting her back.

"Have you seen Tyler?" Madison asked urgently.

"Yes, I think he came in here," Alice said. "But he dematerialized or something."

"Let's wait for Nancy," Madison said. "She's right behind us."

"Obviously a better weight lifter than a runner," Karan said into Alice's right hip. "I'm guessing she's twenty minutes back. The ATV didn't make it up all the way up the hill."

Alice lifted Karan to a wobbly standing position, and she wiped her eyes. Then, feeling crowded, Alice took a step backward, and her foot collided with a pile of rocks. She fell hard onto the wet ground.

She stayed there on her back and stared up at the trees, feeling stupid. And exhausted. It occurred to her that she could just lie there forever.

Then she turned her head away from Karan and Madison with their concerned looks and saw a dead tree left over from a very old burn. Covered in moss, it was broader than the other trees and appeared to be a different species of pine. She didn't know what kind. She didn't care. All she cared about was that it was brightly glowing with prana. The beautiful shimmering substance was the most welcome thing she had seen all day. She closed her eyes and willed it to flow to her, to renew her energy.

Feeling slightly refreshed, she opened her eyes and gazed toward the little pile of rocks she'd stumbled over and saw the same liquid glow dancing and flowing around them.

She rolled onto her side and forced herself into a sitting position. Encouraged that she was seeing prana again, she wondered if its presence meant she was near Nathaniel's hidden meadow. She painfully hoisted herself to her feet and walked over to the shining dead tree.

It was hollow, and inside was another pile of rocks, encircled by a dazzling flow of crystalline air.

Was this supposed to point the way to the hidden meadow? She looked around and saw only more pine trees. Were these little pranic piles of rocks showing her a gateway? Or a keyhole? Elevator? Escalator? Portal? Or what?

"Why the hell are you playing with those rocks, Alice?" Karan asked.

She looked back at the cairn she had tripped over and thought hard. She had seen nothing before kicking it over. No glowing prana near the rock pile or the tree. Perhaps if she disturbed this new pile in the tree, she would see a way forward?

Carefully reaching into the tree, she removed the top stone, warm with pranic energy, and chucked it over her shoulder.

She immediately saw another cairn up ahead, glowing with prana as brightly as the first two. With Karan and Madison following quietly behind her, probably wondering if she had gone insane, Alice approached it, removed a rock, and saw a fourth cairn. With growing excitement, she moved from cairn to cairn, each time watching out for the sudden appearance of a meadow.

"This little forest is way bigger on the inside, isn't it," Karan said. "It's like Endor meets *Doctor Who*."

"What are you talking about?" Madison asked.

As Alice removed a rock from her eighth cairn, Karan gasped behind her. "I can't believe it. The meadow is really here."

CHAPTER 29

SUNDAY, 2:50 P.M.

TEN MINUTES BEFORE THE END

"Alice, you did it!" Madison shouted, brushing past her and into the space that had just revealed itself.

"Wait!" Alice shouted.

But it was too late; Madison ran right into the meadow. About fifty yards beyond her, Alice saw Tyler Toomes, holding a gun in his hand.

What happened next was a blur.

As Alice dashed over to push Madison out of the way of what she assumed would be a flying bullet, Karan plunged into the meadow just ahead of her. Karan dived in front of Madison as a gunshot sounded, and Alice reached out to pull her back while simultaneously pushing Madison forward. Alice missed Karan but connected with Madison, which meant Karan was between Alice and the bullet. But then something orange shot out from behind her as fast as a shaft of light. She heard it strike something metallic, and then a zipping sound as it flew away into the sky. Another orange blur flew past them, and the gun flew out of Tyler's hand.

Then all was still and quiet.

Madison was on the ground; Karan was standing in front of Alice with a defiant look on her scarred face. Tyler was still at the edge of the meadow, near a notch formed by two jagged rocks. They looked unnatural, like a bolt of something stronger than lightning had sliced a boulder down the middle.

Alice turned to find the source of the orange blurs that had saved them from Tyler and was unsurprised to see Dean. She should have known his siddhis would tell him to come here. But she did a double take; he looked much taller, stronger, bigger, more majestic. It was as though he had grown into a seven-foot version of King Arthur. His head was even glowing like he was wearing a gold crown. He had the little kid's bow in his left hand, one matching orange arrow nocked on the string and a few more in his shirt pocket.

Dean was staring ferociously at Tyler.

"Finally," Tyler boomed across the meadow, smiling broadly. Despite having lost his gun and all tactical advantage, his smile seemed genuine, Alice thought with great surprise. Like Christmas had come and the naughty boy had gotten a nice present.

"Finally what, douchebag?" Karan shouted. Her face was just as terrifying as Dean's.

Madison slowly stood up, visibly shaken.

It was a standoff: Dean and three tall, angry girls versus a chameleon. Dean armed with magical arrows, the girls with no weapons except their anger; Tyler disarmed, his back to a precipitous drop-off of at least five hundred feet. Yet he seemed dangerous still.

The silence settled. It was bizarre, Alice thought. There was no birdsong here. Or marmot whistles. Or bugs. As the seconds ticked away, she found herself wondering what pollinated the flowers. Maybe some magical bees were buzzing around. The Harry Potter kids would go nuts over them. Why was she having such inane thoughts at a time like this? She congratulated herself that at least they weren't more of those ridiculous romantic stirrings for Tyler.

"You're a talented man, Tyler," Dean stated in a loud, clear voice, finally breaking the silence. "Only a person with great inner resources could have understood the concealments around this place. But inner resources are not enough when the mind is fractured."

This finally seemed to piss Tyler off, and his smile was replaced with a look of anger that twisted his features.

"I can help you heal," Dean continued. "You are not alone."

"Hey," Karan shouted. "I can make a better offer. Come over here, and I'll kick your stupid ass."

Alice smiled at Karan's bravado. To her knowledge, Karan had never been in a fight. She was athletic and angry but probably had no idea how to throw a punch or a kick.

Alice wanted to destroy this guy too. To keep him from hurting anyone else ever again. (Or maybe to get him out of her head once and for all.) But she suddenly realized she had no idea what to do with him. Should they try to capture him? How?

When was Nancy going to show up?

"Well? What will it be?" Karan shouted.

Tyler just stood there, looking unhinged.

"Where's Wyatt?" Madison shouted, having rediscovered her voice. "Tell us where he is, and we'll leave you alone."

Ignoring Madison, Tyler appeared to recover himself a little, planted his feet squarely, and boomed, "Archer! Who are you, exactly?"

Instead of answering, Dean shot a plastic arrow into the sky. There was a sharp sound like a whip cracking. Everything was silent for a moment as Dean and Tyler stared at each other. Then another crack sounded near Tyler, and a small explosion occurred to his left.

Without flinching, Tyler looked around casually, saw his gun was molten and smoking, and then returned his gaze to Dean.

"Okay, okay, boys," Alice said, stepping forward. She knew this pissing contest was going nowhere.

"Alice, no!" Madison cried.

"It's fine, Mad," Alice replied as calmly as she could. She gestured that Dean should lower his toy bow. Then she held up her hands and started walking as casually as possible across the meadow toward Tyler, observing him.

He smiled and shifted his weight, striking a pose. Alice began to feel something stir inside her, but she shook off the feeling.

She caught his eye and fought her way into his head, reading his thoughts. The sense he had a screw loose persisted, but otherwise his mind was surprisingly orderly. Everything in its place. Plans for everything. Schemes for everyone. Then she sensed that beneath it all, he was hiding a secret. Of course, that secret was what she wanted, and she forced him to show it to her. And there it was: the shining visage of Nathaniel. Not like the graffiti version, but in full color. More than full color— he was like an angel, or even a kind of private savior.

That was when Tyler fought back against her. Furiously. Thrashing and kicking like an angry child, he forced Alice out of his head and broke the connection. Something of the angry child remained in his face as he stood there afterward, breathing hard, fists clenched.

Alice put her hands up again to calm him down. "I'm just here to talk to you about where Wyatt is."

Tyler seemed to compose himself and pointed to the cliff. "Have a look for yourself."

She walked around him, giving him a wide berth, and peered over the edge of the cliff. She saw no caves, no little boys, no traces of crashed drones—nothing. In any event, it was very, very, very far to the bottom of the cliff.

Instinctively, she considered what it would be like to jump. If she angled toward the left, she would have plenty of time to catch enough prana to fly. *If* she could get prana to cooperate. If not ... (Better not to think of it.) Jumping toward the right, however, would be harder. Unless she jumped far out and swam like crazy, she would clip some rocks that jutted out twenty or thirty feet below where she stood.

Looking back at Tyler, she asked, "What happened to him?"

Ignoring her question, Tyler gestured to Dean. "You've done well to attach yourself to that amazing man. He's like Nathaniel. I can see it. Those powers come naturally to him."

"I'm not attached to *anyone*, Tyler." As soon as it came out of her mouth, she knew he would take it the wrong way. She meant she didn't rely on anyone for anything, but Tyler probably thought she was coming on to him.

"You and I are alike," he said, in full control of his voice again. "Neither of us has the abilities they do, but we are wise enough to hang around them, hoping some of their power will rub off. And I can tell you, it does rub off eventually. I can't do everything Nathaniel could, but just by following him around, I learned the art of cloaking physical spaces and how to deceive others. And I can well imagine you've picked up a few tricks from your archer friend the same way."

So, he doesn't know anything about me after all, Alice thought gratefully. She aimed to keep it that way.

"Alice, come with me. I can teach you things. We can find others out there with abilities and learn from them. And eventually, we'll be able to do even more than your friend there. Just imagine what I could do with abilities like that! How easily could I gain wealth and power! I could be president of the United States. Anything. Imagine what they would think ..."

Alice must have betrayed some of her disgust at this typical villain speech and her astonishment that he would make such a proposal to a seventeen-year-old. It was twisted. Or it was just another pile of deception. Probably both. And she also realized when Tyler said "they," he probably meant his dad. How pathetic.

His brow furrowed again, he continued, "I admit, I have done some questionable things. But it has all been in pursuit of abilities like those Nathaniel had. Imagine, Alice, how many kids we could help! If you could tap into the energy that your friend over there has, you could use it to influence kids' minds. You could transform a teen's depression into joy. You could save lives! You might find a way to use that energy to heal your sister!"

"My sister woke up, so she's good, thanks."

"But Alice, that's wonderful news!"

He sounded so sincere. Alice had to work hard to remember that he was, by his own admission, a master in the art of deception.

"Alice," a terrified, high-pitched voice screamed from the other side of the meadow. "Get away from the edge! Now!" Alice looked back and saw Nancy running toward her.

But then the powerful boom of a gunshot rang out, and Nancy reflexively spun around to face the sound. She didn't seem to have been hit, and neither did Madison, Karan, or Dean. They were all staring at a small army of men who had emerged from the trees. About fifteen hunting rifles were pointed at them.

As Nancy shouted at them to put down their weapons because she was a deputy sheriff, Alice turned back to Tyler. He wasn't even looking at the little army; he was gazing longingly over the edge of the cliff. Tyler looked like a child who had lost his best friend over the edge, like he wanted to follow, even if it meant his death.

"Hey," she exclaimed.

When he looked back at her, his eyes were red and tormented. "This cliff took my Nathaniel ten years ago. It was the worst day of my life, and I swore I would not let his memory and his abilities pass from this world."

Then he ran toward the notch in the rocks, shouldered a large backpack that Alice hadn't noticed before, and jumped. As she watched in horror, then amazement, he pulled a cord. As she rushed to the edge to watch, it occurred to her he must have done this before. But this time he screwed it up. A blue parachute unfurled and almost saved him before he struck the first rock that jutted out.

Alice heard the shocking *thunk* of flesh on stone. Then the parachute caught an updraft and carried Tyler away from any further danger. He was going to escape, if his initial collision with the rocks hadn't killed him.

She looked back and saw that Nancy was busy with all the hunters, who had decided disobeying a sheriff deputy didn't bode well for their future careers and lain down on their stomachs. Could Alice risk letting her handle Tyler too? Would Nancy be able to call up other officers to intercept Tyler at the bottom of the cliff? Or was Tyler already calling his dad to sort everything out for him?

Alice turned to Dean, who was looking back at her, wide-eyed. Well, if he didn't already know she could fly, it was about time he found out. She nodded at him, turned, and dove off the edge.

CHAPTER 30

SUNDAY, 3:00 P.M.

THE END

As Alice fell, flailing hopelessly through the air, finding no purchase in prana, she saw a dark hole in the rocks just below the cliff top. She didn't have time to process what she had seen. She was plunging toward a huge talon of granite that jutted out of the cliff wall. At best, there were three seconds before a fatal impact.

Alice closed her eyes, and time stopped. And with it, the sound of the wind and all the fear she felt disappeared. In the luxurious space left by the absence of time, Alice felt surrounded by prana, held aloft and still. It didn't feel like she had entered a dream; it was more like leaving one. Like she had suddenly emerged from a blurry black-and-white nightmare into the real world, resplendent with color.

These were not the colors of red stone, green trees, blue sky, white clouds. It was a million shades of feeling, of clarity of thought, of broad vistas of the mind, the capacity to see well beyond the limits of normal sight. It was how her inner world had been before her life had gotten complicated. Back when all she had was sorrow over the loss of her brother and nothing else. It had been terrible and lonely, but simple, and it had allowed her the space to see and embrace the growth of her abilities. She had forgotten how it felt to be this free.

She knew that as soon as she opened her eyes, time would restart and she would find herself plunging toward certain death.

Unless she could use that split second to regain her ability to fly.

Rather than bracing her body for impact with the granite, she forced herself to relax.

Drawing her senses into her arms and legs and stomach, she counted to three and opened her eyes.

The sharp rocks were much closer than she expected. She had only a millisecond.

She used all of her strength to dig into the prana and give one mighty pull. That was all she had time to do. Her effort adjusted her trajectory just enough to avoid the most jagged of the rocks, but not enough to avoid them altogether. Her stomach took the brunt of it. There was a terrible scraping *thud*, but she bounced and remained airborne. Willing her arms to give another pull, she swam again with all her strength, ignoring a crunching sensation in her ribs—probably broken —and urged her legs into a powerful butterfly kick. Now she felt herself gliding away from the cliff edge, and with another painful pull, she started leveling out. She was going to be okay.

She forced her injured body to continue swimming and began to gain altitude. Below her, she saw Tyler's parachute drifting toward the valley floor. She would have plenty of time to circle around, avoid his line of sight, and land somewhere to wait for him. In the meantime, she needed to explore the hole near the top of the cliff. It could be the eye from her persistent visions the last few days. It could be where Wyatt had been trapped all this time.

Fighting against the pain, she swam back toward the cliff

top. She didn't see the hole again until she was nearly on top of it, because some jutting rocks obscured it.

Suddenly, she heard a desperately loud howling noise, and the newfound energy left her as quickly as it had come.

The hole in the rock became a bleak, nightmarish, sucking void, and she was consumed by it before she even had time to scream.

CHAPTER 31

SUNDAY, 4:00 P.M.

HOPE FOR A NEW BEGINNING

Alice woke up to the worst smell she had ever smelled. She snapped her eyes open and gasped for breath, thinking she was in a toilet or a coffin.

"Relax," a boy's voice said.

She could see nothing and could not relax.

Her head was on sand, and she felt a grainy crunch as she jerked it from side to side. She tried to lift herself onto her elbows but had no strength.

"Stop moving. You may have a neck injury. You at least have a concussion. You've been out for an hour."

"Where are you?" she asked, still unable to see.

"It's dark. There's no light down here. And I used the last of my phone battery to see well enough to get you out of the water."

Suddenly Alice heard the water. It sounded like a waterfall. It was like a volume switch had been flipped on.

Alice turned her attention to herself. She reached her hand up and felt a bunch of loose, crunchy bits under the skin and muscle of her neck. Perhaps the sand wasn't the only thing crunching; maybe she had, in fact, damaged her neck. She turned her head one more time, feeling with her hand. Whatever had gone wrong seemed to have healed okay already.

"Except for you."

"Except for me, what?" Alice asked, finally managing to force herself up on her elbows. They felt like they had been scraped raw, but they were healing too.

"This place was in total darkness, except for you. After my phone died, I saw that you glowed." The boy's voice was coming from about ten feet away. It sounded clear and loud, but forced. Like the speaker was making an incredible effort to sound normal but was in fact brutally injured.

"Wyatt?" Alice guessed.

"I thought you were dying," the voice continued. "I couldn't find your pulse. But then the glowing started. I'd only seen something like that once before."

Alice managed to lift herself into a sitting position but felt like she was about to throw up.

"That's how I found the hidden meadow. That glow. It was on these little piles of rocks. When I moved a rock, the glow moved to the next pile."

Alice swallowed hard to keep from spewing. "Wyatt, are you hurt?"

"Did that glowing stuff heal you? It seemed to be coming from your head and neck. That's where you were hurt, I think."

"Yeah, Wyatt. Don't worry about me." She wondered how the hell she could get him to focus on their escape. "Okay," she said, trying to sound serious. "Your sister said you want to become an astronaut. You like to solve problems. Do me a favor right now, Wyatt. Pretend we're in a spaceship. It's in danger. I'm the pilot, and you're the copilot."

"Cool," he said, a bit too easily, like he was falling asleep.

"Wyatt!" Alice said firmly and loudly. "Full status update! Give me all the relevant facts!"

Alice heard a short gasp, like Wyatt's heart had stopped and started again.

"We're in a cavern. There's no way out."

"If there's a way in, there's a way out."

"We fell in through a long vertical shaft. It's like a waterfall. I tried climbing out, but it's impossible."

"Where's the outflow?" Alice asked. "The water's draining somewhere, or we'd be underwater. Where's it going? And where's the air coming from?"

"The pool empties into small openings in the wall. The air comes from another bunch of small openings. I think this place is like an air vent for the coal mine. You know how the mine is drilling by my house?"

"Yes, but I assumed they were drilling for coal or whatever."

"Nope. I asked my dad ... before. He said they were drilling a new ventilation shaft."

"Why?" Alice felt stupid asking a boy all these mining questions, but they were keeping Wyatt awake and alert while she tried to gather her energy and figure out a way out of here.

"Dad said they have gigantic fans down in the mine, sucking air in for the miners to breathe, and they need lots of ventilation shafts for the fans to work. He didn't know how the mine stayed open after the big vent collapsed ten years ago."

Alice remembered Rama saying something about how the mine had to resolve some technical problems before the big Indian company would make a deal with them. This must have been it.

"But, Wyatt, surely all those engineer people at the mine would know about this shaft?" Alice wondered aloud. Perhaps Nancy was out there right now, telling the mine to shut down the fans.

"I'm guessing they don't even know it's here, because Nathaniel's cloaking hides it. That's why they're drilling a bigger air vent by my house."

Alice noticed Wyatt's voice fading again. "How bad are you hurt, Wyatt?"

Wyatt didn't respond at first, then sucked in some breath awkwardly. "I think I broke my ankles. You came in headfirst, I came in feetfirst."

"Seriously? You tried to climb up that torrential waterfall with two broken ankles?"

"Yeah. I didn't make it far …" His voice trailed away again.

Alice scrabbled over to him on her hands and knees. He was lying down on the gravel. "Wyatt! Stay with me!"

"Oh, sorry about that," he said. "I'm kind of tired."

"Stay with me. What's that awful stench?"

"We're not the only ones who fell down here …" He went quiet, then gasped once, as though his heart had skipped a beat or two. Then he started wheezing.

"Wyatt, my name is Alice. I'm going to get you out of here."

"No," he said, before gasping and fading away again.

Alice began to panic. She didn't know if she was losing him or if he was just falling asleep.

She stood up, fought against dizziness, and walked over to the waterfall. She stuck her hand in, and the powerful current slapped it down. Reaching around behind the flow, she felt the slimy rock wall and found a handhold.

If Wyatt could attempt it, so could she.

"Wyatt, I'll go get help. There are some people just at the top of the cliff."

Alice kept her head out of the water as she tentatively felt for her first footholds. Then she plunged all the way in. Mouth tightly closed, she climbed as hard and fast as she could, feeling blindly for handholds. She made it about ten feet before completely panicking and giving herself to the power of the water, smashing into the pool. Nearly drowning in the swirling currents in complete darkness, she swam in the vague direction of up.

Alice broke the surface and gasped in a breath, and then another. Her cheek hit a lumpy object, and, terrified, she swam toward where she hoped Wyatt and the beach were. There were many more floating things, and she had to just swim through them. She didn't want to know what they were.

Her hands touched gravel; she had guessed right. She scrabbled out of the pool, gasped for air, and went straight to where she remembered Wyatt being.

"I bet I made it higher than you," Wyatt said with a faint giggle.

She was so relieved he hadn't died while she was climbing that she laughed with him. "And with two broken legs, too," she added. She wished she had a light so she could assess his injuries.

Then it occurred to her: she *did* have a light. More than that, she had a phone, which might just be their ticket out of this hole.

She jammed her hand into her back pocket and found it—the brand-new phone her dad had given her. Waterproof. Long battery life.

Pressing the side button, she was hugely relieved to see it had lived up to the marketing hype. It had survived the plunge into the pool.

There was no signal. They must be too deep in the mountain. But the light made all the difference.

In the blinding glow, the horrible little space revealed itself to her. They were in a cavern about the size of a bedroom. Half of it was taken up by a disgusting pool filled with dozens of dead birds bobbing around in various states of decomposition. The waterfall poured into it unceasingly. Behind the churning birdbath, the wall seemed pockmarked with small holes, each only big enough for a snake or a little rat to pass through.

Wyatt was lying next to her on a little gravel beach. His eyes opened wide. Next to him was a pile of broken machinery he'd been tinkering with; it looked like a big drone.

"Who is that?!" Alice cried out, having spied another person on the gravel behind him. "Who is hell is that?!"

"A kid called Nathaniel," Wyatt said, straining now. Perhaps in pain. "What's left of him, anyway."

Alice looked carefully and saw that it was indeed a body, rotted down to a rough, sinewy simile of a human. She had to look away.

She wanted out of there. Dead bodies, deafening noise ... claustrophobia began to hem her in.

She rechecked her phone, but there was still no signal.

She looked around desperately. Behind the body was something else she hadn't noticed.

"Did you make that ... shrine thing behind Nathaniel?"

"No. It was here before me. Nathaniel must have done it before he died."

It was a large heart shape about four feet high, intricately woven from plucked feathers and bird bones. The feathers formed the heart, which held together somehow, and the bones formed a kind of lattice table. It was beautiful but creepy. As she inspected it, she realized Nathaniel must have been less disgusted by the dead birds than she was. He must have eaten a lot of them raw to stay alive long enough to turn their remains into this shrine.

Moving closer, she saw that in the center of the heart was a worn photograph of Nathaniel's dad, Henry Narrow.

Alice turned to Wyatt. "What is all this?"

Without opening his eyes, the small boy began to speak. "I've been thinking about it since I fell in here on Thursday. Well, no, I spent the first day screaming and crying. Then I tried to wrap up my feet enough that I could climb out. When that failed, I cried some more, and then I started thinking about Nathaniel and his dad." Wyatt took a shuddering, wheezing breath. "I think his babysitter put him up to it. Jumping off the cliff, I mean. He gave him a piece of parchment—"

"Your friend Asher showed us," Alice interrupted. "And I think I know who his 'babysitter' was. It's hard to imagine that asshole would make a parchment thing that would inspire Nathaniel try to kill himself ..."

"What?"

"Never mind. Go on.."

"Well, anyway, I think Nathaniel believed the parchment. He must have thought he could jump off the cliff and save his dad from dying of cancer."

As Alice began wishing with renewed passion that Tyler cracked his head open on that rock earlier, she saw a snake in her peripheral vision and jumped away, shrieking.

Shining her light on it, she saw that it wasn't moving. It was still coiled up.

She took a step closer and breathed a sigh of relief. It was a rope. She took it in her hand.

"You think Nathaniel made this too?" she asked, marveling at it.

The rope was beautiful. Intricately woven from the spines of bird feathers, it was light, felt strong, and was quite long. Alice unraveled it and guessed it was about thirty feet.

"He must have been in here for months and months," she said, "to weave a rope like this out of feathers. That kid turned out to be really smart, huh? Amazing. He must have been living off raw dead birds and using their feathers to make this."

But what was Nathaniel planning to do with the rope?

Alice tested its strength by placing her foot on one end and pulling as hard as she could. It was rock solid, like a cable.

"Can you believe this?" she said, turning to face Wyatt.

But he was out cold. She dashed to his side and saw he was still breathing, but raggedly.

She felt his pulse in his neck and found it racing.

Keep breathing, she urged.

Breathe. The word echoed in her head. It was the key now. The problem with the waterfall climb was simply the panic she felt at the lack of air. *You're a swimmer*, she scolded herself. *You can go without air for a long time, you idiot.*

She considered the little boy struggling for life on the damp gravel. What would give him the best chance at survival? Dragging him out with the rope, or climbing out alone and getting help?

His eyes started moving rapidly behind his eyelids. What did that mean?

"Wyatt!" She shook him, hoping to revive him, but he remained unconscious. Supporting his head, she pulled him into a sitting position and propped him against Nathaniel's feather shrine. She ran to the waterfall, brought back water in her cupped hands, and tried to force it into his mouth.

Finally, he sputtered a little and tried to open his eyes.

"Wyatt!" she shouted again.

He nodded weakly.

It occurred to her that he might not have time to wait for a later rescue.

"I'm going to tie this feather rope around you. I'm going to take the other end and climb up the waterfall. Then I'm going to pull you up. Got it?"

He shook his head.

"What do you mean, no? Aren't you supposed to be an astronaut?" Alice didn't know what that was supposed to mean, but it was worth a shot.

He smiled faintly.

"You can do it, Wyatt. I'll pull you up as quickly as possible. You don't have to do anything. Just hold your breath. Can you do that, Wyatt?"

He tried to open his eyes again. When he failed, he simply smacked his lips and nodded.

"Good man. Now, I'm going to carry you over to the water-fall. This is important. When I give you the signal, make sure you hold your breath. The signal will be three tugs on the rope."

He nodded again.

"I'll tell you a swimmer's trick. Just before you go into the waterfall, take ten or fifteen quick breaths. It will help you hold your breath longer. You hear me?"

Wyatt nodded. Alice noticed his eyes were moving rapidly beneath his eyelids again.

She was afraid he didn't have much time.

After tying Nathaniel's rope securely around his chest and under his arms, she tied the other end around her waist.

She propped Wyatt up against the stone next to the waterfall.

"Remember—three tugs, then hold your breath!"

CHAPTER 32

SUNDAY, 5:00 P.M.

THE CLIMB

Pocketing her phone, Alice turned toward the falls, took twenty short breaths, and plunged in. It felt like the water wanted to smash her into the center of the earth. But Wyatt was depending on her, so she reached up, groping blindly for her first handhold.

Hand over hand, she strained against the water. Holding her breath, she climbed more calmly and deliberately this time to keep her heart rate down. The force of the water made it feel like she weighed five hundred pounds. She strained, forcing her fingers to grip each precarious handhold. She made painful but steady progress for about thirty seconds, and then she began to feel the panic rising. This was too hard. She needed to breathe. If she just let go, she could slide back down and breathe all she wanted. But then she would die down there. And Wyatt would die first.

Just when the lack of oxygen was so bad it made her lose control of her bladder and explode with fury and panic, Alice reached for the next handhold and found only air above her rather than water and stone. She fumbled for a ledge and pulled her head above the water.

It was like a miracle. The relief of finding air after having none for so long was bliss. She gasped, breathing in wheezing gasps, getting rid of carbon dioxide.

Her head was pounding, and she knew she needed to rest, catch her breath, and let her hands recover.

Then she remembered Wyatt, sitting down at the bottom of the falls, unconscious. He was in worse shape than she was.

Blinking her eyes free of water, she saw some natural light beckoning her onward. She estimated that she had already climbed about fifteen feet through the water, which meant the rope still had a good ten or fifteen feet of slack. She hoisted the rest of her body out of the rushing water and was suddenly accosted by a ferocious wind. She fought against the hurricane-force air, found a foothold, and wedged herself against the rock.

The wind was deafening. Furious. Easily a hundred miles an hour.

Climbing against this wind probably wouldn't be much easier than clawing her way up the waterfall.

Blinking constantly against tears, Alice surveyed her new challenge. She was in another small cavern about the size of a closet. The water feeding the waterfall was coming from a huge opening in the rock by her feet. The wind, on the other hand, seemed to be coming from above. It was easy to see how she, Wyatt, and Nathaniel had been sucked in.

She couldn't see the opening to the outside, which meant the shaft above her was not straight, and she had no way to estimate the distance she needed to climb. She had hoped the surface would be closer than the rope length so she could climb all the way out, then hoist Wyatt up. Now what was the best option? She could pull him up into this little cavern and then lash him to her back before attempting the rest of the climb. But she looked up, squinting into the blasting wind, and the opening seemed too narrow to pass through with Wyatt on her back.

She thought again of Wyatt down below, sitting where she

had propped him next to the waterfall, perhaps wheezing his last breaths. With time ticking away, she decided to see how high she could climb before the slack in her rope ran out. She started climbing against the furious wind, keeping her eyes closed against it except to find the handholds.

Her progress was painfully slow. One little mistake would send her plunging back into the waterfall and the dead bird pool.

And yet she continued to climb, her hopes building. Until she reached the end of the rope.

She was still about ten feet from a narrow curve in the shaft, her fingers holding onto small pockets in the rock. She looked up and saw it was indeed too narrow for her to squeeze through with a boy strapped to her back. But there was no way to let go of the wall so she could pull up Wyatt. She was stuck. She would have to climb back down to the cavern above the waterfall. But when she started back down, one of her hands slipped, and she almost fell.

Help me, she thought. *Help me*.

No help came.

Her fingers were failing. Turning her head, she searched for a way to wedge herself into position. If she could just reach her leg behind her and touch the other side of the shaft, she could swivel herself around and use her legs to press her back against the wall. It would at least give her ruined fingers a break.

She steadied her nerves, used all the core strength she could find, and twisted one leg awkwardly around while not relinquishing her fragile handholds. When she felt like she had enough pressure on the opposite wall with that foot, she released one hand, twisted further, and managed to plant the other foot next to the first. Pushing her butt firmly against the rock, she released her other hand. Shaking the pain out of her hands, she stole some deep breaths from the rushing wind.

Now what, Alice?

She felt a gentle tug on the rope around her waist. Then again.

Wyatt was still awake! She reached down and pulled it three times quickly. He responded with three pulls.

She untied the rope from her waist and pulled hard, then paused. She imagined she had pulled Wyatt up from his sitting position. The next pull would plunge him into the water and prevent him from breathing, starting the ticking clock.

Hoping he had taken his quick breaths, she pressed her feet firmly against the opposite wall and began a furious race against time.

The line grew instantly taut, and she felt like she was pulling a horse, not an eighty-pound boy. Her back and arm muscles strained against the weight, but she kept pulling, hand over hand, making painful but steady progress.

Five seconds.

Ten seconds.

Twenty seconds.

Her strong back muscles were up to the task, but her hands were almost entirely spent. She felt the rope start to slip a few inches each time she grabbed it. But she had to keep pulling.

Thirty seconds.

Wyatt was not going to make it. There's no way he could hold his breath this long in his weakened condition.

In a surge of adrenaline and desperation, she doubled her pulling speed, and finally she saw his black hair break through the water, then his mouth gasping for breath, his hands groping wildly for something to hold.

She crimped the rope against her leg. Not waiting to see if Wyatt was okay, she shook her free hand wildly, hoping to get some feeling back. Then she switched sides and shook out her other hand.

She saw that Wyatt had drawn himself into a position he might be able to hold for a short time. He had to use his broken feet to brace himself against the wall, she noticed with horror. It must be excruciating. But he looked up, seemed to assess the situation, and gave her a thumbs-up.

Well, she thought, if he could put up with that amount of suffering, so could she.

She tied the rope around her waist again and did the awkward twisting movement in reverse to get back into climbing position. Then she began the last part of the most painful climb of her life.

Her hands quickly fatigued, and she felt like they were simply broken dead weight, no better than Wyatt's feet. She willed them to remain in a claw shape and kept moving upward as fast as she dared.

It took another grueling minute of climbing against the wind, and then she reached the turn in the shaft. With great relief, she saw the twilight through the opening. It was only about ten feet farther.

She hoped there were rescue helicopters out there with teams of guys waiting to rappel down and rescue them.

She wedged her legs into the bend in the shaft and began to haul Wyatt up through the wind. She prayed Nathaniel's rope would hold. It was now sliding against the rock at the shaft's turn, and she was terrified it would snap at any second.

But it held, each second bringing the ailing little boy closer.

Finally, she saw his head, then his shoulders. He seemed unconscious again, and his head was lolling to the side.

"Stay with me, Wyatt!!" she screamed into the howling wind.

At last he was there with her, and she grabbed him with one of her claws. He was limp but seemed to be breathing.

With great difficulty, she lashed him to her stomach and was reminded of how she used to fly Connie around like this.

She just had to climb the remaining ten feet to reach the opening of the shaft. But as she turned to begin, she realized her body had already started to shut down from her injuries and exhaustion. She knew it was over. She couldn't make it.

She looked desperately at the opening, hoping a person would appear to save them.

Then, once again, she remembered her phone.

Clawing it out of her pocket, she nearly dropped it down the shaft before securing it in an atrophied, shaking, and now bleeding hand. She saw there was a signal now, and somehow she got to the calling screen and dialed 911.

The wind was too strong for her to make herself heard, even rasping at the top of her lungs. The dispatcher just kept patiently saying, "Can you please move out of the wind a little? I can't hear you ..."

Alice hung up in desperation. Hopefully they would at least figure out it was her phone number and someone would tell Nancy she was alive.

Then she managed to persuade her destroyed fingers to do one more task. She opened up a text message to Karan and Madison and managed to write: *Jstbbelow Clifford ina hole hirrrhy*

After she pressed send, she lost her grip on the phone and watched it get sucked into the shaft with a distant clatter.

Then she felt her left hamstring threaten to cramp. She had experienced hamstring cramps before, and it felt like someone had taken an axe to the back of her leg. If it happened again, she knew that would be the end of her and Wyatt; she would never be able to hold them in this position, and they'd fall. Drawing all of her concentration into her leg, she closed her eyes and prayed for the healing warmth of prana.

Perhaps prana responded, because the cramp never fully materialized, but she knew it would sooner or later.

There was nothing to do now but hope Wyatt kept breathing and that her legs held out. She kept her eyes closed and concentrated on holding on.

CHAPTER 33

SUNDAY, 6:00 P.M.

RESCUE

" A lice!"
The voice was barely audible over the ceaseless screaming of the wind.

Snapping her eyes open, the first thing Alice saw was a snake slithering toward her through the shaft opening. She could do nothing about it. It wasn't until it passed her face that she realized it was a rope, not a snake.

"Alice!" she heard again, closer this time.

At the top of the hole, she saw a set of legs appear—short and muscular.

"Alice!"

"Nancy!" she croaked back.

Nancy was beginning to get sucked in and was held back only by her rappelling rope. She managed to clamber back out and planted her hands and feet firmly on the outside of the shaft opening.

Straining against the forces pulling her in, Nancy peered down at Alice and shouted, "Can you take hold of the rope?!"

Alice felt her leg threatening to cramp again. She looked at Nancy with wild panic and shook her head. It was all she could do to just hold on to her position. And she was about to fail at even that.

Nancy nodded and looked wildly around. Deciding on a course of action, she slowly lowered her legs into the sucking wind in the shaft and began to rappel through the small space down toward Alice. When she reached her, she crimped her rope, wrapped her strong arms under Alice's armpits, and hugged her tightly.

"Can you hold on to me?"

Alice tried, but she couldn't. Her arms felt rigid and useless, like wood. Even worse, the effort instantly brought on the long-dreaded cramping in both of her legs. It was like some kind of massive seizure. She screamed, and her face crumpled in pain.

Seeing Alice's desperation, Nancy wrapped her legs around Alice and Wyatt and used one hand to reach down to a radio on her belt.

"Pull us up!" she shouted into it.

Someone pulled hard on Nancy's rope, and they twisted around in the hole so that Nancy's back struck the ceiling of the shaft. Alice heard a tremendous cracking noise over the screaming of the wind. Or was that Nancy's screaming? Or her own?

But Nancy's hold on her didn't slacken. Wyatt was sandwiched between their bodies, and she willed him to stay alive.

Alice's legs were cramping so hard she began to jerk and twist violently against Nancy's body. She was terrified she was going to crush Wyatt, but there was simply nothing she could do. Her body was out of her control.

She screamed again, and felt Nancy's body grind and bounce against the rock as they were pulled up the shaft.

Finally they were out, and the wind abated.

Something about the quiet allowed Alice to dig deep within herself. With all of her concentration, she willed the cramps in her legs to subside. One leg obeyed, and the relief allowed her to shift all of her focus to the other one. There were five more seconds of terrifying pain before the cramping in that leg finally released.

"You're safe, Alice!" Nancy was shouting.

Alice realized she was still screaming at the top of her lungs, and as soon as she stopped, the whole world grew quiet.

Alice relaxed completely and allowed herself to rely on Nancy's arms and legs to hold her and Wyatt in place.

"That's it, Alice. I've got you now."

It seemed like ages before they were pulled to the top of the cliff, even though it was only about twenty feet farther up. She heard a machine—a winch, perhaps—and saw half a dozen hands reach out to help.

Soon they were safely over the edge.

The scene that awaited Alice was a complete shock. There were dozens of people, and she heard a helicopter in the distance. Overhead were at least six drones.

As she lay there on her back, she called out for her dad.

"I'm here," she heard him say, and felt his hands on her cheeks.

She closed her eyes and wept. She felt other hands trying to release Wyatt from the feather rope, which was still so strong it resisted all of their efforts.

"Someone get a sharp knife!" a voice called out urgently, and soon Wyatt was cut loose from her stomach.

She heard them shout, "He's alive!"

And then she let her consciousness disappear into her father's arms.

CHAPTER 34

MONDAY, 8:00 A.M.

THE INVITATION

Alice awoke to the unmistakable hushed beeping noises of a hospital room.

"Dad?" she said as she opened her eyes and saw him sitting next to her.

"My darling, beautiful girl," was all he managed to say before reaching out and hugging her tightly.

Why was she in the hospital? "Is Connie okay?" she asked stupidly.

"Connie?" he asked, pulling away. "Yes, of course! She's with Mom outside. Don't you remember? Connie woke up just before—"

Then it all came back to her—the leap from the cliff, falling into the hole, and the horrific ascent.

"How is Wyatt?"

Dad's face became grim. "He's not good. But he's alive."

Just then, the door burst open, and Karan and Madison rushed in.

"Alice, you are such an idiot!" Karan blurted with a huge smile.

"Easy, girls," Dad said. "She just woke up."

There was an awkward moment of silence as Madison and

Karan tried to find space in the crowded room to get near Alice's hospital bed. After they settled, Dad announced fondly, "We have Karan to thank for your rescue, you know."

Karan started to deny it, but Madison scolded, "No, Karan, he's totally right. You were the one who insisted Nancy call in all those search and rescue guys immediately and got them to focus on that mine shaft. Nobody knew it was there but you."

"Yeah," Karan said, "I knew that Eye of Sauron thing Alice dreamed about must have been there. Where else could it have been but a mine shaft?"

"When we got your text, Alice, the rappelling equipment was already in place."

"Almost. Remember when some guy tried to tell Nancy he wanted to move the winch to a safer spot before she could rappel down? She literally picked him up and chucked him out of her way."

Noticing Karan was carrying the whiteboard suitcase Asher had given them, she quickly asked, "What's that for?"

"Oh, I just brought it in case you wanted to watch TV. It's got awesome resolution."

She suddenly wanted to be alone with Madison and Karan. She wanted to be able to speak freely about what really happened. To ask them what became of Tyler Toomes, and Dean, and whether anyone had seen Alice fly.

The room grew quiet. "Dad," she finally said, "can you get me some coffee?"

"Absolutely," he said, rising. "It might be a few minutes, though. I know you don't like instant."

After Dad left, Madison turned to Alice. "Tyler hit his head as he parachuted down to the ground," she said. "He's here in the hospital too, but they don't think he's going to make it."

"I poked my head in there," Karan commented, "and his head totally looks like that potato-headed god. Divine justice, if you ask me."

Madison continued, "Nancy's here too. She tore a biceps muscle and cracked some ribs, but she's probably up and about by now. I'll call her."

"No," Alice said, fearing the dressing-down she knew was coming. "Let's just save that for later."

Karan turned to Alice. "They caught the incel boys, and they confessed to planting those vicious rumors about us on the internet. They blamed it all on Tyler, though. Said he ordered them to do it. They believed he was acting in patriotic defense of the mine, an American institution."

"What about Tyler's dad?"

"We have no idea," Madison said. "That's above my pay grade."

Karan looked at her wide-eyed. "Did you just make a frickin' joke?!"

Just then, the door opened slowly.

"Ladies," Dean said in his proper English accent. He looked two feet shorter than he had when they'd faced off with Tyler in the meadow. Dean had also lost his majestic vibe and had gone back to his hard-faced cowboy look. Perhaps he could switch it on and off at will?

He tiptoed in, carrying three large coffees in cups bearing the Bitches Brew logo. Looks like they would end up with two rounds of coffees from Bitches today. Madison took hers reluctantly, clearly still suspicious of him.

"How are you?" he asked Alice.

"Fine," she said, then drank half of the latte down.

A doctorly knock sounded through the room, and a white-coated man came in.

"Dean," the stout doctor said, nodding.

"Ladies," Dean announced, "Doctor Blake is a friend of mine. He wants to run one more test on Alice's neck."

"There's nothing wrong with my neck, dude."

"Nevertheless, please indulge me," the doctor said. "It won't take long."

Looking at Madison and Karan, Dean smiled and said, "Please join us. You can help Doctor Blake push Alice's bed."

Having finished her double latte, Alice felt like moving her body. "Don't bother," she said, swinging her legs out of bed.

"Lie back down immediately, young lady," Dr. Blake commanded firmly. "You've completely torn both hamstrings."

Ignoring him, Alice stood up effortlessly and bounced a few times on her legs, testing them. They were fine. She pulled the IV bag off its stand. "Cool, let's go."

Dr. Blake looked at Dean, and a moment passed between them. Like they shared a secret. Or like they knew Alice's secret.

"Lead the way," Alice said, feeling suspicious but grateful to be up.

Dr. Blake led them down a hallway and through a doorway. It wasn't until the doctor had left them alone in the room and closed the door that Alice began to realize something was not right.

Madison's eagle eyes bored into the doctor, and she shielded Alice with a long arm. "Alice, let's go back. Immediately."

Alice hesitated. She had expected to be led to an MRI room, but this was just an office. There were cute family photos on the desk, and one of them had Dr. Blake in it.

She looked squarely at Dean. "What's going on?"

Dean pulled out his phone and looked at each of them in turn. "Alice, Madison, and Karan," he began, clearing his throat awkwardly, "I brought you here so we can speak in private for a few moments."

Karan picked up two of Blake's family photos and held them up like weapons. "One wrong move, and I'm slicing you, got it?"

"Yes, of course," Dean said, backing away. "Your suspicions are completely understandable."

He tapped on his phone, and it began to ring. It was answered instantly, and the phone screen resolved into the image of a woman.

She had dark eyes, light skin, and jet-black hair, probably dyed. It gave her a goth look. She looked a bit like Madison, but maybe twenty years older. She wore the smile of someone who had experienced everything in the world and come back to share it all. Her eyes glowed with fierce intelligence, even with the poor resolution of the video call. Behind her was a very old-fashioned collection of office items on a shelf fitted into an old stone wall, like something in a castle.

"Good afternoon, ladies!" she said in a posh British accent like Dean's.

Alice looked at Dean and lifted an eyebrow.

"Let me introduce you," he said. "Alice, Madison, Karan, this is Pippa Thrasher, Dean of the London Institute for Siddhis."

"You mean that school you told me about before?" Alice asked, astonished that he was speaking about it in front of Madison and Karan.

"The same," he said.

Alice had a million questions and didn't know where to start. "Ms. Thrasher," she stuttered.

"Just call me Pippa," the woman said with a laugh. "I understand you've been through quite a trial, Ms. Brickstone."

"Just call me Alice," Alice said.

Pippa gave her a warm smile.

Madison had maneuvered herself protectively between Dean and Alice and seemed about ready to pick Alice up and run away.

Meanwhile, Karan seemed to have completely lost all of her suspicions. She set down the picture frame weapons and started unfolding the whiteboard. "Give me that, Dean," she said, indicating his phone. Karan powered up the whiteboard, touched a few buttons on Dean's phone, and Pippa's image appeared on the bigger screen.

"Well, let's get down to business, shall we?" Pippa said. "I want to personally extend an invitation to the three of you to come visit our little campus."

Wide-eyed, Karan turned to Madison, whose mouth was hanging open, and then to Alice.

She saw prana circulating around her friends—perhaps a sign that everything was going to work out this time? Maybe she could consider having roommates after all.

"When?" Alice asked, smiling.

REVIEW REMINDER
YOU CAN MAKE A BIG DIFFERENCE!!

Reviews are the most powerful tools I have when it comes to getting attention for my books. I don't have the financial muscle of a New York publisher. I can't take out full-page ads in the newspaper or on the sides of buses. But I do have something much more powerful and effective than that, and it's something that those publishers would kill to get their hands on.

A committed and loyal bunch of readers.

Honest reviews of my books help bring them to the attention of other readers.

If you've enjoyed this book I would be very grateful if you could spend a few minutes leaving a review (it can be as short as you like) on the book's Amazon page.

Besides Amazon, there are many other places you can leave reviews: goodreads.com, Apple Books, barnesandnoble.com, kobo.com ... Wherever is easy for you. Don't put it off!

Reviews don't have to be intellectual ramblings. The best ones are just a quick, honest, personal thoughts. Your aim is to help someone decide if they want to buy the book, nothing more. Thank you!

WHAT'S NEXT FOR ALICE?

The next book in the Alice Brickstone series will hit the shelves in mid-2021. Sign up for Tyler's email newsletter for updates and sneak previews.

Quick signup at www.tylerpikebooks.com

Tyler has also written a novella about Alice and Nancy's journalist friend, Rama. (Remember in chapter 20, when Rama told Alice he was about to "do something foolish?") Rama's adventure will be made exclusively available to Tyler's newsletter subscribers in late 2020. Sign up now and we'll send it to you the minute it is available.

**THE ALICE BRICKSTONE
SERIES**

Have you read all of them?

Girl in the Air (note: an updated second edition hits the shelves late 2020!)

The Feeling of Water

Alice's Secret

Rama's Adventure

Turn the page to read the first chapter of *The Feeling of Water*, a novella set after *Girl in the Air* and before *Alice's Secret*. The story unfolds from Karan's point of view. Enjoy.

It took only five minutes for the temperature to dive dramatically. Karan hated this time of day when the sun abandoned her. She felt healed and whole with the dry warmth of the Colorado sun on her skin, but when the day suddenly turned to night, she felt damaged and alone again.

The icy bluster of the river made it worse. It ran alongside the restaurant where she ate every evening with her dad. The rushing waters terrified her and made her shiver, but it was better to stand out here on the riverside deck than to sit inside in silence with her brooding father.

She watched the pine trees and tried to fall into her usual fantasy. It was comforting to imagine she had traveled long and far to reach a secret valley high in the Himalayas. It was the abode of an unimaginably wise and powerful woman whose existence was known only to Karan. She would find her in a temple built into a towering cliff, meditating on the infinite, and would be welcomed like a long-lost daughter. The woman would lovingly teach Karan everything she knew.

Today the fantasy just wouldn't gel. Karan's heart wasn't in it. She looked around as the other people on the deck covered bare shoulders and put on jackets—everyone but the huge, muscular woman on the far side of the deck.

Karan had been watching her and noted that she was well into her second or third milkshake and appeared oblivious to the cold. She leaned on the wooden railing, shunning company, staring at the rapids below. Or maybe she wasn't looking at anything at all.

She turned and caught Karan staring.

Karan realized she had misjudged the woman's age; she could be as young as twenty. Maybe younger. Karan noticed an angry scar on her forehead.

She looked away, embarrassed to have been caught staring. Karan herself was always attracting stares because of her own scars, and she knew how oppressive it felt.

"Beautiful evening," came a deep male voice from the opposite direction. Karan turned, expecting to face a huge mountain of a man, and she was surprised to find a skinny, short guy wearing a white T-shirt, holding a beer and smiling at her.

"I guess," Karan replied, though she felt it was just cold. She knew she should be flattered to be spoken to by any man, especially given her condition—she could hardly look at herself in the mirror—but this guy was not her type.

"It gets dark in this valley so early," he said. "Up here we get sunset during happy hour, while all the poor souls in the bars down in Denver have to wait."

"I guess," she said, though guessing was all she could do. She had no memory of any bars in Denver, no memory of anything before the accident six months ago.

"The river is running clear and low. It's been a dry spring." He stood on his tiptoes and leaned over the railing to see better.

"Whoa." His voice grew even deeper. "Will you look at that. Hey, come here—check it out."

Karan reluctantly stood up from her chair, resolved to give a cursory look to whatever he wanted to show her, then use the opportunity to get away from him and walk back inside.

"That's a rainbow trout hovering behind those rocks right there." He pointed. "He just jumped for a mayfly. They often hatch in the late afternoons."

When she glanced at the icy-white water, Karan's vision fractured, and she was no longer standing safely on a deck during happy hour. She was suddenly transported into the freezing, violently disturbed water. She was fighting to breathe, struggling against certain and fast-approaching death, surrounded by water colored pink by her own blood. Her chest was pierced with something, and her face was so badly smashed she wasn't even confident she still *had* a face.

Two heavy hands were forcing her head deeper into the water. She managed to catch a glimpse of her murderer through the disturbed river mud and bubbles—a man in a backward baseball cap that clung to his head despite the force of the current. It looked like her father.

She had to ask him why before she died. She decided she would use the last ounce of her life's energy to take him by the throat, draw him toward her ruined face, and scream the single word: *Why?*

She reached out to grab him, and suddenly she knew he was dead. He had been dead the whole time; it was only the current pressing his hands against her. She would die with him, her question unasked and answered.

His body drifted away, but then he returned, or was it a different man? It must be her father. He had the same cap, worn backward. Perhaps the other man hadn't been her father after all; this one was the real one. This one was alive, pulling her out of the river.

"Easy. Easy. Are you okay?" a deep voice was asking her. The skinny man was standing above her, and they were back on the bar's deck overlooking the river, droning its freezing hush as it pushed against rocks and rolled toward the plains. Beside him was the milkshake girl, looking down at Karan with a face full of disdain. Karan rolled her head to the left and right to confirm there were no dead people anywhere. She pushed herself up again, and milkshake girl rolled her eyes and walked away. She must have thought Karan was drunk.

"Let me help you sit up," the skinny guy said. "You just kind of fell over. You passed out. What's your name?"

"Karan," she said without thinking. "With an *AN* instead of an *EN*." She immediately regretted divulging her name to this creepy guy.

When Karan tried to stand, he pushed her down. "No, no, no. You gotta relax. I'll call an ambulance."

Karan collapsed under the sudden pressure of his hands, and the milkshake girl dashed over quicker than a squirrel and swept him away with the back of her left arm, knocking him toward the glass doors of the bar.

"Here," she said to Karan, holding out a hand.

Karan took her hand and was pulled up. Looking into her eyes was like looking at a miniaturized astronomical event. They were blue green, like the river, but the irises spindled outward in a starburst pattern until they were met by a deep blue circle bordering the clear whites of her eyes.

"You don't remember anything, do you?"

As Karan lifted her chin to respond, she realized how tall milkshake girl was. At five foot ten, Karan was tall, but her eyes were level with this girl's mouth.

"What do you mean?" Karan asked, unsure whether she was being asked about what had just happened or what had happened some time ago.

"Never mind. You okay? I gotta go."

"No, I'm not okay, but thanks for chasing that guy off." Karan looked around and saw he had shuffled off, scowling, to the bar.

"I don't think he's coming back," milkshake girl observed. "You black out often?"

"No."

"Okay."

"Actually, I didn't black out just now. I think I was hallucinating."

"Sucks," milkshake girl said, her eyes wandering again. She seemed to be getting bored.

"I think looking at the water brought it on. I've always been terrified of water."

"Oh. That's weird. I thought you couldn't remember anything. Hey, how old are you?"

"That's an odd question to ask someone you just peeled off the deck."

"Sorry. Okay, see ya," she said, and started walking away.

Karan realized she didn't want the girl to leave.

"I'm twenty-one," she told the back of milkshake girl's head.

She turned and said reluctantly, "I'm Alice."

Alice stared at Karan, and time seemed to slow down. Karan felt herself zone out, and her mind wandered back to the scene she had hallucinated a moment earlier.

"Hey, listen," Alice said, breaking the spell. "I'm seventeen, and I need someone who's at least twenty-one to sit in my car while I drive. I gotta get fifty hours of supervised driving logged in before they'll give me my full driver's license."

Now it was Karan's turn to look skeptical. "You have got to be kidding me. You look at least twenty." When Alice didn't seem to understand, Karan added, "I bet you get that all the time."

"Whatever," Alice said after an awkward pause. "Anyway, I think I can help you with the water thing. I'm kind of a good swimmer. If you sit with me in my car for a few hours, or at least say you did, I'll teach you how to swim. Also, you seem to be one of the few people on this planet I can talk to."

"What do you mean?"

"I have selective mutism. I can only speak to certain people. You're the first stranger I've ever had a conversation with. There's something about you."

Karan didn't know anything about selective mutism, but considered the odd request as she looked inside the restaurant where her father, with his backward baseball cap, was looking at her wide-eyed. He didn't like for her to socialize; he said it was bad for her recovery to get too worked up. Apparently he had been too busy with his beer to notice her passing out on the deck.

He rushed out, as she expected, and put himself between Karan and her new "friend."

"You okay, honey?" He was squinting, wary.

"Yeah, Dad, I'm fine. This is Alice."

"Pleased to meet you," he said, though he clearly didn't mean it.

Alice didn't respond.

"We should be heading home." Dad was already guiding Karan toward the doors. It had been months since she had actually needed help walking. She felt fine now physically, but old habits die hard, and she didn't mind her dad doting on her now and then. But now was not one of those times.

"Hey, Dad," she said with a firmness she didn't feel, "I'll catch up with you at the car. I just want to say goodbye to Alice."

He looked at Alice skeptically, smiled with only half his face, and went back inside to pay.

"I'm sorry about that," Karan said to Alice. "He's overprotective."

"That's your father? The one you thought was drowning you?"

Karan paused, confused. A tingle ran up her spine.

"What the hell?" she exclaimed. "How do you ... I didn't tell you that. I just said I hallucinated."

Alice said nothing, just kept looking at Karan with her mesmerizing eyes. Something about them was calming.

"It was just a hallucination," Karan said.

"Okay. So do you want my help getting over that water phobia or not?"

Karan looked at her dad, who had finished paying for their dinner and was looking through the window at her expectantly.

"All right. Where is your pool?"

"Don't worry about it. I'll pick you up at five tomorrow morning. Where do you live?"

"*Five* a.m.? Tell me you don't swim at five a.m."

"I don't swim at five a.m. I'm used to being in the water by six. I'm only here for a few weeks, and I'm trying to maintain the same training schedule as my swim team back in Hardrock, where I live. I do an evening session too. I'm about to head to the pool, if you'd rather come now."

"No, I gotta get home. Okay, pick me up in the parking lot here."

"Cool. See you tomorrow at five."

Karan frowned as she watched Alice stride purposefully away. Karan didn't fully trust her, but she seemed like someone who knew where she was going. Maybe some of it would rub off on Karan.

As she walked toward her father, Karan realized Alice didn't even know her name.

Read the rest of this book for free by signing up for the Tyler Pike mailing list. You will immediately receive The Feeling of Water *to enjoy on your devices.*

Quick signup at www.tylerpikebooks.com

ABOUT THE AUTHOR

Tyler Pike writes young adult novels full time. Before his writing career took off, he taught literature, film, and Mandarin Chinese at the University of Sydney for ten years. Tyler was academically confused, earning a PhD in Chinese and a physics degree before that.

He grew up reading anything he could find, under the covers, way past his bedtime, and now he needs thick glasses. Let that be a lesson for you.

Tyler Pike lives with his family in Australia. He surfs with his Aussie wife Tamsin and likes to pummel himself in the gym before picking up his daughter from school.

For more books and updates:
www.tylerpikebooks.com.
Email: tyler@tylerpikebooks.com

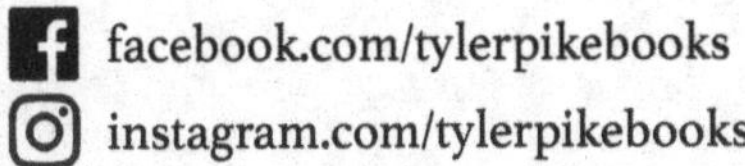

facebook.com/tylerpikebooks
instagram.com/tylerpikebooks

**IN CASE YOU WERE
WONDERING...**

This book is a work of fiction. All characters are drawn from
the author's imagination and are not to be construed as real.
Any resemblance to actual persons, living or dead, is coin-
cidental.

COPYRIGHT PAGE